HOT

Other Avon Books by
John Lutz

Bloodfire
Flame

JOHN LUTZ

AVON BOOKS NEW YORK

AVON BOOKS
A division of
The Hearst Corporation
1350 Avenue of the Americas
New York, New York 10019

Copyright © 1992 by John Lutz
Published by arrangement with Henry Holt and Company, Inc.
Library of Congress Catalog Card Number: 91-3153
ISBN: 0-380-71447-7

First Avon Books Printing: July 1993

AVON TRADEMARK REG. U.S. PAT. OFF. AND IN OTHER COUNTRIES, MARCA REGISTRADA, HECHO EN U.S.A.

Printed in the U.S.A.

RA 10 9 8 7 6 5 4 3 2 1

FOR BARRY N. MALZBERG

When the sun sets, shadows, that showed at noon
But small, appear most long and terrible.

—NATHANIEL LEE
Oedipus

| 1 |

BEAUTIFUL! CARVER thought. He was sitting by his office window, watching two women walk past on the other side of Magellan. They were young and elegantly built, and the warm breeze off the Atlantic molded their lightweight dresses to them as they leaned forward gracefully and tried in vain to hold their hairdos in place. If I were a painter, he thought, I'd do a "Women in the Wind" series of canvases. But he wasn't a painter. A couple of rooms long ago, and a house once. That was it.

As the women passed from view beyond the cream-colored stucco Del Moray courthouse and jail, Carver wondered if really he appreciated them because of his bad leg, because they moved so beautifully and with an ease he now felt only in the water when he took his therapeutic morning swims in the sea.

"I knocked," a voice said, "but nobody answered."

Carver turned away from the window and the outside glare, swiveling slightly in his desk chair. The man who'd entered his office was tall, lanky, gray-haired, with pale blue eyes and a ruddy complexion. He had broad shoulders without much meat on them, and thick wrists with veins like fire hoses. He had to be pushing seventy, an aged Viking.

"You Fred Carver," the man asked, "the detective that used to be in the Orlando department?"

Carver said he was.

"You got shot in the knee by a punk holdup man, I hear, and had to pack it in and go private. Walk with a cane now."

"That's the way it is," Carver said, wondering why the old man had researched him.

"I got shot myself once, but not so serious it made me change my line of work."

"No kidding?"

"Henry Tiller, here." The man shuffled closer and extended a huge hand. Carver shook it. Tiller's grip was dry and powerful. He had about him the smell of stale tobacco. "I was a cop in Milwaukee for a while, then in Lauderdale. Made sergeant. Worked plainclothes for the last couple years in Lauderdale, before I took retirement. I'm living down in the Keys these days."

Carver waited for Tiller to get to the point, but the raw-boned old man simply stood and took things in for a long moment, his flat cop's eyes scanning the office in the way Carver knew so well. Once a hunter always a hunter.

"Can I help you some way, Mr. Tiller?"

"Hope so. A mutual friend, Lieutenant Desoto, told me I should maybe look you up as the answer to my problem."

Carver's interest heightened. Lieutenant Alfonson Desoto of the Orlando Police Department didn't refer people to him lightly. Tiller must have something the police couldn't or didn't want to deal with, but which shouldn't be ignored. That was the classification most of Carver's Desoto-referred cases fell into. Or maybe Tiller was here because he was an ex-cop, a lifetime member of the fraternity just like Carver, and Desoto figured there was a debt to be paid here.

"Wanna sit down and tell me your problem, Mr. Tiller?"

"Call me Henry, and I'd just as leave stand. Been sitting the last couple hours driving up from the Keys."

"And your problem is?"

"I'm not sure. But I'm damned sure there *is* a problem. Since I retired from the department three years ago I been living down in Key Montaigne, little island halfway down the string of keys. Only way to get to it's by a narrow bridge off Duck Key."

Carver said he knew where Duck Key was.

"I bought a little cottage down there," Tiller went on, "and I been living there alone. Wife cut and run from me fifteen years ago. You know how it is, cop's wife."

"Uh-huh." Carver's own marriage had broken up five years ago, probably for some of the same reasons Tiller's had come unraveled. But there were other reasons as well, reasons he knew were his fault. Maybe he'd make the same mistakes even now.

Tiller stood with his giant's ruddy hands at his sides and leaned toward Carver. He seemed to fill the room. "Even an old cop like me, Carver, I still got the instincts, you know what I mean?"

"Sure."

"I spent a lotta years on the force in Milwaukee, then served down in Lauderdale, plainclothes the last couple years. Rank of sergeant."

Tiller had already mentioned that to Carver, but Carver didn't point that out. What the hell, Tiller was an old man, and old men repeated things. "Them instincts tell me sure as snow in Buffalo something's wrong on Key Montaigne."

Carver assumed he meant Buffalo, New York, but he decided not to ask about it. "Wrong how?"

"My cottage is right near the water, and I can look out my window and see things happen on some of the neighbors' grounds. One of them neighbors ain't right."

"Why do you think that?"

"Like I said, an old cop's instincts."

At least he remembered telling me that, Carver thought.

"Best I first tell you about Key Montaigne," Tiller said. "It's about halfway down the Keys. Population's not even a thousand, with the ritziest places fronting the ocean. Small fishing industry. Lots of tourist trade, resorts, fishing cabins with boats, that sorta thing." He absently waved a big hand, first and second fingers slightly extended and a cigarette-width apart. A longtime smoker. "Condos, condos, condos, and a couple of retirement communities. One town, Fishback, but it ain't much—service station, a few restaurants, a strip shopping center, some tourist traps and places that sell bait. Also got the Southeast Oceanography Research Center down there, with an aquarium and all, so tourists can help pay for that, too."

Carver said, "Sounds like a nice place to retire to," wondering if that was true of any place.

"Would be," Tiller said, " 'cept for Walter Rainer. He's got a big estate near my cottage, and I can see the back of it, including his boat dock, out my window. Things are going on over there, Carver."

"Things?" Tiller was sounding more and more like a paranoid old man, but Carver reminded himself Desoto had directed him here.

"That Rainer smells corrupt as a four-day-old trout," Tiller said. "Lives in his big house with his wife name of Lilly, 'bout young enough to be his daughter. Got some employees, Hector Villanova, a Latino seems to be the do-everything whatchamacallit."

"Factotum?" Carver suggested.

"Yeah. Then there's Davy Mathis, a geeky bunch of muscle got tattoos all over him, s'posed to be Rainer's bodyguard, far as I can tell."

"Why's this Rainer need a bodyguard?"

"That's one of the things I wanna hire you to find out, Carver."

Carver said, "I need to know some specifics."

Now Tiller did sit down. He settled into the black vinyl chair near the desk and crossed his long, bony legs. He was wearing brown loafers with tassels on them, the kind that should be golf shoes but aren't. His baggy gray socks had bunched down and there was some sort of rash on his ankles, which were actually thinner than his wrists. He fumbled with a pack of cigarettes in his shirt pocket, not pulling it out, and said, "Rainer's got hisself a boat, the *Miss Behavin'*, about a sixty-footer. It leaves his dock like it's sorta sneaking away every once in a while in the early morning hours, when only an old man with insomnia might be awake. Rainer and that Hector and Davy do a lotta hurrying around in the dark, then the boat puts to sea, don't come back till a couple nights later, so's it can dock in the dark, just like when it left.''

Carver thought about that, ''Tell you the truth, Henry, I don't see much we can do with what you've told me. No law against when to put to sea, and maybe you only *think* Rainer and his employees are sneaking around. There's a lot to the way we look at things.''

Tiller's shaggy gray eyebrows knitted in a fierce frown. ''Don't patronize me, goddamnit!''

Carver shrugged and said, ''Okay, I won't. I was, I guess, and I'm sorry.''

''Those people are into some bad shit, Carver. I heard Rainer talking a few times after I knew for sure he'd been gone to sea, and he lied when he was asked where he'd been. I heard him tell somebody that boat hadn't been away from the dock for a couple of months, but I knew better. He's lying to cover up something illegal. Every atom in my brain tells me that.''

Carver absently drummed his fingertips in sequence on the desk. *Thrrrrump! Thrrrrump!* He said, ''Well, I see what you mean there.'' But he wasn't sure if he did. If lying was against the law, who'd be left to run the country? So far Henry Tiller hadn't given him much in the way of hard facts.

''Then there's the dead boy,'' Tiller said.

Carver looked at him. ''Huh?''

''Dead kid. Thirteen years old. Washed up on the beach.''

''Rainer's beach?''

''No, no, farther down the island.'' Impatiently. Carver just couldn't catch on.

''How'd the boy die?''

''Drowned, they say. I say cocaine killed him. There were traces of it in his blood.''

''Maybe he was tripping,'' Carver said, ''and went for a swim, got too far out.''

''That's what Wicke says.''

"Wicke?"

"Key Montaigne police chief, Lloyd Wicke. The kid was just another runaway got hisself fucked up on drugs, the way he sees it. The boy's parents came from somewhere up north and claimed the body, and that was the end of it."

"You don't think it should be accidental death?"

"Hell, I dunno! But pieces don't dovetail, you know what I mean?"

"No," Carver said, getting exasperated. Henry Tiller had plenty to tell, but he had an oldster's difficulty in getting it out in logical and comprehensible order.

"Evening after they came to Key Montaigne to claim the kid's remains, I seen the boy's father talking to Rainer in Rainer's big gray Lincoln parked outside Fishback."

Carver stopped drumming his fingers. The sound was getting on his nerves. "Could be coincidence. Or maybe they even knew each other from some time back, and Rainer was driving along and saw the guy. Or maybe the father's rental ran out of gas and he was hitchhiking."

"Coincidence and the Easter Bunny," Tiller said angrily, fumbling again with his pack of cigarettes, this time so violently Carver could hear the cellophane wrapper crinkling.

"Okay, okay. You tell any of this to the Key Montaigne law?"

"Sure, to Chief Wicke hisself. Bastard didn't take it too serious. Told me what I wanted to hear, then sent me on my way. I tell you, I got old and learned what it is to be a member of an oppressed minority."

Carver said, "You think Rainer's mixed up in drugs?"

"It's sure as hell possible."

"More possible than the Easter Bunny," Carver admitted. "So what do you want me to do, Henry?"

"Go down there and investigate on the sly, find out what's going on. I know *something* is."

Carver leaned far back in his chair, extending his bad leg beneath the desk. "Why are you so interested, Henry?"

Tiller looked mystified for a moment, in that panicky

manner of only the very young or very old, the momentarily or forever lost. "Why, I told you, I used to be a cop. Up in Milwaukee, then for a while in Lauderdale. I was plainclothes for a—"

"I see," Carver interrupted.

Tiller stood up; he must have been an intimidating and powerful man when he was young. "You gonna give it a go, Carver?"

"You haven't even asked about my rates."

"I asked Desoto. Figured I better know that before I drove over here. Don't you worry, I got money saved. I can pay."

"When you driving back to Key Montaigne?" Carver asked.

"Soon's I walk out your door."

"Leave me your phone number and I'll give you a call. I'd like to talk to Desoto before I tell you yes or no."

Tiller looked suspicious. "Why would you wanna do that?"

"I don't want to steal your money, Henry."

"Fuck you, Carver. You figure I'm some old fool thinking with my prostate gland?"

"No, no, I don't. That's nearer the center of judgment for young fools."

"Fuck you," Henry Tiller said again. "I spent a lotta years on the force in Milwaukee, and a few more in Lauderdale. I know what's going on around me. You'll take the job or you won't."

A little puzzled, Carver said, "Yeah, that's where it stands."

Tiller yanked a plastic ballpoint pen from his shirt pocket and scrawled a phone number on an envelope on Carver's desk, then stomped from the office. A minute later Carver saw him drive from the parking lot in a ten-year-old Buick, the cigarette he'd been denying himself jutting from his lips. When the car turned onto Magellan, Carver noticed a "Support Your Local Police" sticker on the rear bumper.

He sat looking out at the glaring heat for a while. A gull circled on rigid wings and swooped low over the courthouse's red tile roof, then flapped away toward the open, glittering sea. No more beautiful women walked past in the ocean breeze.

Carver had the feeling he was on the edge of something better left unexplored. It was a sensation seldom in error, a sixth sense that increased the odds on survival, and that he too often ignored. Was he dumb enough to ignore it again?

Finally he sighed, dragged the phone across the desk, and called Desoto.

| 2 |

AFTER A five-minute wait Desoto came to the phone. *"Amigo,* what can I do for you?" Soft Latin music played in the background. Carter knew it was from Desoto's portable Sony perched on the windowsill behind his desk. He could picture Desoto in his office on Hughey in Orlando, spiffily dressed as always, probably in shades of cream, plenty of gold jewelry, black hair flawlessly combed, handsome as the movies' idea of a romantic bullfighter. Looking more like a dance instructor than a tough cop, but a tough cop nonetheless.

"It's what you already did for me," Carver said. "You sent me Henry Tiller."

"Ah, Henry. Yeah, I talked to him yesterday, thought you were the man he should see. He tell you what was troubling him?"

"He told me," Carver said. He found himself staring at the chair where Tiller had recently sat. "I'm not so sure about it, though. He seems vague."

"You do police work in Florida, my friend, you deal with a lotta old people. You know that. The human mind changes with the years. Sometimes following Henry's logic is like following a bus in traffic, start, stop, detour, but you stay with it and eventually it reaches a destination."

9

"Then you agree with him? There's something going on down on Key Montaigne needs looking into?"

"It's possible, *amigo.*" Desoto was quiet for a moment. Then: "Let me tell you about Henry Tiller. He was cop in Milwaukee for a long time, then came down here and was on the force in Lauderdale."

Carver looked out in the distance.

"Made sergeant and worked plainclothes," Desoto said. "His wife left him a long time ago, but they had a son, Jerry. Jerry got married and had a son name of Jim, but everybody called him Bump. Three years ago, when Bump was fifteen, he became a runaway and died of a drug over-dose up in Panama City. Turns out he'd been hooked on cocaine since he was twelve. That was bad enough, but Henry's son, Jerry, couldn't take what had happened to *his* son and hanged himself. It all got to Henry, and that's when he took his retirement over in Lauderdale. He aged ten years in six months, they tell me."

Carver thought about the dead boy found on the beach in Key Montaigne. About his own son, much younger, who'd been a murder victim three years ago. It was some-thing he tried not to think about often, but he could imag-ine how Henry Tiller must have felt. Must still feel. First his grandson, then his son. Jesus!

"Casualties in the war on drugs, *amigo,*" Desoto said sadly.

"You got anything on Tiller's neighbor, Walter Rai-ner?"

"I did check, here in Florida and with VICAP. Rainer's clean. The employees, Hector and Davy, are a bit smudged. Hector came with his parents from Cuba and grew up in the Miami slums an orphan after they deserted him. Did two years in Raiford for assault, but that was five years ago and he seems to have been a good boy ever since. Davy's got a long sheet, from joyriding cars in Cleveland as a kid to getting court-martialed out of the Navy for stealing. He worked for a while as a seaman on cargo ships outa New Orleans and got in some kinda trou-ble there, too. Word is he's don't-give-a-damn tough and not to be messed with. Supposed to have killed two men in a brawl in some South American port, but nobody knows for sure. Carries one of those pointed steel cargo hooks the way other thugs carry a knife or gun. Thinks he's Long John Silver or somebody, and it's unwise to argue with him. Of course, you're unwise in that respect, aren't you, my friend?''

"Sometimes, in some ways," Carver admitted. Desoto knew him too well. But then, he knew Desoto.

"That was my one reservation about sending Henry Tiller to see you," Desoto said. "Davy Mathis."

"I'll try to avoid him," Carver said, realizing he'd made up his mind. He was going to call Henry Tiller and tell him he'd investigate whatever might be happening on Key Montaigne.

"You'll avoid him like a mongoose avoids a snake," Desoto said. "Still, Henry needs help. After what happened to his son and grandson, he deserves help. If he had anything concrete, the Key Montaigne police, or even the DEA, could jump into the game. But he's only got his intuition, what he calls his cop's instincts. That's enough for me, 'cause I got my own instincts about Henry. But instincts don't count in court."

Carver said, "If Rainer's got two bona fide hard-asses like Hector and Davy working for him, maybe he really is into something illegal."

"Could be. But there are no outstanding warrants for those two now, so they're solid citizens in the eyes of the law. In fact, they've been clean as soap itself the last three years."

"Or they haven't been caught during those years."

"You're going to work for Henry, right?" Desoto said.

"Yeah, I suppose I am."

"Keep me posted and I'll help when and how I can. Even here in Orlando, I might be able to do something. According to Henry, the Key Montaigne police might not be the most reliable. The chief there, Lloyd Wicke, thinks what he's got is a case of senility on his hands."

"Henry acts in a way that makes it seem a reasonable conclusion," Carver said, watching a tractor-trailer rumble past out on Magellan. The trailer had on its side a vast print from Michelangelo's Sistine Chapel ceiling, the one of God and Adam with their hands almost touching. In this version, God was handing Adam an orange. In Florida that kind of advertising might be meant seriously. How out of touch could Henry Tiller be? "Know anything about Wicke?"

"I checked around. Didn't find out much, but he's supposed to be a good cop. I'm not saying he's wrong about all of this being in Henry's mind, but after talking to Henry, I'm not so sure. Anyway, like I said, Henry's got a favor or two coming from the system. In this case, you and I are the system."

"I'm the one going to Key Montaigne," Carver pointed out.

"But I'd go if I could," Desoto said. Carver believed him. "You work on your own, so you got certain advantages."

"You mean like irregular income?"

"Anyway, *amigo,* you're supposed to be a detective, so detect, eh? Worry this till you know everything and too much about it. Isn't that what you do in life? Your calling?"

"It's what I do," Carver said, thinking maybe "calling" wasn't too strong a word. The music coming over the phone had changed. A woman was singing now; Carver couldn't make out the words, but it was a sad song with slow, syncopated rhythm.

"Go extra cautious with this one, all right?" Desoto said. There was concern in his voice. Instinct again.

"Sure, always."

"How's the lovely Beth?" Ever the gentleman, Desoto was considerate of women, especially beautiful ones. Even though he still wasn't entirely approving of Beth, her gender alone was enough to earn his gallantry.

"Soon as I get off the phone," Carver said, "I'm gonna drive up the coast and find out."

"You're a lucky man, *amigo.* But remember, you be careful."

"I'll buckle up."

"I didn't mean on the highway, my friend."

Carver was about to ask him what he did mean, but Desoto had hung up.

Carver let the receiver clatter back into its cradle. There was no point in trying to call Henry Tiller until he'd had time to drive back to Key Montaigne.

He removed the life insurance pitch from the envelope Tiller had scribbled his phone number on, stuffed the envelope in his shirt pocket, and used his cane to lever himself to his feet. Then he limped from the office, wincing when he met the June Florida heat, and made his way across the parking lot to his car.

Leaving the canvas top up on the ancient Oldsmobile convertible, he coaxed what he could from the balky air conditioner as he drove north on the coast highway toward his beach cottage and Beth Jackson.

3

CARVER MADE love to Beth before telling her about Henry Tiller's visit. He knew if he'd told her first, she'd have been distracted. Was that male chauvinism? Maybe. His former wife, Laura, had pointed to that kind of attitude as part of the reason for the dissolution of their marriage. Carver figured she might be right and had tried to modify his thinking. He was still trying.

Beth lay beside him now on her back, her hands clasped behind her head, considering what he'd said. The window was open and the breathing, sighing sound of the surf was in the room, punctuated by the lazy metallic ticking of the slowly revolving paddle fan on the ceiling above the bed. A breeze was playing over their nakedness, evaporating perspiration and purging the room of the musky afterscent of sex. Carver looked over at Beth's smooth, dusky body, long and lean as a high-fashion model's but with an obvious wiry strength. There was firm definition to her stomach muscles, and her long thighs curved with the musculature of the distance runner. She'd been running when Carver first met her, from her drug-czar husband who'd been bent on killing her.

Staring at the ceiling, she said, "Tell you about the war on drugs, Fred, it obscures other things. People in power use it to advance their own agendas. The news media give the public wrong images, wrong impressions.''

''What's obscured, for instance?'' Carver asked. He was aware Beth knew plenty about drugs, having been married to the infamous late Roberto Gomez. She'd grown up in a Chicago slum and gotten out the only way she'd known how—with her sex and beauty. Then slowly she'd turned her life around, even while living with Gomez and regrets, got an education, escaped from Gomez and his world bought by drug money, and fell in love with Carver. Called herself Jackson again, her maiden name. It bothered Carver sometimes that what she'd seen in Gomez, she might see in him.

''Main thing that's obscured,'' she said, ''is the fact there is no drug problem.''

Carver wasn't surprised; she was always saying things like that, setting little conversational traps, and he'd learned not to jump in and argue. He said, ''Explain.''

''The powers that be act like there's some substance, some *stuff*, causing all our problems, and if we just stop most of it at the border, things'll get better. They say guns don't kill people, people do, then they think it's the junk itself that's causing drug addicts. Get rid of the white powder and the weed that can be smoked, and the problem'll be solved.''

''Hasn't worked so far,'' Carver said.

'' 'Cause it's bullshit. You stop most of the drugs, and their street price'll go up and so will the crime the addicts commit to pay for their habits. Stop every bit of drugs and people'll grow their own, or develop new designer drugs. Hell, a good chemist could walk around this place and figure out some way to cook up something gets folks high. And there's always somebody who'll buy it and sell it. Problem's not drugs, problem's that people wanna do whatever to escape the reality of their lives.''

Carver thought her reasoning was sound. He propped himself up on his elbow and stared at her dark, highlighted features. There was a softness to them, a gentleness, that belied how tough she was. Toughness from deep down wasn't always obvious.

She stopped looking at the ceiling and glanced over at him. "So the government declares war on drugs by saying, 'We're gonna come down hard on you people if you don't stop using that stuff we've made illegal 'cause you can't stop using it.' Makes no sense. An addict'll check in for a cure only after hitting absolute bottom, Carver, and then they put him on a waiting list so he has months before he can get treatment. So he goes back to drugs and thinks everything's fine again, and he's no longer interested in treatment. Big surprise. Thing they do then is arrest and convict him and toss him in jail with some real hard cases that'll teach him tricks and stay in touch with him the rest of his life. Turn him into one of them. Sometimes I wonder who those government assholes talk to when they get their ideas about drugs."

Carver said, "They talk to each other."

"What I'm trying to tell you," Beth said, "is whenever drugs might be involved, don't take for granted things are what they seem. Or even that they're about drugs at all. What they're about is somebody getting money or getting elected or both. That's the way it is. I goddamn know."

"I love you," Carver said, "because you're so ambivalent."

"It's just that I happen to know about drugs and what goes on around them."

"I guess you do."

"So what you're getting into here might be more dangerous than you think. You best be careful."

"That's what Desoto kept telling me."

"He's your friend, and I'm more'n that to you. So listen to us. We care about your hide more'n you do. You're like a combination bloodhound and pit bull, and that's unhealthy."

Carver said, "Grrrr," and pretended he was trying to bite her right nipple. Well, not entirely pretending.

She laughed and shoved him away, and they both lay still for a moment. Then she moved languidly in the bed, rustling the cool sheets, and kissed him, using her tongue. One of her long dark legs curled over him, warmer than the breeze. Her foot hung off his side of the bed.

She rested her head on his chest and said, "You gonna need me?"

He knew she wasn't talking about more sex.

Beth sometimes acted as Carver's business partner as well as lover. She'd gotten tough during her hard years, knew martial arts, could handle firearms. He didn't need to worry much about her. But he remembered what Desoto had said about Davy Mathis.

"I'm not sure," he told her. "Let me sniff around down on Key Montaigne for a while, get some sense of things."

"If that's what you want. But when you're ready to tilt at the windmill, let me know." She unwound herself from him and stood up. Stretched, arching her back. "I'm gonna take a shower." She padded barefoot across the plank floor, her slender body undulating like dark flame. Carver enjoyed watching her walk. He wondered how she'd look in a light summer dress, luxuriating in the wind. Again he wished he could paint. Maybe he'd take it up. She stopped and turned, smiling at him. "You coming?" she asked.

After showering together, they drove in the Olds to the Happy Lobster, a restaurant on the coast highway. It was a place where Carver and Edwina Talbot, the previous woman in his life, had often spent time, but that didn't bother Carver or Beth. Neither was the type to wallow in sentiment.

Carver ordered the swordfish steak, and Beth devoured a lobster with mannered and precise enthusiasm.

Over coffee and cheesecake she said, "From what you've told me, it seems possibly this Henry Tiller's mind has been affected by age."

"Desoto doesn't think so, and he's seen more of Tiller than I have."

"What do *you* think?"

"I'm not so sure, but I trust Desoto enough that I need to go to Key Montaigne and find out."

"I'm not as devout a believer as you are in those cop's instincts you talk about. I've seen them wrong plenty of times." Her dark, dark eyes became serious. "I've seen them get cops killed."

Carver stared out the wide, curved window at the dark-

ening Atlantic. The horizon was almost indistinguishable
from the gray-green sea. So much distance out there, so
much emptiness. Anything might be lost in it. Anything.

Beth took another bite of cheesecake. Chewed, swallowed, then sipped her coffee. She extended her little finger when she sipped from a cup. Where had she learned
that? Not in the slums of Chicago, or from Roberto
Gomez.

She placed her cup in its saucer with a faint and delicate
clink, then reached across the table and rested her long,
graceful fingers on Carver's bare forearm. She dug in
slightly with her painted nails, demanding his full attention. "You need me, you'll call me. Promise?"

"I promise," he said. "But first I better call Henry
Tiller and tell him I'm driving down to see him in the
morning."

BUT BACK at the cottage, when Carver punched out the
number scrawled on the envelope from his office, it wasn't
Tiller who answered the phone. It was a woman's voice
that uttered a tentative hello.

"Can I talk to Henry?" Carver asked. Beth was leaning
on the breakfast counter, pouring a couple of after-dinner
brandies and staring at him.

"No way. I mean, I'm afraid you can't do that," the
woman on the phone said. She sounded young now, maybe
a teenager.

"Why not?"

"He ain't home. He's in the hospital."

"What hospital?"

"Faith United, in Miami."

"Who is this?" Carver asked.

"My name's Effie. Sometimes I come in and clean for
Mr. Tiller. You Fred Carver?"

"I am."

"Mr. Tiller said you might call. I was to tell you he's
in Faith United. A car hit him. I think he's in serious
condition."

"Car hit him how?" Carver asked.

"I ain't sure. All I know is he said he stopped and ate

supper in Miami, and he was crossing the street to go back to his car and got run down."

"Who was the driver?"

"I dunno. You could talk to the Miami police, I guess. Or the hospital."

"Did Mr. Tiller himself phone you?"

"Yeah. We're friends. He trusts me, and he knew I'd be here cleaning up."

"I'll call him at the hospital," Carver said.

"I don't think you can. He told me he was about to be operated on, that's why he wanted me to let you know where he was and why. He left a message on your office answering machine, he said, but he was afraid you wouldn't get it. Mr. Tiller don't trust anything with a microchip in it."

"Me, either," Carver said.

He thanked Effie the cleaning girl and hung up. Told Beth what had happened.

"Still driving to Key Montaigne?" she asked, crossing the room and handing him a brandy snifter.

"First thing tomorrow," Carver told her, passing the glass beneath his nose and breathing in the sharp alcohol scent, like a head-clearing warning. "With a stopover in Miami."

4

FAITH UNITED Hospital was on Hoppington Avenue in west Miami. Its main building was a five-story arrangement of pale concrete and arched windows, but onto this had been added long, three-story wings of pink brick and darkly tinted glass. The architecture clashed, making it look as if an old building had dropped from the past and landed in the center of a modern one.

At the information desk in the lobby, which was in the original building, an elderly woman behind a marble desk told Carver that Henry Tiller was in Room 504 and could have visitors, but Carver was to stop at the nurses' station and let someone know he was there.

Carver thanked her, limped past a hideous piece of steel modern sculpture looming in the lobby, and rode the elevator to the fifth floor.

He didn't like hospitals, and this one was no exception. The hall smelled faintly of disinfectant, and there was a hushed and impersonal efficiency in the midst of disease and suffering, as if Death were merely a member of the staff. White-uniformed nurses and occasionally people in pale green surgical gowns bustled meaningfully about the halls. Patients' relatives slumped in plastic chairs and read dog-eared magazines, or wandered about with studiously nonchalant expressions, trying to come to terms with the

20

realities of institutionalized illness. Carver told himself at least it was cool in here; outside it was ninety degrees even though it was only eleven o'clock.

There were two beds in 504, but Henry Tiller was the room's only occupant. His upper body was slightly elevated, and his right leg was in a cast and raised on a thin cable draped over a stainless steel pulley contraption above the bed. A thin white sheet covered his lower body, and he had on a blue hospital gown tied with a drawstring at the neck. There was an opaque plastic tube fitted through one of his nostrils, and something clear was being fed to him intravenously. His eyes were closed, and he didn't seem to be in any pain. He was much paler than he'd appeared in Carver's office yesterday. Carver thought he looked dead, only his chest was rising and falling.

Carver stepped all the way into the room, which smelled like spearmint and was dark green on the bottom and pale green from halfway up the walls to the white ceiling. A nightstand with a phone sat beside the bed, and nearby was a traylike arrangement on a stand with wheels. A green plastic pitcher sat on it, and an upside-down clear plastic glass. There was a beige vinyl chair near the foot of the bed, with a pillow and folded blanket on it. Outside in the hall a couple of nurses hurried past, giggling softly. A job was a job.

Carver approached the bed, stood leaning on his cane, and Henry Tiller sensed he was there and opened his eyes.

Carver said, "I got your message. The girl, Effie, said you'd been hit by a car."

"Effie Norton."

"Guess so. She didn't tell me her last name, only about you and the car."

"Goddamned hit and run," Tiller said. His voice was slow, a bit slurred, but his eyes seemed focused and knowing. He was making sense—for Henry Tiller anyway. "I was crossing the street after I stopped for supper, out shoots this big car away from the curb, and *ka-blam!* I was on the pavement 'fore I knew what'd happened. Hell of a jolt, I can tell you."

"I'll bet. Get a glimpse of the license plate?"

"Didn't even think about it till it was too late," Tiller said disgustedly. "Figured it was an accident, then I realized the bastard drove off and left me."

"Might still have been an accident," Carver said. "Driver might have panicked."

"Or knew just what he was doing," Tiller said. He was probably right. "It was a Chrysler New Yorker or Fifth Avenue, all white, like the ones car rental agencies got by the thousands here in Florida. White, I said."

Carver knew what he meant. Hitting a human being with a car often caused very little damage to the vehicle while smashing hell out of the victim. White paint was easy to match, so if minor damage to the car was quickly repaired by someone in on the crime, or who wouldn't ask questions, after a short drive down a dusty road the car rental agency wouldn't be able to tell the vehicle had been in an accident.

"See the driver?" Carver asked.

"Yeah, but it was all so fast I couldn't give you an ID. A man, I'm pretty sure, but there was glare on the windshield and I can't even be positive of that. I do know the bastard had both hands on the steering wheel and was staring straight ahead, at me. I got a mental image of that, all right."

"You figure Walter Rainer's behind what happened?"

Tiller snorted. "Whadda *you* figure?"

"How badly you hurt?" Carver asked. "I mean, how long they say you're gonna be in here?"

"Weeks, the way it looks. Busted leg, cracked pelvis, and some internal injuries they ain't quite sure about yet. They did some minor exploratory operating yesterday, and they're gonna get into me good tomorrow morning. Know where that leaves us, Carver?"

"I know where it leaves you: right there in that bed, probably for the next month."

"Where I'd like it to leave you," Tiller said, "is in my cottage down on Key Montaigne."

A young nurse came in, smiled at Carver, and walked directly to Tiller. She had blond hair pinned up off her neck, and wore one of those old-fashioned starched white caps that look like the newspaper hats kids make in grade school. After a concerned and appraising glance at Tiller, she adjusted the angle of his suspended leg slightly, then she peered at the glucose bottle as if it might be changing form before her eyes.

Gazing up at her, Tiller said, "You don't come back in about ten minutes, I'm gonna yank all these tubes out and get outa bed so I can hop to the bathroom on my good leg."

She grinned. "I'll be back in nine minutes, Mr. Tiller."

"Call me Henry," he said as she sashayed out. He looked at Carver. "Whaddya say, Carver?"

"I think she'll be back."

"You know what I mean."

Carver didn't have to think about it for long. "Well, I was gonna call and tell you I was on my way there."

Tiller's right hand, the one with the IV needle in it, rose and fell feebly. A gnarled forefinger pointed. "My clothes are in that closet, key ring in a pocket. Take the brass key with the square top; that's the one to the cottage. Address is number ten Shoreline Road. You remember that?"

"Sure." Carver went to the locker-size closet and fished the key ring from Tiller's pants pocket, then worked the brass key off the ring. He returned the cluster of keys to the pocket and left things the way they'd been in the closet, so Tiller's clothes would be as little wrinkled as possible in two weeks or a month or whenever he'd put them back on.

"Tell me more about Effie the cleaning girl," he said.

Tiller tried to shrug but only managed slight movement that obviously hurt. "She's a fourteen-year-old kid lives nearby. Her daddy runs a gas station in Fishback, mentioned to me she was looking for work, asked if, being alone, I needed somebody to come in once or twice a week to clean. I told him sure, I'd help the kid out—not that I need anybody. I can damn sure look after myself."

Carver considered pointing out Henry's present position, then thought he'd better be quiet. After all, he'd made a mistake himself and was limping around with a cane.

"It was a white Chrysler that hit me," Henry said. "I mention that?"

"You did."

"I never got so much as a peek at the license plate."

"Uh-huh."

Tiller let out a long breath and looked up at the pipe-work and pulley system elevating his broken leg. An expression of infinite sadness passed over his features, for a moment making him look a hundred years old. "I forget some things these days, Carver, I know that. But I also know I'm a long ways from senility. I guess that's another reason I want you to go on down to Key Montaigne and prove I'm right about something not being as it should there, prove I'm not some paranoid old man just a shell of what he was. Maybe in the same way, after you was shot, you had to prove you was more'n just a cripple people could write off. You understand that?"

"I understand my big problem was writing myself off, Henry. It took me a while to understand it, but now I do. Don't get down on yourself because you've got a lot of miles on your odometer."

"If you tend to forget things, Carver, how do you know? I mean, how do I know how *much* I forget?"

Carver said, "Well, how much is worth remembering, anyway?"

"All I wanna remember for now," Tiller said, "is that I got some good years left in me. Not many, but a few. It ain't easy holding on to that thought when there's people treating you like you're halfway in the grave. It works like voodoo or something; they give up on you, so you give up on yourself. You wither and die like a plant that gets no water."

Carver knew what Tiller meant. He'd seen it happen. He patted Henry Tiller gently on the shoulder and told him he'd move into his cottage and poke around Key Montaigne. Not to worry, if Rainer was up to anything illegal, he'd tumble to it.

"Let me know if and when," Tiller said.

"Sure. I'll stay in touch by phone."

Tiller gave him a feeble wave, bumping a tube and causing his glucose bottle to sway on its steel pole, making Carver worry for a moment that the IV needle might pull from the back of his hand. "I give you the key?" he asked.

"I've got it," Carver assured him. "Try to get some rest, okay?"

"Not much else to do here." Tiller closed his eyes.

Thinking about his dead son, maybe, Carver thought. Remembering. The way Carver remembered.

Or maybe just thinking about the pretty blond nurse due back with the bedpan.

Clutching the key tightly in his free hand, Carver limped from the room.

5

SOUTH OF Miami, U.S. Route 1 trails like a thread unraveling from the sleeve of the Florida peninsula. It connects the Florida Keys, a string of small islands that curves gently southwest to end at Key West, only ninety miles from Cuba.

Route 1 was constructed after a hurricane in the thirties had devastated the Keys and swept an Overseas Railroad train and all its passengers out to sea, forever ending rail service from the mainland. The highway, built in part over the remaining railroad trestle, was a safer, more durable way to connect the islands to each other and to southern Florida. For the first several miles from the north, it cuts through flatlands and is mostly a level two-lane road, where passing slower traffic is almost impossible. Farther south it's flanked by water, the Gulf of Mexico on the west, the Atlantic on the east, and has long four-lane stretches. The islands, some of them almost too small to appear on a map, are sometimes so close together only the highway signs let the driver know he's bridged open water and passed from one key to the next. Some of the keys, like Marathon and Isla Mirada, are larger and well populated. Even many of the smaller islands support condo developments, retirement communities, and fishing re-

26

sorts. And tourist shops. Even ahead of fishing, tourism ranks as the Keys' primary industry.

The bridge from Duck Key to Key Montaigne was a narrow, arced ribbon of concrete that still had the fresh, sunwashed look of new construction. Studying it through the windshield, Carver thought that probably an older bridge had recently been replaced.

Key Montaigne wasn't exactly kidney-shaped; it more closely resembled a miniature Africa, one that barely showed up on the standard road map. According to the more detailed map Carver had bought when he'd stopped for gas at a Texaco station on Marathon Key, Key Montaigne was slightly more than half a mile across at its widest point, and about a mile from its northern to southern tip. It was flat, like the rest of the keys, and heavily overgrown with lush tropical foliage that concealed the condo developments and single-family residences.

Carver was driving the Olds with the top up and all the windows down. Key Montaigne was hot, but there was a wind off the sea that might be more or less constant, like farther south in Key West. Outlying reefs prevented incoming waves from breaking into surf, leaving the offshore waters calm. And there didn't seem to be any beach, except for a stretch of public beach that a sign proclaimed was built with sand trucked down from the north. A few sunbathers were lounging on the beach, and two sailboats leaned into the wind not far from shore. In the brilliant sunlight the transplanted sand appeared almost white and looked unnatural in its setting.

It was easy enough to find Shoreline Road, and just a few minutes on it brought Carver to a narrow driveway meandering off through palm trees and undergrowth toward what a rural mailbox proclaimed to be Henry Tiller's cottage.

Gravel crunched beneath the Olds's big tires as Carver followed the driveway to the sea and a small weathered structure with a screened front porch and an almost flat roof. He recognized it as the sort of building Key Westers called Conch houses, solid homes built by nineteenth-century ship's carpenters to withstand hurricane-force winds. Modest but enduring structures that ignored time.

Carver parked the Olds beside the cottage, climbed out and set the tip of his cane in the sandy soil. He squinted out at the Gulf, which was undulating and glittering with silver sparks in the glaring sunlight. To his left the shoreline curved and he could see, some distance away, a manicured stretch of green land sloping gradually to a dock where a large white-hulled private yacht rested as if posing for a postcard. Carver figured it must be the *Miss Behavin'*, Walter Rainer's boat.

A mosquito droned close to his ear, and he raised a hand and brushed at it. He hadn't seen it, but if volume was any indication, it was large enough to fly mail. He wiped the back of his wrist across his perspiring forehead, hoisted his scuffed leather suitcase from the trunk of the Olds, and limped up the wooden steps to the cottage's front porch. Behind him the cooling metal of the Olds's engine ticked like a bomb.

The screen door was unlocked. He opened it partway, then shoved it wider open with a corner of the suitcase and stepped up onto the shaded and noticeably cooler porch. The plank floor creaked beneath his weight. There was a green AstroTurf carpet on part of the porch, and a chipped yellow-enameled metal glider. Instead of a porchlight, there was a paddle fan mounted on the rough wood ceiling. Carver used Henry Tiller's key on the front door and went into the cottage.

The interior was small but neat, with matching white wicker furniture that looked as old and serviceable as the cottage. There was a multicolored braided oval rug on the floor, a bulky old air conditioner mounted in a side window. On the cream-colored walls were oil paintings that were probably done by local artists—a flower arrangement, a stormy seascape, three domestic cats posing in tall grass as if they were a pride of lions. Carver liked that last one. He could see into the tiny kitchen with its dated white appliances. A door led to what he assumed was the bedroom. Another door, half open, was to the bathroom.

The air in the cottage was hot and still and smelled like lemon furniture polish. It took the fun out of breathing.

He limped across the braided rug to the air conditioner and switched it on High. It screamed shrilly and went *Thunka! Thunka!* before the compressor kicked in, then it settled into a steady hum and emitted a stream of moderately cool air he could only hope would grow colder.

He lugged his suitcase into the bedroom and tossed it onto the double bed with its tufted white spread. The bedroom was small, with only a dresser and nightstand in addition to the bed. The walls were the same off-white as the walls in the rest of the cottage. One of them had a dark smear on it where an insect had been swatted. The floor was wood, with a gray throw rug beside the bed. There were a few oil paintings in here, too, but none as good as the one with the cats. Carver was glad to see another window unit, this one smaller but newer, and a ceiling fan like the one on the porch. June nights in the Keys could emulate Hell.

On top of the oak dresser was a display of small framed photographs. Carver stepped closer and examined them. There was Henry Tiller, accepting what looked like an award in front of a group of people, shaking hands with a gray-haired man in a dark suit. There were no women in the photograph, and everyone looked like a cop. Maybe this was Henry retiring. There was a black-and-white shot of a much younger Henry Tiller, standing next to an attractive woman with dark hair and an overwide smile. The ex-wife, perhaps, whom Henry professed not to care about. And there in a bronze frame was Henry about the same age, dark hair like the wife's, posing with a lanky boy about ten years old in front of a lake. A slightly older Henry with the same boy, this time in his teens and looking something like Henry but with his mother's smile; they wore heavy coats and there was a half-melted snowman behind them in this photo. Next to it was a shot of a man in his twenties, the boy grown up, with a heavyset blond woman standing next to him, one leg studiously in front of the other to make her appear thinner. She was holding an infant. Son Jerry again, and his wife, and *their* son

Bump years before cocaine and death. All of them now out of Henry Tiller's dwindling life.

A squeaking sound from the front of the cottage made Carver turn. At first he thought it might have been the ancient air conditioner, but a shadow wavered in the short hall outside the door.

He edged to the side, leaned with a palm against the wall and gripped the shaft of the hard walnut cane just below its crook. He focused his concentration, ready to rumble if he must.

A redheaded girl about five feet tall moved into the doorway and stood with her stick-thin arms crossed. She was wearing shorts, clompy red and white jogging shoes, and a sleeveless blouse, a green sweatband around her forehead. She was in her early teens and was pale and had freckles on every part of her that was visible. She didn't seem surprised to see Carver, and stared inquiringly at him with guileless and friendly green eyes. Danger would be the farthest thing from her mind, until she grew up. She said, "You Mr. Carver?"

He straightened up and planted the tip of his cane back on the wood floor, feeling slightly silly at having brandished it for use as a weapon if necessary. "I'm Carver." This had to be Effie Norton, the teenager who did Henry Tiller's cleaning, but he thought he'd let her tell him that.

She did. Then she said, "Mr. Tiller told me what a great investigator you were, how you were probably better'n anyone in most police departments."

Maybe Desoto had oversold Henry. Carver said, "Sometimes I can help, sometimes not."

She grinned, crinkling the flesh around her eyes. Like a lot of redheads, she'd look old before her time, but until then she'd be a coltish charmer. "You're being too modest."

He said, "Yeah, Effie, I guess I am." He wondered how much Effie knew about Tiller's suspicions. How much she knew about Tiller. Well, there was a direct way to find out. "If you don't mind my asking," he said, "what do you think of Mr. Tiller?"

She arched an almost nonexistent eyebrow. "In what way?"

"Any way you feel like talking about."

She uncrossed her arms and let her hands dangle at her sides, standing like a schoolgirl getting ready to recite in front of the class. "He's nice. He reminds me of my grandfather, who's been dead three years now. When I say something, he listens. He don't treat me like some kinda feeb just because I'm young. Hey, did you see him in the hospital?"

"Yeah, for a short time."

"So how is he?"

"Some broken bones, and the surgeons are gonna do some work on him tomorrow. But I think he'll be all right."

"I sure hope so." She was plainly concerned, maybe recalling the pain of losing her grandfather. Fourteen was young, all right.

"Do you think there's anything to Mr. Tiller's suspicions?" Carver asked.

"Suspicions?"

"About something being wrong here on Key Montaigne."

"Of *course* there's something to those suspicions." Now she propped her fists on her narrow hips, ready to defend Tiller. "Mr. Tiller used to be a policeman, you know, in Milwaukee and then in Fort Lauderdale."

"I know."

"I mean, if he sees smoke—"

"Okay, okay. Then you believe he's—thinking okay these days?"

"Ha! I know what you mean, but you take the trouble to listen and wait when Mr. Tiller tells you something, you'll see how smart he really is. He sorta stops and starts and gets off on side roads when he talks, but don't you ever bet he don't know what he's saying."

Carver remembered Desoto's bus-in-traffic analogy. Henry made a lot of U-turns, too.

"The person who ran over Mr. Tiller," Effie said, "you think they did it on purpose?"

"I'm gonna find out," Carver told her. "In fact, if any-body asks you, that's what I'm here to investigate—Mr. Tiller being hit by a car that kept going."

"You bet!" Her eyes widened brightly; she liked secrets.

"Have you discussed Mr. Tiller's suspicions with any-body else?"

"Oh, no! He asked me not to. Only ones who know about them are Mr. Tiller, me, and the police chief, Lloyd Wicke. Mr. Tiller said it'd be best not to let anyone know somebody was suspicious of 'em; that way they'd destroy evidence or whatever, and might even sue for slander."

"Something to remember," Carver said. "Mr. Tiller must trust you a lot."

Her freckled chin lifted. "He does."

Carver smiled. "I guess I will, too, then."

"You gonna be staying here awhile?"

"Probably."

"I been coming in to clean three days a week. What I dropped by for was to ask if you wanted me to keep doing that."

"Sure," Carver said. "That's what Mr. Tiller would want."

She smiled and started to back away.

"Effie," Carver said, "you never did tell me what you figured was wrong on Key Montaigne."

She looked thoughtful. "I only know Mr. Tiller *thinks* there's something. Could be a lotta things, I guess."

"Drugs?"

"Huh?"

"Is there much drug use on the island?"

She didn't hesitate. "There's some, even among kids my age. I don't know as there's more here than anyplace else, though."

"What about the boy they found drowned, washed up on the beach? He was about your age."

"He was lots younger." She sounded indignant. "At least a year. And I didn't know him. He was from up north."

"Miami," Carver said.

"I only drove—been driven through—Miami now and again. Don't know a solitary soul there." When she saw he was finally finished questioning her, she started backing away again. Maybe shyly, but Carver wasn't sure; few things were harder to read than a fourteen-year-old girl. She wore her joggers untied, with the shoelaces trailing. He wondered how she kept from tripping over them. "I got a door key," she said, "so you don't have to worry about letting me in if you wanna be someplace else. And my number's circled in Mr. Tiller's directory in by the phone, case you make a mess and need spur-of-the-moment cleaning. I live not far down Shoreline and can get here on my bike pretty fast."

"You charge extra for emergencies?" Carver asked, half jokingly.

She took him seriously and a calculating expression came over her freckled, girlish features. She'd apparently never considered the idea of overtime pay. "No," she said, "cost is just the same." Youthful virtue had conquered greed.

He grinned. "Okay. See you later, Effie."

She crossed her arms again, stood the way she'd been standing when he first saw her. "If you need any help around Key Montaigne, I mean, need to know anything only somebody lives in this place might be able to tell you, I'll be glad to help that way, too, Mr. Carver."

"You can do that right now," Carver said. It was almost five o'clock; he'd taken care of some business by phone from Miami, had a long but light lunch with an old friend, then hadn't stopped except for gas on the drive south. "Where's a good place in town to eat supper?"

She gnawed her lower lip a moment, considering. "Ain't a lotta choices, but mine'd be the Key Lime Pie. That's what they call it, like the actual pie only it's a restaurant."

"Thanks, I'll try it."

She smiled, bobbed up and down on her thick-soled jogging shoes as if building momentum, then swept away in a dash. He heard the reverberating slap of the screen door echoing out over the water.

He walked to the window and watched her mount a balloon-tire Schwinn bike with a rusty wire basket attached to its handlebars, then build up speed, her boyish body whipping back and forth as she stood high on the pedals.

Carver removed slacks and shirts from his suitcase and put them on wire hangers from Henry Tiller's closet. Henry had one of those space-saving fold-down multihanger plastic gizmos in his closet; it came in handy. Carver hung it on a brass hook on the outside of the closet door and placed all the hangers on it so his clothes were draped in descending layers. Neat, he had to admit. He left socks and underwear in the suitcase and placed it in a corner with the lid closed but not latched. His shaving kit he carried into the bathroom and set on top of the vanity, over to the side, where it wouldn't get wet. There was a large white towel embossed with SUNCREST MOTEL folded over a rack in the bathroom, that had on it stitched in red, "Hi, I'm Mr. Towel and I live here. If you take me away from home, please bring me back." Henry must have abducted Mr. Towel. Carver saw himself smiling in the medicine cabinet mirror, a tan, bald man with a fringe of curly gray hair that had grown too long in back. Lean, with a powerful upper body from exercise and walking with the cane. A scar at the right corner of his mouth. Pale blue eyes that were oddly catlike. As soon as his strikingly beatific smile faded, his was a brutal face rather than handsome. He knew the abrupt contrast could be unsettling.

He went outside and stood in the heat for a while, gazing across the expanse of glimmering water at the *Miss Behavin'* rocking gently at her moorings. He could only see about half of the back of the large white clapboard house with red canvas awnings, a corner of a swimming pool behind a chain-link fence, a round blue table with a fringed umbrella sprouting from it at an angle. There was no sign of anyone at the Rainer estate.

Listing sharply over his cane, Carver shielded his eyes from the sun and his cupped hand and looked westward over the Gulf. A pelican flapped low above the surface, seeking its dinner. A large vessel that had the look of a cruise ship haunted the hazy, distant horizon like a wavering ghost. Henry Tiller had retired to beauty if not peace.

The sun wouldn't be setting for a long time, but Carver was hungry.

He locked the cottage door, then he drove toward Fishback to look over the town in daylight. After that, he'd eat an early supper at the restaurant Effie had recommended.

There were a number of things he wanted to find out. One of them was why anybody would name a town Fishback.

6

No ONE seemed to know. The waitress, a stout, broad-shouldered woman named Fern, said she thought Montaigne got its name way back in the nineteenth century when the Keys were a haven for pirates. So serious was the problem that a U.S. naval base was established in Key West to stop piracy. It was successful only up to a point. As to who named Key Montaigne's population center Fishback, and why, Carver would have to ask somebody who knew about pirates, Fern said.

He was sitting in a window booth in the Key Lime Pie restaurant, eating the day's special, broiled shrimp with salad and a baked potato. He'd driven through the town, consisting primarily of a main street, called Main Street, on which were lined weathered, low buildings housing bait shops, bars, a hardware store, Laundromat, barber shop, supermarket, and various other assuagers of needs and yearnings.

At the foot of Main was the town marina, where dozens of docked pleasure boats bobbed on the gentle waves, along with several commercial fishing boats and a lineup of charter boats for tourists to hire for deep sea fishing. There wasn't a lot to do on Key Montaigne other than fish, eat, and drink, and the tourists the island attracted usually weren't interested in theme parks and water slides. Plenty

of tourists walked the streets, skin still pale from northern
climes, sporting souvenir T-shirts with cameras slung
around their necks, but there were few young children
with them. The families with kids were farther north, seeing Disney World and Universal Studios and learning about
the wonders of citrus.

Where Carver sat he could see a section of Main Street,
the small, flat-roofed building that called itself Food Emporium Supermarket, and on the corner a freshly white-
washed service station with a single work bay and two
pumps. NORTON'S GAS 'N' GO, read the sign over the
pumps. Effie's father's place. It was a self-service station.
A bearded man in a sleeveless gray shirt was pumping
unleaded into a dusty black pickup truck, glaring at the
pump's price and gallon meters as if he held a grudge
against them. There was a pyramid of Valvoline oil cans
at a corner of the building, the kind of display you seldom
saw anymore. The work bay's overhead door was open,
and a Ford Escort was up on the rack getting its oil
changed. Carver was glad he hadn't ordered anything fried.

Loud voices drew his attention back inside. The Key
Lime Pie restaurant was long and narrow, with round tables on one side and a counter with red vinyl stools on the
other. Struggling air-conditioning and half a dozen ceiling
fans kept the temperature down and cast flitting shadows
over the red-checkered tablecloths and green and brown
tiled floor. Beyond the counter was an arch with a swordfish mounted above it. Through the arch Carver could see
into the adjoining lounge, where several men sat or stood
at the bar. Most of them were wearing jeans or shorts and
T-shirts and had deep tans. One of them, a short, stocky
guy with an oversized blond mustache that lent him a fierce
expression, was arguing vehemently with a man wearing
a loud red and yellow tropical shirt with a parrot pattern,
who was slouched on a bar stool facing away from Carver.
Yellow Mustache was getting madder and madder, while
the man in the garish tropical shirt seemed to be ignoring
him. Carver couldn't understand what was being said.
Something about shipwrecks, he thought. He popped his

last broiled shrimp into his mouth and sat chewing, waiting to see what would happen.

The man on the stool slowly swiveled around and stood up. He was about average height, built blocky, and wore his hair shaved almost short enough to classify him as bald. His loud tropical shirt was untucked and might conceal a weapon. The thick, tan forearms that protruded from the wildly colored short sleeves were so covered with tattoos they almost looked like an extension of the busy-patterned shirt. A colorful snake coiled up one arm. The other arm sported what looked like an anchor and a topless hula dancer.

With the tattooed man standing staring at him, Mustache suddenly was quiet. The evening had turned serious. The guy with the tattoos grinned at him, then in a quick motion grabbed his belt buckle and lifted and twisted, drawing Mustache's pants tight into his crotch. Mustache screeched in pain, and Tattoo snapped a thick-wristed forearm up below his chin and pressed. The screeching became a series of strangled pleas for mercy. Tattoo shoved Mustache out of sight, toward the street door, then swaggered after him with a deliberate bow-legged gait, as if he were on a ship in high seas. Carver could no longer see either man, but in a few seconds Mustache appeared out on Main, limping bent over and in obvious pain toward a parked four-wheel-drive Jeep. With a hand cupped to his crotch, he climbed into the Jeep and got the engine started. He glared angrily but with terror in the direction of the Key Lime Pie, then drove away, the Jeep's knobby tires spinning and throwing gravel. The conversation and noise level of the bar increased to what it had been before the trouble started.

"The boys get frisky sometimes when the charters are back for the day," Fern said, " 'specially if the fishing ain't been good." She was standing near Carver with her order pad in one hand, yellow stub of a pencil in the other.

"Who're the boys?" Carver asked.

"Some of 'em are commercial fishermen, others are

charter boat captains and crew. You can always tell if it's been a good day by the way they behave.''

The tattooed man had returned to his bar stool. "Who's the guy in the parrot shirt?" Carver asked, figuring he knew the answer.

"Some of those are cockatoos."

"Yeah, I can see that now you point it out."

"Anyway, that's Davy inside the shirt. He's part of the crew of a yacht belongs to some rich fella out on Shoreline. That joker that was arguing with him I never seen before, and if he hadn't been a stranger, he wouldn't have crossed Davy. That Davy'll argue anything from baseball to politics, but he won't stand for no badgering. He just wants to be let alone, is all, but if people push him just a little bit, they pay. He's the sort that likes to make 'em pay. That fella he shoved outa here's lucky it didn't get more serious.''

Carver watched Davy calmly drinking his beer. No one was talking to him, or near him. He didn't seem to notice. "So Davy's a bad boy?"

"I dunno for sure, as he never caused any real trouble in here. Or anyplace else, far as I know. But I been told he's bad, all right.''

Carver thought the mustached man might regard what had happened as real trouble.

"Don't repeat this," Fern said, "but he gives me the creeps. Maybe it's all those tattoos." She gave a mock shiver, almost dropping her pencil. "They tell me you're a private detective of some sort."

"Who tells you?" Carver asked. He shoved away his plate so he'd no longer have to breathe in the shrimp smell of the leftovers. He wished Fern would clear the table.

Fern shrugged. "That's one of them questions like why's the town named Fishback. Word just gets around, is all. They say you're staying up at the Tiller place. You here about whoever it was run over Henry Tiller?"

"That's it," Carver said.

"How *is* Henry?"

"I think he'll be fine, but it'll take some time."

"Shame what happened. He's a nice old bird. A little vague at times, but ain't we all?"

Carver agreed we all were. "There anyone here you think might feel strongly enough about Henry to try running him down?" he asked.

Fern shook her head. "Everyone figures he's harmless, you know? Ask me, I'd say he was just the victim of an accident. But I guess, with a hit and a run like that, the law's gotta investigate."

"That's what I'm doing," Carver said. If she wanted to think of him as the law, that was okay. Even convenient.

"Get you anything else?" Fern asked.

"A refill on the coffee." He swished around the mud-colored inch of liquid left in his cup to draw it to her attention.

"How about some dessert?"

He looked up at her. "What's good here?"

She laughed. "You kidding? There's only one item on the menu."

"Then I'll have it," he said.

She licked the point of her stubby pencil, added the slice of key lime pie to his check, then scooped up his dirty dishes and ambled away toward the kitchen. A few minutes later she returned with the round glass coffeepot in one hand and the wedge of pie on a white china plate in the other. She refilled Carver's cup, laid his check in a puddle on the table, then went around the restaurant topping off everyone's coffee.

The pie was a delicate and delicious combination of sweetness and tartness. Carver ate it staring at the garish parrot-and-cockatoo pattern shirt stretched over Davy's broad back, wondering if the wildly colored material concealed a steel cargo hook tucked in Davy's belt.

One thing he did know, he shared Henry Tiller's cop's instincts about Davy. He was a bad one.

7

THAT NIGHT Carver sat on Henry Tiller's screened-in porch, smoking a Swisher Sweet cigar, listening to the screaming lament of a thousand crickets, and looking out over the water at the lights of the Walter Rainer estate. There was movement over there, for a few seconds what appeared to be a man walking with a flashlight down by the dock. But the *Miss Behavin'* itself stayed dark. Carver blew a smoke ring he couldn't see but imagined as perfect in the darkness, and wondered if the boat would still be at its moorings in the morning.

IT WAS. As soon as he'd climbed out of bed he limped onto the porch and checked, saw the sleek white hull with the red trim, the rising sun shooting sparks off the bright-work. For a moment he found himself speculating, if Henry were here, would he see the boat, or the unoccupied dock he wanted to see?

After getting dressed, Carver burned two eggs and three strips of bacon in a heavy iron skillet in Henry's kitchen. His cooking was heating up the kitchen, so he switched on the air conditioner. That helped some, but the tropical climate was gaining. When he was finished eating, he turned on a paint-speckled radio on top of the refrigerator and listened to local news while he sipped a second cup of coffee.

Apparently not much happened on and around Key Montaigne. A couple of wedding announcements; the Holy Rock of the Keys Baptist Church was planning a fish fry next weekend; an octogenarian named Ida Fletcher had died in her sleep; and the Fishback Dinner Theatre was doing *A Midsummer Night's Dream.* After the news, it was time for music, a medley of numbers from *Cats.*

Carver washed the breakfast dishes and left them on the sink to dry, then switched off the radio, even though he liked *Cats.* Slow as things were on Key Montaigne, it would be a good time to extend the professional courtesy of dropping by to meet Chief Lloyd Wicke.

KEY MONTAIGNE police headquarters was a squat clapboard structure near the marina on Main. There was a steeplelike antenna next to a satellite dish on the roof. At the front curb was a dust-coated blue Ford Taurus with red and blue roofbar lights and an official-looking gold badge decal on its door. Through the windshield Carver could see a twelve-gauge riot gun mounted to the dash. Once, that had seemed a formidable weapon, in the time before drug dealers had taken up AK47 and Uzi automatic weapons. Beyond the police cruiser a dented tow truck and a maroon Toyota station wagon were parked at an angle in the small lot alongside the building. The lot was layered with chat, small white stones the size of gravel, which was used often in Florida. It was the reason for the pale coating of dust on the vehicles, like talcum powder.

Carver parked the Olds next to the Toyota, then narrowed his eyes against the sun and limped around to the front of the building. Down the block, at the marina, the commercial fishing boats had already left, but the charter crews and tourists were preparing to set to sea. A large sailboat, canvas lowered, putted on diesel engine power across Carver's field of vision, trailing wisps of black exhaust in the clear morning air.

It was cool inside headquarters. The building had once been a house, but most of the interior walls had been removed to form a rectangular area sectioned off by low wooden railings. An elderly woman with a blue hairdo sat behind a big walnut desk near the door. There were four gray metal desks beyond her. At one of them a man with sun-bleached curly blond hair, wearing a yellow Bart Simpson T-shirt, was studiously working at an old gray IBM Selectric. He was a nifty typist; the venerable Selectric *tupita-tupita-tupita—dinged!* its contentment to be in such capable hands. Three identical closed doors, in a neat row beyond the desk, probably led to back offices, and maybe the holdover cells. There was a control panel and microphone near the blue-haired woman's desk. Aside from her other office duties, she was apparently the dispatcher.

"Help you?" she asked, smiling at Carver. She had a round face and soft, pliable skin much younger than her eyes.

Carver told her who he was and that he'd like to see Chief Wicke.

"You the one staying at the Tiller place?" she asked, still smiling warmly.

"The same."

She nodded. He thought she'd press a button on the control board and announce him on the intercom, but instead she excused herself and left her desk. She was overweight and wide-hipped and moved with effort, her labored breathing audible. Without pausing, she knocked perfunctorily and entered the middle door behind the desks. The guy at the Selectric had stopped typing and was staring at Carver. Carver nodded to him. He nodded back solemnly. Kept staring with his cop's flat blue eyes. Maybe he remembered Carver from the last time the Fishback bank was robbed.

"Chief'll see you," the blue-haired woman said, bearing down on *Chief* and making it sound like a gentle-but-firm command. She left the office door open and trod heavily back to her desk.

Carver used his cane to push open a gate in the low rail, then limped toward Chief Wicke's office. He thought the cop at the gray metal desk would still be staring, but behind him he heard the Selectric start clattering again.

Chief Wicke was standing up behind a wide oak desk that took up most of the office. It was a messy desk. File folders were in a jumble on one corner, a dirty ashtray was poised to fall off another. A four-line phone sat on top of another stack of folders. Papers and two thick ringbinders lay near the chief, and he had one of those green felt desk pads with brown leather borders. Small slips of paper, business cards, and opened envelopes were tucked beneath the overlapping leather on each side. Chief Wicke was either a very busy or a very lazy public servant.

The chief himself was average height but wide all over, as if he'd been compressed by a great force. He might have been a long-ago high school football player too small and slow for college. His blue uniform shirt was bulging over his belt. His gold badge hung down above his shirt pocket like a flower wilted by the heat. He had a fleshy face but narrow, sharp features, as if nature had been guilty of a genetic mix-up and combined fox with fat cells. Salt and pepper hair had receded and was cut short and combed straight back. Wicke's gray eyes were neutral yet appraising, like the eyes of the cop out at the typewriter. Like Henry Tiller's eyes, and Carver's, and the eyes of every cop everywhere who ever lived. Central Casting might have done worse suggesting him as the frustrated southern sheriff in one of those yokel chase comedies.

Carver introduced himself, and Wicke pumped his hand, saying, "Lloyd Wicke. I understand you're staying up at Henry Tiller's place." Wicke's eyes hadn't so much as flicked toward Carver's cane; he already knew things about Carver, so maybe he was more on top of his job than those yokel sheriffs in the movies. And there was no trace of a southern accent.

Carver leaned on the cane. "I'll be there for a while," he said.

"So how's old Henry doing?"

"Not bad, considering. He'll be laid up for some time, though. I'm here to look into the hit and run." Among other things.

Chief Wicke frowned and nodded. "Hell of a turn for Henry, but I guess that's what happens when you get old, your hearing and eyesight go bad, and you can't see or hear a car coming at you." He ran beefy fingers lightly across his chin, as if checking to make sure he'd shaved that morning. "Kinda problems we're all gonna run into sooner or later."

"That how you see it? Henry got nailed by some drunk driver who kept on going?"

"Sure. Or some variation of that. What other way is there to see it?"

"Henry thinks maybe it wasn't an accident. Maybe it had to do with some suspicions he has about a neighbor of his, Walter Rainer."

Chief Wicke chuckled and shook his head. "Now why ain't I surprised?"

"Henry said he'd been to see you," Carver said.

"He sure has. 'Bout a week ago. I told him he better not go around spreading such theories unless he expects to be sued. There's no evidence Walter Rainer's anything but just another middle-aged man with money living his Florida dream. Got himself a younger, good-looking wife, a couple of steady employees to take the load off his shoulders. So what if he does go out in his boat at night—*if* he does, which I doubt. Hell, he's one of the least eccentric rich folks we got living on the island. You wouldn't believe some of the oddball shit goes on here. Or maybe you would." The chief squinted at Carver and leaned forward over his cluttered desk. "What exactly'd Henry tell you, Mr. Carver?"

"He wasn't very specific. He seems to have added up everything he's observed, and doesn't like the total, even if he doesn't know exactly what it is. Mainly, he figures a longtime cop can sense when something's not what it oughta be."

"I guess he's right on that one, but there comes a time when that cop gets too old and too far away from the work. Listen, last thing I wanna do is bad-mouth old Henry, but my actual belief is that he's rounded that bend, like a lotta old folks, and his imagination's doing a job on him. It ain't unnatural, either, for a man his age to get kinda paranoid.''

''You'd have a tough time convincing him of that.''

''Don't I know it? What I tried was to convince him to quit spying on Walter Rainer, and to try and forget his crazy suspicions. Take up goddamn basket weaving or some such.''

''I bet he took to that suggestion with a smile.''

Chief Wicke grinned. ''Well, you probably ain't noticed any baskets around his place. He cussed a lot and then tromped outa here. Tell the truth, I don't guess I blame him. It can't be easy admitting the string's about played out. Maybe working up suspicion about Walter Rainer is Henry's way of trying to make himself meaningful.''

''Exactly who is Rainer?''

''Man about fifty, said to have made his fortune in the car business up north. Lives out on Shoreline and manages his investments. Now and again him and his wife, Lilly, come into town for dinner or what have you, though usually they pretty much keep to themselves. Rainer's well-enough liked, or at least not *dis*liked, and no trouble to anybody far as I can see.''

''His man Davy Mathis looks like a rough character.''

Wicke spread his hands on his desk and nodded. ''Yeah, I know about Davy. Even mentioned his background to Walter Rainer, 'case he didn't know. But he did know. He said he'd gotten to like and trust Davy when Davy worked for him up north, and felt he deserved a chance despite his background.''

''So he's a humanitarian.''

Wicke's broad but foxlike face creased in a smile. ''Now you sound like Henry.''

''Yeah, I guess I do. Sorry. I'm working on not being so cynical.''

''Well, in our line of work, that ain't easy. Which is maybe why an old cop like Henry needs a crime to look into, and the truth is, other'n tourist con games and an occasional fight, there ain't much crime here on Key Montaigne. Maybe Henry shoulda gone back to Milwaukee or retired to the South Bronx.''

"So you didn't do anything to investigate his suspicions?"

"Oh, I didn't say that. I asked around a bit. Even drove up to the Rainer place and talked to Walter Rainer. He was surprised. He don't even know Henry. I think his feelings were a little hurt; it ain't pleasant to be suspected of God knows what. He even offered to let me search the house grounds."

"But you didn't."

The chief lifted his broad shoulders helplessly. "I honestly had no reason, Mr. Carver."

"Other than the Walter Rainer matter, is there anyone on Key Montaigne who might have reason to do Henry harm?"

"Hell, no. Ain't nobody takes him all that serious." Wicke rested his palms flat on his desk and faced Carver squarely. "Look, you're making too much of this. What happened is some DWI or scared-shitless tourist accidentally ran over Henry in Miami, then panicked and fled the scene. I've asked Miami police to set up checks on the car rental agencies in the area, notify me if they report any suspicious damages. But you know how it is, a car can hit a human being and not sustain near as much damage as the person. All depends on how it happens."

"You're probably right," Carver said, "but I owe it to Henry to ask around. Maybe, if nothing else, I can put his mind at ease."

"I sure hope so," the chief said. "I wouldn't want his fixation about Rainer to run outa control, maybe prompt him to do something really foolish. Henry still got his service revolver?"

"He probably does," Carver said.

"Great." Wicke waved a hand. "But then, what the hell, every nut case in Florida's got a gun, so why not Henry?"

Carver couldn't answer that one. He thanked Chief Wicke for taking time to talk to him, then limped from the office. The curly-haired cop at the Selectric stared at him on the way out. The woman behind the desk smiled at him like a grandmother who'd just fed him cookies. Smalltown life.

It was much hotter outside. The sky was cloudless and the sun was having its way. There was a slight breeze off the ocean, but it was warm and created the effect of a convection oven. As he set the cane on the loose chat and limped back to the Olds, Carver could feel the sun's heat on his bald pate. Probably he should buy a hat.

When he got back to Henry's cottage, he punched out Effie's number on the cheap digital phone. A woman answered. Effie's mother? Carver asked if he could talk to Effie, for a moment feeling like a nervous tenth grader working up the nerve to ask for a date. "Just a minute," the woman said suspiciously. It was more like three minutes before Effie came to the phone.

In the interest of propriety, Carver kept the conversation short. He asked Effie for the names of people on Key Montaigne who were particularly friendly with or had dealings with Henry. Sounding as enthusiastic as if he'd provided a last-chance date for the prom, she said she'd make up a list and bicycle over and give it to him.

After thanking her and hanging up on her boundless energy, he called Faith United Hospital in Miami and asked about Henry Tiller's condition.

Satisfactory, he was told. Mr. Tiller had been on the operating table three hours while surgeons explored and treated his internal injuries. Soon he'd be able to accept brief phone calls and have visitors, but not today or tonight.

After replacing the receiver, Carver found a can of Budweiser in the back of Henry's refrigerator and sat on the front porch, sipping beer and looking out at the sea. At the sleek white form of the docked *Miss Behavin'*. He thought about his conversation with Chief Wicke, who seemed a competent and sensible man with no ax to grind, though maybe something of a toady for the island's rich residents who no doubt kept him in office, politics being politics.

Maybe the chief was right, and Henry was in the gray area between reality and the tricks advanced age played on body and mind. The place where past and present mixed with never.

The beer can was empty, and Carver was still considering Henry's questionable instincts, when he heard bike tires crunching in the driveway and Effie pedaled into view on her weatherworn Schwinn.

8

ONE OF the names on Effie's list was Katia Marsh, an employee of the Oceanography Research Center. After lunch, Carver found the handful of tourist brochures he'd picked up before crossing the narrow bridge to the island. The research center had its own brochure, a slick foldout that showed a low, buff-colored building perched on the edge of the sea. There were several fenced-in areas near it that reminded Carver of enclosed tennis courts, but he saw that inside the cages of chain-link fencing were rectangular pools that must contain sea life. There was a shot of a room where various tidal-pool creatures could be observed and handled by visitors. The back wall of the room was a glass window looking in on a tank wherein a large shark swam. A dark-haired man in a white smock and a stoop-shouldered woman with a pinched nose and pointed chin were smiling and observing the observers. Carver wondered if the woman was Katia Marsh.

It took only about ten minutes to drive the Olds down Shoreline and then follow the signs to the research center. It looked exactly like its photo in the brochure, but there was also a businesslike, functional feel to the place that gave the impression it existed primarily for research, and the tourist angle was merely a side endeavor to provide financing.

Carver noticed immediately that the research center provided an almost clear view of the Rainer estate, certainly a better view than from Henry's cottage. It was no mystery to Carver why Henry had spent time at the center and gotten to know one of its employees.

He left the Olds parked in the shade of a grouping of gigantic palm trees with their lower trunks painted white. Beyond the palms was a low buffer of what looked like old telephone poles laid out horizontally and fixed in place with heavy stakes, then a stretch of rocky soil and a wooden pier jutting out to deep green water. A dock was built perpendicular to the pier, but no boat was there. Old truck tires were lashed to the weathered wood of both pier and dock to prevent damage when hulls bumped against them.

Carver turned his back on the sea and limped through the sun's glare to the research center. He pushed open a door that led to a cool, gray-carpeted room whose walls were lined with information charts and underwater photographs. A thirtyish couple dressed like tourists was staring at some of the photos, moving in the trancelike shuffle of people combining vacation and edification. The man was holding an infant who gazed at Carver with incredibly round, curious eyes. In the back wall was a door lettered TIDE POOL ROOM. PLEASE TOUCH.

A small stuffed hammerhead shark was mounted in a glass case in the center of the room, swimming perpetually toward the door. The guy carrying the infant glanced at it, then left the woman and ambled over to stand and stare. Other than that, not much seemed to be happening here among the posters and enlarged photos of sea horses and sharks. Carver limped over and opened the door to the Tide Pool Room.

He was on a square steel landing from which half a dozen black-enameled metal steps descended to a concrete floor. The Tide Pool Room was blue-painted cinder block, the bottom half of which was below ground level. Not the usual sort of construction in southern Florida, but Carver figured it was to lend strength to the sides of the tank where the big shark swam in endless circles, eyeing the

outside world with the unconcerned expression of an expert poker player with aces in the hole. What, me wanna
get out and devour a couple of tourists? Naw!

The seaward wall was thick glass from top to bottom to
provide a view of the shark. Lined along the other three
walls were what looked like large trays on wooden legs.
There were a few inches of seawater in the trays, and coral
and plant life. And an assortment of creatures that might
be found in the shallow reaches of the sea and in tide pools
left by receding waves. Two elderly women were standing
near one of the trays. They wore baggy knee-length shorts
and identical blue T-shirts lettered LAST HETEROSEXUAL
VIRGIN ON KEY WEST. The larger of the two was poking
an exploratory finger at the top of a starfish. The other
woman was glaring with distance at a large crablike creature that was furiously waving its antennae as if warning
her to keep hands off, it had had enough of people like
this for one day.

Watching this all with an expression as unreadable as
the shark's was a blond woman in her twenties, wearing a
white smock like the ones in the brochure photos. But she
wasn't at all like the woman in the brochure. She was
enticingly on the plump side and almost beautiful, with a
squarish face, large blue eyes, and a ski-jump nose. Her
blond hair was cut short and hung straight at the sides and
in bangs over her wide forehead. It was a simple, convenient hairdo, just right for jumping in the water and frol-
icking with the dolphins, then shaking dry, but on her it
seemed stylish.

She noticed Carver on the landing, smiled at him, then
looked back at the tourists to make sure they didn't hurt
the starfish. Carver set the tip of his cane and descended the
steel stairs. He was wearing moccasins as usual, since
they had no laces to tie, and the only noise on the steps
was the clunking of his cane. Down in the room now, he
could hear the throbbing hum of a filter pump, or maybe
simply the air-conditioning. It made him feel as if he were
in a submarine.

He stood before the nearest display and stared at the
largest snail he'd ever seen. The elderly woman got tired

of the starfish, volunteered without being asked that she and her friend were from Canada, then left. Carver continued to stare at the snail. For all he knew, it was staring back at him.

The blond woman in the white smock said, "You can touch anything you'd like."

He thought he'd better not touch the answer to that. He said, "Are you Katia Marsh?"

"You asking me or the sea snail?"

He turned to look at her. She was smiling. "You," he said.

"You're not really interested in the snail, are you?"

"Why do you say that?"

"I'm not sure. You don't strike me as a tourist. Or a scientist."

"Maybe I just like French cuisine."

She looked slightly ill but her smile stayed.

"I'm a friend of Henry Tiller."

"Oh." She took a small step toward him. "How is Henry?"

"He's doing all right. He'll be in the hospital in Miami for a while, though."

"I want to send him a card. Can you tell me what hospital he's in?"

Carver told her, along with the room number. She carefully wrote down the information in a spiral notebook she'd removed from one of the smock's big square pockets. Water flowing into one of the trays made a soft trickling sound.

"Now," she said, retracting the tip of her ballpoint pen and slipping it and the notebook back in the pocket, "you're Fred Carver."

"How'd you know?"

"Word gets around Key Montaigne in a hurry." Behind her the shark was circling, circling, easily ten feet long, and streamlined and deadly. "You're staying at Henry's cottage."

"Sort of house-sitting," Carver said.

"I thought you were investigating the hit and run."

"My, my, word really does get around." He used his cane to point to the circling shark. "Doesn't he ever rest?"

"No," Katia said, "they never stop swimming. If they do, they drown."

"Drown?"

"The water forced through their system by their forward motion is what provides their oxygen."

"Interesting."

She brightened. "Really?"

"Sure. I know people who can only breathe during forward motion."

She cocked her head and looked him up and down as if he were interesting sea life. Her gaze snagged for a moment on the cane and stiff leg, then moved on. "Would you like me to give you the tour?"

"That's why I came here," Carver said.

She smiled in a way that let him know she didn't believe that for one second.

She stood next to him and they moved along the displays while she identified each sea creature, some of them by their Latin names. Most of them she merely pointed to, but a few she picked up so Carver could view them more closely, or look at their undersides.

"You're a biologist?" he asked, when they'd made the circuit of the room.

"Oceanographer, actually. However, I'm interested primarily in the habits of sharks, which is Dr. Sam's field."

"Dr. Sam?"

"Dr. Samuel Bing. He's very big in shark research. Dr. Sam's what everyone calls him. He's chief researcher and director of the research center and aquarium. When I graduated from college last year, one of my professors suggested I write him and ask if he needed an assistant. I was surprised when I got an answer, even more surprised when I got the job."

"Why sharks?" Carver asked.

Katia crossed her arms, hugging herself as if chilled, but she was smiling. "Did you know there are sensory areas all over them that pick up distress signals of prey? In fact, their entire bodies are sensors, with a compulsion to feed. They're like living fossils, as primitive as anything on land or in the sea, yet so little is actually known about them. It's the mystery that attracts me, I suppose.'' The shark behind the glass glided close, gazing out with the round, merciless eyes that had seen the Paleolithic era.

''They intelligent?'' Carver asked.

''Not in the way we think of intelligence. But they're ideally suited for what they do.''

''Which is?''

''They're perfect predators. They eat and eat and eat.''

''I remember that from the movie.'' Looking at the shark's torpedo-shaped, powerful body and toothy, underslung jaw, he could believe everything Katia told him, and almost share her fascination. Something about predators. ''This Dr. Sam, does he live here at the research center?''

''Almost. He and his wife, Millicent, have a house about quarter of a mile down Shoreline. Practically next door.''

''She the woman in the brochure photo?''

Katia seemed confused for a moment, then said, ''Oh! Right. That's Dr. Sam and Millicent.''

''When I drove up,'' Carver said, ''I noticed this place affords a clear view of the Walter Rainer estate. Henry ever ask about that?''

She hesitated, carefully sizing up Carver before sharing. He liked that. ''I'm sure Henry doesn't want me spreading it around, but yeah, he wondered if I'd seen anything suspicious going on over there.''

''And had you?''

She looked down at a display of anemones. ''I'm not sure. I live in town, but occasionally I stay overnight here. There's a lot of activity over there some nights. Early mornings, actually.''

''What kind of activity?''

''Can't tell from here. All I ever saw were lights, people moving around. And that big boat over there puts to sea now and then at odd hours.''

''Any of it mean anything to you?'' Carver asked.

She laughed. ''I thought you were the detective.''

''That's why I asked. I'm a snoop.''

''No, it means little to me. But on the other hand, I haven't given it much thought. My mind's on my work.''

''Sharks,'' Carver said.

''And my other duties. I'm a scientist, not a busybody.''

''You think Henry Tiller's a busybody?''

She slid her hand into a pocket but wasn't reaching for anything. Left it there. ''No, Henry gets a little befuddled at times, but he's not someone I'd take lightly.''

''But you're not concerned about his suspicions.''

Her square chin jutted forward aggressively, though her voice remained pleasant. ''I told you, I'm interested only in my work. That might sound cold, but it's what's important to me at this point in my life. It's why I moved here.''

''You could never be cold,'' Carver assured her. ''I'd like to talk with Dr. Sam.''

''Can't do that for a while,'' she said. ''He's on his way to Mexico on the *Fair Wind*, to buy for the research center.''

''The *Fair Wind* his boat?''

''The center's, actually. It used to be a fishing boat, but Dr. Sam converted it to a diving platform for research at sea.''

''You're not one of those people who go down in metal cages and stir up the sharks, are you?''

''You guessed it,'' she said. ''Of course, we also use the *Fair Wind* to collect aquarium specimens. Tourism's what keeps this place in the black.''

''Well, I'll talk with Dr. Sam another time.''

''Millicent might be home, if you wanna talk to her.''

''I think I'll do that,'' Carver said. He took a step toward the exit, then stopped and leaned with both hands on the crook of his cane. ''I appreciate the tour. I learned something.''

''About sea life?''

He smiled. ''I'm single-minded about my work, too.''

''I could sense that in you,'' she told him. ''That's why I liked you right off. But then, I like sharks.''

She watched him as he clomped up the steel steps with

his cane and shouldered through the door to the upper
level.

THE BINGS' house was constructed of the same beige brick
and cinder block as the research center, and probably built
at the same time. It had a green door and shutters, and
bougainvillea with lush red blossoms climbing a trellis in
front of the picture window. Bees droned and darted in
among the blossoms. There were three small date palms
in the front yard, and a larger palm tree that leaned over
the side of the house and touched the roof. The sea wind
rattled their fronds. The drapes were closed behind the
trellis, and no one answered Carver's ring.

He stood patiently in the sun, listening to the big tree's
palm fronds scrape the roof tiles, watching a brown and
lavender butterfly flit about and sample the bougainvillea,
unmolested by the bees. A rivulet of sweat ran from his
armpit down the inside of his right arm, almost making it
to his wrist before evaporating.

The brass plaque on the door was engraved DR. SAMUEL
AND MILLICENT BING. Carver was at the right house, but
Millicent simply wasn't home. He didn't mind too much.
He could catch up with Dr. Sam or his wife within the
next few days. It probably wasn't important to talk to them
anyway. They weren't on Effie's list.

He limped back to the Olds and lowered himself behind
the steering wheel. Even in the short time he'd been out
of the car, the sun-heated leather upholstery had become
almost too hot to sit on. He started the big V-8 engine
that was now as prehistoric as sharks, shoved the hot metal
gearshift lever to R, and backed out of the driveway onto
Shoreline. As he drove away, he glanced in his rearview
mirror and saw a black van with darkly tinted windows
parked on the shoulder near the Bings' driveway.

A short distance down the road, he looked again in the
mirror.

The van was following him.

9

THE GAME seemed to be intimidation. The black van accelerated to within a few feet of the Olds's rear bumper. Even the windshield was tinted so dark the driver was visible only as a vague and ominous form. Darth Vader on wheels.

Carver goosed the Olds, and the van stayed on its bumper as if being towed. To his left was a shallow slope to the sea. Flashing past on his right were driveways, fence posts, shrubbery, terrain he'd rather not test in a straight line at high speed.

The Olds was roaring along with speed in reserve, but the way the van had stayed with it suggested it had plenty of power, too. Probably a modified engine. It was questionable that the Olds could simply outrun the van, even if the island were large enough to allow it.

Carver tapped the brake pedal and gradually slowed to thirty, tensing his body and waiting for impact as the van tried to force him off the road.

But the van's driver was skillful and had other ideas. It slackened its speed in perfect synchronization with Carver's and continued to fill the rearview mirror. The sun glinted dully off its blunt black nose. The shape of the driver was as still and remote as an obscure reflection in the dark glass.

Carver braked the Olds hard, twisted the sweat-slippery steering wheel and made a skidding right turn onto a narrow gravel road that led through dense foliage. The van followed, but fell back to about a hundred yards behind Carver. Maybe the sudden maneuver had spooked the driver. Nice to know he might be human. Though the terrain was flat, the road snaked and became even narrower.

It ended at a faded, red and white diagonally striped barrier that was almost overgrown with bougainvillea.

Carver stopped the Olds a few feet from the barrier, sat with the motor rumbling and stared into the rearview mirror. Heat from the exhaust system was building beneath the car; he could feel it rising through the metal floor and going up his pants legs. The sole of his left moccasin was growing warm against the rubber floor mat.

The van had also stopped, about a hundred yards back. It, too, simply sat with its motor idling.

The two vehicles stayed that way in the bright sun for almost a full minute. Perspiration was trickling down Carver's face, stinging the corners of his eyes. His jaws ached and he realized he was clenching his teeth. The van stayed in his rearview mirror as if painted there. Its headlights reminded him of malevolent, unblinking eyes.

Time dragged. The haze of dust raised by the braking vehicles slowly settled in the sunlight, like particles after an explosion.

"Hell with this!" Carver said aloud, and jammed the transmission into Reverse.

He twisted his torso and slung his arm over the seat back, feeling his sweat-plastered shirt peel away from the upholstery. His palms were moist, but he got as firm a grip as possible on the slick steering wheel and tromped the accelerator. The Olds snarled and shot backward, raising more dust that partially obscured his vision and rolled in through the windows so he could feel its grit between his teeth. The car swayed and bucked as he aimed it with difficulty at such high speed, but despite the delicate reverse steering, he was able to stay dead on course. The driver of the black van was about to get a face full of vintage Detroit.

Dust billowed from the van's back wheels. For an instant Carver thought it was going to speed forward to meet him. Then he realized it was moving in reverse, too.

The Olds got to within ten feet of it before they reached the coast highway. The van didn't pause as it roared backward onto the paved road; its driver's guess that there'd be no cross traffic was right. With a screech of tires, the van leaned hard to the right and skidded in a sharp turn so its blunt nose was pointed north on Shoreline. Carver stood on the Olds's brake pedal, yanking the steering wheel to the left.

But his sweating hands slipped from the wheel and it spun out of control, bending back his thumb. The Olds shot across the road and skidded sideways on the soft gravel shoulder, met the grade and rocked up on two wheels. Higher, higher, tilting the view out the windshield. Carver hooked an arm through the steering wheel and braced himself.

The car hung poised for what seemed like minutes, while his heart stopped beating and he didn't breathe.

Too heavy to turn over, the Olds dropped right-side up with a heavy *Whump!* as the suspension bottomed out. Carver's teeth clacked together as he bounced from the seat. The safety belt kept him from bashing his head on the roof.

He shook off his disorientation, seeing the black van disappear around a curve on Shoreline. His arm or leg must have hit the transmission lever as he'd been jounced around, forcing it in Neutral. He crammed it into Drive, stomped on the accelerator, and realized the engine had died.

By the time he got it started again, he knew he'd never catch up with the van.

As he pulled slowly back onto the road, he saw that the temperature light on the dashboard was winking red. He drove cautiously and found if he kept the big car at around twenty-five, feeding it very little gas and letting the ocean breeze sift through the grill and play over the radiator and engine, the light blinked less frequently. If it didn't glow red steadily, he figured he wasn't doing the engine permanent harm.

He nursed the Olds into Fishback, then down Main to Norton's Gas 'n' Go. Norton was nowhere in sight, but a cheerful teenage boy with greasy blue overalls and a thousand pimples replaced a sprung hose clamp that had pulled loose when the big engine had rocked on its mounts. Apparently that was the only reason the Olds was running hot.

Carver splashed cold water over his arms and face while the car was being worked on, then paid the kid with Visa and drove down Main to police headquarters.

The grandmotherly receptionist-dispatcher recognized him and gave him a milk-and-cookies smile. A gangly uniformed cop he hadn't seen before was bent over at the waist and rooting through a bottom file drawer. His legs were long, his blue uniform pants creased too sharp to touch. Chief Wicke was standing nearby watching him with his fists on his hips, as if he'd just chewed out the skinny cop.

Carver told Wicke he'd like to talk to him, and Wicke glared at the cop and said, "Don't give up till you find it, Dewey!" He motioned with a jerk of his head for Carver to come into his office.

Wicke listened silently as Carver told him about the encounter with the black van. He rocked far back in his padded chair and stared up at the ceiling, as if maybe pictures accompanying Carver's words were up there.

"Davy Mathis has such a van," he said, when Carver was finished. He let the chair fall forward. The breeze from his sudden descent stirred papers on his cluttered desk. "Was it a Dodge?"

"I don't know," Carver said. "Production model full-size vans look pretty much alike, and I was busy trying to stay alive. Except for the black-tinted windows and missing license plates, it was just a van."

"Well, it mighta been Davy's, all right, but I gotta tell you there are a lotta vans like that running around the Keys." Wicke stood up out of his chair and paced around the massive desk, dragging his fingertips on its surface as if testing for dust. "I think I better drive out and talk with Davy nonetheless. If it was him driving the van, he'll have a solid alibi. Probably playing cards with ten people a hundred miles away, or doing charity work for the world's unfortunates." Wicke grinned. "I'd say the better the alibi, the more likely it is he was the one in the van."

Carver said, "I like your approach."

"What's your plan now?"

"I'll try talking to Millicent Bing later today. Other than that, I'm not sure."

"Millicent was probably home," Wicke said. "I wouldn't call her a recluse, but she's shy."

"Too shy to answer the door?"

"Sure. It'd be just like her." Chief Wicke chewed on the inside of his cheek, staring at Carver. "The business with the van don't scare you, huh?"

"It scares me," Carver said. "A nautical nasty like Davy's a scary guy."

"If it *was* Davy."

Carver said nothing.

Wicke played with a massive turquoise ring on the middle finger of his right hand. It looked like cheap souvenir-shop jewelry, but it would be as formidable as brass knuckles if Wicke punched someone. "I talked to a few people I know up north, Carver. Inquired about you."

"What'd these people say?"

"Not to be fooled by the fact you walk with a cane. That you was one tough sonuvabitch. They right?"

Carver said, "Tough's relative."

"Uh-huh."

Wicke tucked his shirt in beneath his meal-sack stomach paunch and ambled toward the door, a signal that he had matters to attend to and Carver had taken up enough of his time. Fair enough, Carver thought, and braced with his cane and stood up.

Wicke said, "I'll give you a call after I talk with Davy, let you know what he said."

"If it was Davy," Carver told him, "it means there might well be something to Henry Tiller's suspicions."

"Could be. Davy's a real piss-cutter, though. Running interlopers off the road might be his idea of sport."

"Interlopers?"

"That could be how he sees you. You can bet he knows about your staying up at Henry's place, getting around the island and asking your questions."

"It's the hit and run I've been asking about," Carver pointed out.

"But Davy sees the connection between you and Henry, and he might know about Henry's suspicion that Walter Rainer's up to no good. Davy might add that together and figure his employment's in jeopardy. Or maybe he'd do something crazy like trying to throw a scare into you just because of loyalty to Rainer. After all, Rainer was the one gave him a chance in this world when nobody else'd give him spit."

"You make it sound like him killing me on the highway would've been an admirable act of servitude."

"Now, now, it ain't that bad, Carver. But keep in mind we're standing here just *assuming* it was Davy in that van to begin with."

"Davy or the Easter Bunny," Carver said, remembering what Henry Tiller had said about the likelihood of coincidence.

Wicke knew what he meant. "That bunny don't have a valid Florida driver's license, far as I know. In my capacity, I can't afford to lean on the wrong man."

Carver wondered if he meant Walter Rainer had too much money and local clout to risk going up against. It was people like Rainer who kept an appointed chief of police like Lloyd Wicke in office, and people like Rainer who could start a political ball rolling that might knock a cop all the way back to civilian. But Carver didn't know for sure that Wicke was intimidated by Rainer, so he said nothing.

"I'll just clean up some paperwork here," Wicke said, "then I'll go talk to Davy. Maybe we can throw light on this thing."

Carver thanked him and limped from the office. There was no point getting on the wrong side of Chief Wicke, but he didn't think he could count on him for a lot of help. The incident had convinced Carver that Henry was on to something. Carver, younger and taken more seriously than Henry, would pose a genuine threat, so Davy, on his own or on Walter Rainer's orders, had attempted to scare him off the case.

He slid in behind the Olds's steering wheel and sat with the windows up and the engine and air conditioner off, thinking and perspiring. It would be necessary to move in on the Rainer estate and watch it carefully, and for that he'd need help. It was time to ask Beth to drive down and join him.

Carver was aware he tended to be too independent, to become obsessive and develop tunnel vision to go along with what Desoto often referred to as his dog-with-a-rag neuroses. Once committed to anything, he found it very difficult to give up, even when logically he should. Obsession could be his weakness as well as his strength; a dog tugging on a rag sometimes lost a tooth and the rag.

He was sure he wanted Beth on Key Montaigne because he needed somebody reliable to spell him staking out the Rainer estate. It couldn't be because he missed her and needed her in ways other than professional. Sitting there on the sweat-moistened upholstery and suffering in the heat, that kind of need must be the farthest thing from his mind.

Right.

That settled, he started the engine and got what he could from the laboring air conditioner.

10

It was late the next morning before Carver was able to contact Beth. She'd been at the library working on a paper for a post-graduate communications class at the University of Florida, but she told him it would be no problem to set it aside and help him in Key Montaigne. She'd leave soon as possible, she said, and should be able to drive south and join him by that evening. "You and I got a dinner date," she told him.

He said he'd make reservations at the Key Lime Pie.

"I gotta dress up for that place?" Beth asked.

"Casual clothes are de rigueur there," he assured her, wondering what Fern the waitress would think if Beth strolled into the Key Lime Pie on Carver's arm, looking like a high-fashion model for *Ebony*.

"Bring the infrared binoculars," he added. "Some of what we'll be doing's at night."

"I'll just bet." He liked her tone of voice.

"Incidentally," he added, "bring my gun, too."

" 'Incidentally,' huh? You step in something nasty down there, Fred?"

"I'm not sure yet. The gun's in a brown envelope taped to the back of my top dresser drawer."

"I know where it is, and I'll bring it with me. You just try'n stay alive till I get there to take care of you."

65

Carver said, "Bring along some extra ammunition."

"Never leave home without it."

After hanging up on Beth, Carver rummaged through Henry's refrigerator and came up with the ingredients of lunch: some oat bran health bread Henry kept in there so it would stay fresh longer, extra-lean sliced turkey that smelled edible enough, some Heartline low-cholesterol cheese, a half-used jar of vitamin-enriched diet mayonnaise. Henry apparently feared slipping physically as well as mentally in his old age.

Carver built a sandwich that was probably no more than two or three calories, then washed it down with three beers from the six-pack of Budweisers in the back of the refrigerator. He reminded himself he'd better stop by the Food Emporium Supermarket in town and pick up some more beer and food. He and Beth might get tired of romping through the culinary delights of Fishback's eateries.

Before returning to the Bing residence, he decided to give Millicent Bing a call. Shy as Chief Wicke said she was, she might be more likely to answer the phone than the doorbell.

The Bings were listed in Key Montaigne's thin phone directory. It took ten rings, but finally Millicent picked up the receiver and uttered a tentative hello.

Carver told her who he was, then said, "Katia Marsh over at the research center assured me you'd talk with me."

"Katia said that?"

"Just this morning."

"Talk with you about what?" She had the wary voice of a hostile witness at her own trial.

"Henry Tiller."

"You mean his accident?"

"If it was that."

A pause while she thought things over. "You're not from an insurance company, are you? Trying to trick me?"

He laughed at the absurd notion that he might be devious; maybe he'd sell her some magazine subscriptions while he was at it. "No, no, honestly, I'm just a friend of Henry's who promised him I'd look into what happened. I can be at your place within fifteen minutes, Mrs. Bing, and I won't take up much of your time at all. I thought I'd just stop by for a few minutes before lunch, while I was out.''

The connection was silent for so long he wondered if she'd hung up. Then: "Oh, I suppose it'll be all right, if it's soon as you say."

"It will be, Mrs. Bing. Thank you." He hung up before she could change her uncertain mind. She seemed the type who reconsidered everything, always combed her hair twice.

Less than fifteen minutes later he was standing on the shaded porch of the Bings' house by the sea, hoping the dozen or so bees circling among the bougainvillea wouldn't get it into their collective mind to swarm in his direction before his knock was answered. One of them made a darting, circling pass at him, like an armed reconnaissance plane.

Before the bee had a chance to return with friends, the door swung open and Carver saw that Millicent Bing was indeed the sharp-faced woman in the research center brochure. She was thin, and slightly stoop-shouldered despite the disguising oversized shoulder pads beneath her silky gray blouse. She had narrowed and suspicious blue eyes and a marvelous pale complexion. Her sharp, elongated nose and receding chin gave her the look of a pretty but nervous ferret.

"Mr. Carver?" Her voice sounded even more tentative in person than on the phone.

He smiled at her and confirmed who he was, then thanked her again for letting him take up her valuable time. That seemed to make her feel guilty, and she hastily invited him inside.

"I notice you've got a bee problem on the porch," Carver told her.

"They're like sentries," she said. "They discourage unwelcome visitors."

She could sure put a guest at ease.

It was almost cold in the living room. The severe modern furniture and chrome-framed, surreal-looking color photographs of sea life didn't add one degree of warmth.

Millicent invited Carver to sit down, and he shifted his weight over his cane then lowered himself into a white vinyl chair with bleached wood arms. It was hard as cold concrete, but it enabled him to extend his bad leg out in front of him comfortably. He could get up out of the chair easily, too, which was always a consideration for a man with a cane.

Millicent perched on the edge of the low vinyl sofa as if poised for the start of a race. She would have tripped and fallen at the sound of the starter's gun, though, because her beige skirt was wound like a shroud around her legs. Carver asked her a few perfunctory questions about Henry to put her at ease, then said, "Henry seems to think something might have been going on over at the Walter Rainer estate. I noticed there was a clear view of the grounds from the research center, and I wondered if you or your husband ever observed anything there worth mentioning."

She looked flustered for a moment, then puzzled. "What on earth do you mean by 'something might have been going on'?"

"Well, Henry wasn't specific, so I thought I'd ask you and your husband."

"Dr. Sam's in Mexico," she said, "buying specimens that can only be found along the coast in that area."

"Katia Marsh told me that's where he is," Carver said, wondering if she called her husband "Dr. Sam" in bed. "About the Rainer estate—"

"Neither my husband nor I are nosy people, Mr. Carver," she interrupted. She raised her pointed but almost nonexistent chin in a futile effort to look haughty. "Nor would we like anyone nosing into *our* business."

"I'm not asking you to be nosy," he assured her. "Or to gossip. Henry's been run down and almost killed, and the car sped away. A crime's been committed."

She looked astounded. "And you assume it has something to do with Walter Rainer?"

"I don't assume anything, Mrs. Bing, I'm only asking."

"Well, the answer's no, I've never observed anything

unusual there, and my husband's never mentioned to me that he has, either.''

"Are you also a research scientist?"

She seemed amused by the question. "Not I, Mr. Carver. I played the faithful faculty wife for years, until Dr. Sam got the funding to start the research center and aquarium." She sounded oddly bitter. Must have realized it, and smiled. She had an overbite but an unexpectedly nice smile. "It's Dr. Sam who's the biologist, and that's fine with me. Early in my academic endeavors, I found that science bored me." She stood up and smoothed her skirt over her thighs. Carver was boring her, too, the gesture suggested; why didn't he leave?

He couldn't think of a good reason not to, and the base of his spine was beginning to ache, so he set the tip of the cane in the Berber weave carpet and stood up from the uncomfortable chair. "I'd like to ask Dr. Sam some of the same questions," he said. "When will he be back?"

"When he gets back," Millicent said. Her Adam's apple bobbed in her long throat. "I mean, he doesn't keep to a regular schedule when he goes on buying trips." She moved toward the door. He noticed that she had almost no breasts, but an elegant lower body. "If you don't mind, Mr. Carver, I've got a great deal of work to do."

"I didn't think you worked."

"I do the bookkeeping for the center."

"I see." He limped toward the door. She was alongside him, then ahead of him, holding it open. Warm air rolled in from outside. "When your husband returns," he said, "would you or he phone me at Henry Tiller's cottage?"

"Certainly, but I don't know when that'll be."

Carver smiled and said, "Whenever. Thanks for seeing me, Mrs. Bing."

She didn't answer. Her mind seemed to be far away as he stepped out onto the porch and she closed the door behind him.

A bee followed him as he limped back to the Olds. He used his cane to bat it like a baseball, and didn't see where it went, so he hurriedly got into the car.

He was sure Millicent Bing was watching him from the

window behind the bougainvillea-strewn trellis as he backed out of the driveway onto Shoreline.

She was obviously nervous about something, maybe even afraid, but it wasn't necessarily connected with Henry Tiller or Walter Rainer. Carver cautioned himself not to see something sinister where there was no proof. Fear could become habit, then personality. As with a lot of people, Millicent Bing's unease might be about something relatively innocent that had ingrained itself as dread, maybe even something that could be traced back to her childhood.

The Easter Bunny?

11

CARVER DROVE back to the cottage and called Henry Tiller at Faith United in Miami. Henry answered the phone on the third ring. He sounded weak.

"How're you making it, Henry?" Carver asked.

"They got inside me with their knives, took out some of this, some of that, sewed me up where I was tore. What there's left of me's gonna be okay, I think. They gave me a CAT scan yesterday and now they say I got a head injury. Hell, that's just what I need, the way people think of me already."

"They're gonna have to start taking you more seriously, Henry."

"Ah! You're on to the bastards?"

Carver filled Henry in on what had occurred since his arrival on Key Montaigne. He tried not to make it sound as if they had enough to send Walter Rainer to the gas chamber.

When he was finished, Henry sounded stronger, exhilarated. He said, "Gotta be that shit-bum Davy tried to run you off the road, Carver."

"Wicke thinks so, too, I'm sure, only he won't admit it."

"Wicke'd be a good cop if he wasn't running so scared of his job. But the fact is, his position's a political appointment, so he kisses ass to keep it. And Walter Rainer's ass is one of the kissed. I up and told Wicke that one time. Got him irritated, I think."

Carver smiled. He could imagine.

"I figure it was Davy in a rented car tried to do me in, too," Henry said.

"Wouldn't doubt it," Carver told him. "Proving it's the hard part. You know police work."

"Sure as hell do. From years in the department in Milwaukee, then later in Lauderdale. You give me a call when you learn anything else, you hear?"

"I hear," Carver said.

"I think you oughta find out about that dead boy, too. The one washed up on the beach. Did I tell you there was traces of cocaine found in his blood?"

"You told me."

"Something like that happens, and that ass-kisser Wicke's got the nerve to tell me there ain't no drug trafficking to speak of on Key Montaigne."

"Effie seems to agree with him," Carver said. "She told me there's a fair amount of drug use, but nothing bigtime happening."

"Hell, Effie's just a kid. She don't run in the kinda major money circles that'd deal hard stuff."

"The boy found washed up on the beach was just a kid, too. Younger than Effie, in fact."

"Younger in years, maybe," Henry said, "but he was a runaway. Two months on the street and Effie'd be ten years older, God willing it never happens."

"You're right about that," Craver said. He'd met too many kids not old enough to shave or have regular periods, whose lives were set on unalterable courses to hell. Drugs were always involved. Always.

"There was cocaine in that dead boy's blood, Carver. I figure we oughta find out what that means."

"We will. You get some rest, though, Henry. Best thing you can do is get well enough for them to release you so you can come down here and help with the investigation."

"You're right, damnit! You keep in touch with me, you hear, Carver."

"I hear," Carver said again.

"This phone call was better painkiller than them little

white pills the nurses give me. I might disconnect these tubes they got plugged into me and check myself out.''

Carver didn't know if he was serious. ''Listen, Henry, just rest. Recuperate.''

''Aw, that's what I'll do,'' Henry said. ''You stay in touch, Carver, you hear?''

Carver said he heard. Hung up. Drank the last beer in Henry's refrigerator.

He'd go nuts waiting in the little cottage for Beth to arrive, so he decided to drive into Fishback and pick up the beer and groceries, then go by police headquarters and see if Chief Wicke was around. Carver was working for Henry, and Henry was right again: It was time to find out more about the boy who'd mixed cocaine and seawater.

THE FOOD Emporium was hot, humid, and crowded. Every resident and tourist in the area must have decided to go shopping today. Carver limped along with his cane, bumping with his grocery cart and getting bumped in return. The cart's left front wheel squealed and hopped with regularity, exactly the way they manufactured them. Every other passing cart was equipped with a squawling, grasping infant in the wire basket-seat where produce normally went. A fat woman in a frilly white sundress nudged Carver aside with her hip and snatched the last jar of dill pickles from a top shelf. ''I got a coupon,'' she explained.

Finally, after checking out behind a man with twenty items in the ten-items-or-less express lane, he limped behind the squeaking cart to his car and slung the plastic bags into the trunk. Shoved the cart out of the way and drove from the lot feeling like a commando who'd just raided an enemy storehouse.

Deciding that fifteen or twenty minutes in the Olds's trunk wouldn't spoil anything that needed refrigeration, he drove to police headquarters, where the mayhem was less frequent and more controlled than at the Food Emporium. He parked in the side lot, in the shade of the building, and struggled out of the car to lean on his cane.

The Toyota station wagon he'd seen there yesterday rolled into the lot and braked alongside the Olds. Today it had a magnetic cherry light stuck on its roof. Chief Wicke climbed out. Every hair on his head was in place and he looked dry and cool, even had his dark blue uniform tie tightly knotted. The Toyota must have a terrific air conditioner. Not like the Olds.

"Mr. Carver again," Wicke said, walking around the Olds and showing a smile as frosty as the rest of him. "Here to see me, I presume."

"Am I getting to be a pest?" Carver asked. He could feel rivulets of sweat trickling down his back; they felt like insects crawling toward his belt.

"I'll hide behind the Fifth Amendment," Wicke said. "C'mon inside."

Carver followed Wicke into his office and told him what he wanted, and Wicke had the skinny cop he'd been lambasting yesterday pull the file and bring it in.

"Thanks, Dewey," Wicke said amiably. They were on the best of terms today.

Dewey withdrew, poker-faced, and closed the door behind him. He'd been chewing candy or breath mint and left in his wake the scent of peppermint.

"Dead kid's name turned out to be Leonard Eugene Everman," Wicke said, staring into the open file folder. "Just turned thirteen before he died. Coroner's report says death by drowning, traces of cocaine in the blood but not nearly enough to make him an O.D. victim. Enough to fuck up his judgment and swimming ability, however."

"Any other marks on the body?"

"A few bruises, some abrasions on his ankles, from where he mighta been tossed around on the rocks before he died. Or he coulda been in a fight before he drowned." Wicke shook his head sadly. "The kid was a runaway, but at least he had a family cared enough to claim the remains. His mom and dad. They were plenty broken up, too. Obviously cared a lot. Maybe the poor kid coulda got his life straightened out eventually." Wicke lifted a pencil between his stubby fingers, then let it fall and bounce on the desk. A gesture of frustration, seen more and more in the War on Drugs. "Narcotics are a goddamn curse from hell on this country, burning up the young folks."

Carver agreed. Plenty of older folks were burning, too. No one seemed to know how to extinguish the fire. "Who found the body?" he asked.

"Couple of tourists from Atlanta, out jogging one morning and saw it floating in shallow water near shore. No clothes on it, so we were puzzled about identity at first. Then the parents read in a Miami paper about the kid being found, and drove down and identified and claimed the body."

"The boy was from Miami?"

"Yeah. He'd run away before and been mixed up with drugs. Thirteen, Jesus! Anyway, the parents' names are Frank and Selma Everman. You want their address?"

"Yeah, I think I'll talk to them."

"I don't see what any of this has to do with Henry Tiller getting run over."

"It might have to do with Walter Rainer," Carver said, "which might have to do with Henry being in the hospital."

"The drug angle?"

"Sure."

"I'm not naive, but I can't see Rainer involved in drug trafficking."

"He's got a boat and is within easy turnaround distance of the Mexican coast."

"There're thousands of people like that in Florida," Wicke said. "Even me."

Carver smiled. "You're lucky Henry doesn't suspect you."

"I am at that," Wicke said, "since he's got a persistent peckerhead like you working for him." He wrote down the names and address of Leonard Everman's parents on a memo sheet headed "From the Desk of Chief Wicke" and handed it to Carver.

Carver folded it, slipped it into his damp shirt pocket and thanked the chief.

"Anything else?" Wicke asked wearily.

"No," Carver said, standing up. "I better get outa here before my milk sours."

Wicke gazed at him strangely as he limped out. You meet all kinds in this work, the look implied.

Wasn't that the truth?

12

A FEW minutes before five o'clock, Beth arrived. Carver was sitting in the shade on the screened-in porch, drinking a beer, when he heard tires crunching in the driveway and her white LeBaron convertible pulled into view and parked behind the Olds.

She didn't notice him on the porch as she got out of the car, placed her hands on her hips and glanced around. Standing next to the LeBaron with its top down, she seemed even taller than her five feet, ten inches. She was wearing Roman sandals, loose-fitting khaki shorts, a baggy sleeveless blouse, and had a wildly colored bandanna wound around her head to keep her hair from getting mussed in the convertible. After the long drive in the wind and heat, any other woman would have been a mess, but Beth seemed to be modeling a trendy look for a high-class fashion magazine. Would she gaze haughtily into the distance?

She wrestled her bulky Gucci suitcase from the backseat of the car and lugged it up onto the porch. When she saw Carver, she looked surprised for a moment, then let the suitcase rest at her feet.

He smiled and said, "Want a beer?"

"Sure."

He limped past her into the cottage. When he came

back out on the porch a few minutes later carrying two Budweiser cans and a glass, she'd dragged a nylon-webbed aluminum chair over next to the yellow metal glider and sat down in it. Her long dark legs were crossed at the thighs; they looked fantastic. So did the rest of her. She was a woman who froze glances and inundated minds. His glance, his mind, anyway. He gave her the glass and one of the beer cans, then sat down in the glider and watched her pour beer, tilting the glass to achieve a precise head of foam.

He looked out through the screen at her mid-size convertible. Nice wheels, but nothing like when she was chauffeured around in a stretch limo when she was married to Roberto Gomez. She never seemed to miss the luxury of her life with the late drug lord, maybe because early in her own life she'd learned to exist without it. She'd finally found out who and what she was, and wanted out of Gomez's world. With Carver's help, she'd made it.

"Drive straight down?" he asked.

"Yeah, the wind felt good." She sipped her beer, somehow avoiding a mustache of foam. "That the place needs watching?" she asked, motioning languidly toward the Rainer estate and the *Miss Behavin'* riding gently at its dock. Perspiration gleamed on the well-defined but gentle angles of her cinnamon-hued face, lending her a sculptured air of nobility. In the colorful bandanna, she looked like a cross between a Zulu queen and British aristocracy.

"That's the place," he said.

"Can't make out much from here."

"That's okay. I scouted out a place closer in where we can observe most of what goes on outdoors, and maybe see in through the windows. I put together a blind like duck hunters use."

She took a long swallow of beer and looked around at the dense foliage beyond the screen. "Well, I brought mosquito repellent. Anything particular we're looking for over there?"

Carver told her everything he'd learned since arriving on Key Montaigne.

"Must be dealing drugs," she said when he'd finished.

"I'm not so sure," Carver said. "Maybe your background makes you think drugs are more pervasive than they are."

"Hah! Don't you listen to the drug czar in Washington? Half the country's high, other half thinks it's a tragedy but don't wanna pay to do anything about it. Drugs are everywhere, Fred, that's what I think."

"You were close to it," Carver said.

"Part of it."

"Okay, part of it. So you see drugs everywhere."

"Hmm. You saying the drug czar don't know shit?"

"I'm saying that. Takes a former addict to know about drugs. They're the *only* ones who *really* know."

"You're right about that," she said. "But what you told me, and that big-hulled boat sitting over there, it all smells like a dope operation. And I've got a nose for them, no pun intended."

"It probably is drugs, but I don't wanna see it that way without knowing for sure. You bring the night-vision binoculars?"

"Sure. Brought your gun, too. And the extra rounds of ammunition. It's all in my suitcase."

"Why don't you unpack, then we'll take a drive and I'll show you the town?"

She stood up with elegant slowness on those long, long legs, then bent from the waist and kissed him on the lips. He tasted the salt of her perspiration.

"Let's keep our priorities straight," she said. "Unpacking's third, driving into town's second. Know what's our first priority?"

He was sure she didn't really want to play a guessing game. Neither did he. He got up from the glider and went with her into the bedroom.

IT WAS seven o'clock when they drove into Fishback in Beth's LeBaron. After a two-minute familiarization cruise around town, they went into the Key Lime Pie. The air-conditioning had lost its battle with today's heat, and the restaurant was uncomfortably warm. The ceiling fans tick-

ing and rotating overhead seemed only to rearrange the
heat. The seats of the booth where Carver and Beth sat
were sticky and soft to the touch, as if the warmth might
be dissolving the mottled red vinyl upholstery. They studied the dinner menu. Carver noticed it was identical to the
lunch menu only with boosted prices. At least dress was
optional.

"Ain't cheap," Beth remarked.

"Consider the atmosphere," Carver told her.

"Humph. Atmosphere's hot, what it is."

Carver glanced around the restaurant. Customers sat at
about half the tables. Florida had a nasty fundamentalist
religious streak in it, and occasionally he and Beth had
run into trouble because she was black. But apparently
there was enough tourism on Key Montaigne for an inter-
racial couple not to be all that remarkable, and no one
seemed to be paying much attention to them. Carver was
glad. Beth could get combative over that sort of thing.

Fern wasn't on duty. A scrawny young waitress who
looked overheated enough to drop took their orders and
plodded back to the kitchen.

Carver noticed that a hugely fat man had moved onto
one of the bar stools visible through the archway and was
staring at them. He was average height but easily three
hundred pounds, with gray hair neatly framing a puffy yet
symmetrical face. A hundred pounds ago he must have
been handsome. Oddly enough, he looked quite cool,
wearing a cream-colored unstructured sport jacket and a
white shirt open at the neck to reveal a thick gold chain.
His pants were a blue so pale they were almost white, and
he was wearing immaculate unlaced white tennis shoes.
Carver imagined that with all the weight he carried, he
had foot trouble. His expression was neutral, but there was
something calculating about his intense blue eyes, as if
they had a life and intelligence all their own and were
assessing him and Beth. His back was to the bar, and one
of his elbows was propped on the smooth mahogany to
help support him on the stool. A highball glass was min-
iaturized in his bloated free hand, his wrist resting on his
knee.

Beth noticed him, too. She said, "Who's the fat guy eyeballing us?"

Carver said he didn't know.

Beth said, "Hope he ain't the leader of the Fishback chapter of the Ku Klux Klan." Uh-oh. Was she pumping up some anger?

"He's probably an equal-opportunity ogler," Carver told her, trying to head off trouble.

"I dunno. All he needs is the white hood to complete his ensemble."

The heat-plagued waitress arrived with the Budweiser Carver had ordered, and Beth's mineral water. Carver was glad to see her. She set the glasses on the table and said, "Lord, but it's hot in that kitchen."

"Bet it is," Carver said.

"Wouldn't you know they got me baking pies?"

"You happen to know the big fella at the bar? The one in the white jacket?"

She took a quick glance in the direction of the bar, which was all that was necessary, considering the size of the subject. "You must mean Mr. Rainer."

"Walter Rainer?" Carver asked.

"Uh-huh. He's a well-to-do gent, lives in a big fancy place out on Shoreline. Don't come in here very often."

Beth said, "Maybe it's an occasion."

The waitress looked at her curiously but said nothing. Instead she wiped her arm across her forehead and trudged resignedly toward the swinging doors leading to the hell that was the kitchen. With each step her rubber soles sounded like wet kisses on the heat-softened composition tiles.

"So that's our man," Carver said. He suspected Rainer had been apprised of his actions, and come into the Key Lime Pie so he could have a look at the troublemaker staying in Henry's cottage.

"Man's got eyes like a pig that can reason," Beth observed.

"Spoken like a communications graduate."

Rainer continued to study them dispassionately until the waitress arrived with their food, then he turned back toward the bar and hunched over his drink. The material of his tent-sized jacket stretched tautly across his shoulders as he raised his glass to sip from it.

Carver had the tuna steak again, the meal he'd had for lunch yesterday, only the more expensive evening version was decorated with parsley. Beth had blackened redfish with a salad, baked potato with sour cream, and several huge buttered dinner rolls. Her metabolism made dieting no concern of hers.

After dinner they had coffee and key lime pie. With the first bite, she licked her lips and arched her eyebrows in surprise. "This is really good! Better'n any pie I ever had in Key West."

"I wouldn't take you someplace served lousy food," Carver told her.

"Well, that's a subjective point of view." She forked another large bite of pie into her mouth, chewed and swallowed with enthusiasm. "One thing, with Walter Rainer here, we probably don't need to be watching his place."

"Probably not," Carver said, "but don't forget Davy and Hector. They do the muscle work."

"I can see why," she said, glancing at Rainer's corpulent form overflowing the bar stool. "Shame to let yourself get that heavy."

Carver thought that was easy for her to say; she could probably eat whale blubber and it wouldn't show up as fat. But he didn't feel like an argument, so he kept quiet. Beth could be difficult. The late Roberto Gomez had found that out in a big way.

"What's the plan tonight?" she asked.

"I drive up to Miami so I can talk to the drowned boy's parents tomorrow. You use the infrared glasses and set up surveillance on the Rainer estate, particularly the boat dock." He ate the last bite of his pie, savoring it. "Rainer's seen you with me, so be extra careful. Don't stray from your vantage point with the idea of working in closer for a better view. These people are as bad as the folks you met when you were with Roberto."

She nodded. "That's what I was trying to tell you earlier. Don't waste energy worrying over me, Fred. You know I can do whatever's necessary.''

He did know. Doing what was necessary, no matter how difficult, was what she was all about. It was what had enabled her to escape from an opulent but corrupt existence she knew was consuming her soul like cancer. Other women would have given up, drifted on the currents of cash and stayed with the animals that were Roberto and his associates. But Beth had fought and thought her way out of the slums of Chicago long before she'd met Roberto. Not giving up was her religion. Carver's, too. Which was why they got along so well. They gave each other room. They had to. But at times they could work together almost as beautifully as they made love, obsessive personalities sharing an obsession.

The sun was still blazing well above the horizon when they left the restaurant and crossed the baking street to where the LeBaron was parked. Half a block down from the car was a dusty black van with tinted windows. Now it was wearing a Florida license plate. Davy was leaning against the van, the faithful servant waiting for his master to come out of the bar. He nodded to Carver and smiled. The smile reminded Carver of the shark in the observation tank at the aquarium.

Beth noticed Davy and her body stiffened. She didn't have to ask who he was; she recognized evil when she saw it, and Davy wore it like a disease he took pride in.

Carver was relieved when the van didn't follow the LeBaron as they drove out of Fishback.

But then it wasn't necessary for Davy to follow. He knew where to find them.

13

CARVER SHOWED Beth the foliage-concealed vantage point from which she could maintain surveillance of the Rainer estate. He didn't have to familiarize her with the army-issue infrared binoculars for night vision; she'd used them before. She knew the tools of her late husband's trade.

After leaving her with the night glasses, her spray can of bug repellent, and a thermos jar of black coffee, Carver got in the Olds and started for Miami. He drove north on Route 1 until well after dark, and checked into a Days Inn on the outskirts of the city.

In the morning he ate a leisurely breakfast in the motel restaurant, then he sat on a concrete bench outside in the shade, smoking a Swisher Sweet cigar and reading *USA Today*. The world's problems were plainly visible in colorful bar graphs that suggested solutions might be equally as simple. He wished he could reduce the swirl of questions on Key Montaigne to a similar graphic display. Maybe it was in fact possible; maybe he should buy some crayons.

When he figured it was late enough, he drove the rest of the way into Miami to see Frank and Selma Everman, the drowned boy's parents.

The address Chief Wicke had given Carver turned out to belong to the Blue Flamingo Hotel on Collins Avenue in South Miami Beach. It was an area of old art deco buildings being renovated to comprise what the developers were ambitiously describing as the "Florida Riviera." Lots of pastel stucco and rounded corners, garish neon signs and neo-Egyptian decor of the sort seen in late-night TV movies from the twenties and thirties. An Al Capone/King Tut ambience. Carver thought that when it was finished, when the seediness had disappeared to leave only the reborn art deco essence, the Florida Riviera would be impressive indeed. Right now, the Blue Flamingo was still on the seedy side of that gradual gentrification.

It was a twenty-story building that, true to its name, was pale blue. Its peeling wooden window frames badly needed a coat of paint. But there were new tinted glass double doors beneath an ornate entrance arch with flamingos in bas-relief. Or possibly they were some sort of Egyptian bird. Carver limped through the doors and felt the welcome coolness of the lobby.

The interior renovation hadn't caught up with the building's exterior. The lobby floor was yellowed square tiles that long ago might have resembled veined marble. There was a long wooden counter with fancy brass bars beneath a cashier's sign. More brasswork ran along the front edge of the counter, broken only here and there to allow room for the registration book to be signed and money or credit cards to pass from hand to hand. The lobby furniture was gray, overstuffed, and threadbare. So were the two old men slouched in armchairs and gazing wistfully out through the entrance glass at the brightness of Collins Avenue and long-ago youth. The potted ferns in the lobby were artificial and looked as if they thrived on dimness and shunned the light. Like the old men. Probably the Blue Flamingo was still primarily a residence hotel, catering mostly to retirees without the money to play out the last act of their dwindling lives in anything like luxury.

Both men glanced emotionlessly at Carver as he limped across the lobby to the desk, as if between them they'd seen about everything and he was nothing new. The desk clerk was potbellied, middle-aged, had greasy black hair that looked dyed, and an ugly mole beneath his left eye that made Carver think of cancer. He noticed Carver and said, "Be with you in a sec," and finished leafing through what looked like invoices while Carver leaned against the desk with his elbow near a placard that said, VISIT OUR FLAMINGO LOUNGE!

"Okay," the man finally said, after more than a sec, smiling and walking over to the break in the fancy, tarnished brasswork.

"What room are the Evermans in?" Carver asked. "Frank and Selma."

The desk man gave him what might have been a surprised look, then raked his fingers through his impossibly black hair and consulted the registration book. "Five-oh-five. If you wanna call upstairs, house phones are over there." He motioned to a lineup of dreary gray phones mounted on the wall near the desk. "Just punch out the room number."

Carver used one of the phones and waited through ten rings on the other end of the connection. He hung up, stood for a few seconds, then decided since he'd driven all this way, he'd go upstairs and see if he could rouse the Evermans by knocking on their door, just in case they were late sleepers. If they asked who was there, he could yell in that he was from room service, come to give them their complimentary champagne-and-omelet breakfast. They might believe that.

The desk man was wrestling with paperwork again as Carver limped to the elevators.

The floor indicator's brass dial above the middle elevator lurched numeral to numeral from 12 to 1. When the doors opened, a bedraggled woman with a preschool child that might have been either sex hurried out and through the lobby. Carver stepped in and watched them push out into the bright day as the elevator doors glided closed.

The fifth-floor hall was warm and smelled musty, and the white paint on the gently rounded walls was mildewed in places and beginning to flake. Every ten feet or so tarnished brass chandeliers cast dim pools of light. Carver had to be careful not to let his cane snag in a loose thread on the worn and faded blue carpet that should have been replaced a decade ago.

He knocked softly on the door to 505, then loudly with

the crook of his cane. Tried the knob to make sure the door was locked. Knocked again. The door to 508 across the hall opened and an old woman with wild white hair glanced silently out at him, but no one came to 505's door. Carver smiled at the woman and said he was sorry if he woke her. She smiled back and closed the door gently, as if *she* didn't want to wake *him*.

So maybe the Evermans had gone out for breakfast or their morning walk. He decided to drive to the hospital and see Henry, then return later in the morning and try again to catch one or both of them in their room.

He took the elevator back down to the lobby, thought better of leaving a message for the Evermans, and limped outside past the old men in the armchairs. One of them was reading a crinkled *Miami Herald* now. It looked like yesterday's edition.

When Carver arrived at Faith United Hospital, he was afraid visiting hours might not have begun, so he acted as if he belonged and limped purposefully past the nurses' station without stopping and talking to anyone.

The door to Henry's room was closed. He worked its large push-handle, like something on a theater exit, and eased it open so he could peek inside. He didn't want to embarrass Henry by charging in when the nurse was removing the bedpan.

But the bed was empty.

Carver felt a cold apprehension.

"You looking for Mr. Tiller?"

He turned and was staring at the inquisitive features of a nurse approximately his size. The name tag on her white uniform said she was Pru, short for "Prudence," Carver assumed. He said he was looking for Henry, then added, "He isn't . . . ?"

"No," the nurse said, with something like a smile, "he's become comatose and was taken to ICU this morning."

"ICU?"

"The intensive care unit."

"But how'd that happen? He was doing so well."

"Are you family?"

"A friend. Can I see Henry?"

"You can look in on him. I'm afraid he won't know you're there." She shot a glance at a large round wall clock with oversized black numerals that looked as if they belonged on an antique watch. "Listen, the doctors are due to make their rounds soon. Why don't you wait in Intensive Care and I'll have Dr. Montrose talk to you."

"All right," Carver said, "where's—"

She interrupted him and gave directions to Intensive Care. Pru wasn't a woman with time to spare.

"Doctor'll see you soon as he can," she assured him, then strode down the hall and disappeared into one of the other rooms.

It was permissible only to view Henry through an observation window. His eyes were closed and he was pale. He looked untroubled and oddly younger, as if his mind had been wiped clean, worries and all. One of his fingers twitched regularly, but that was the only movement in the small green room. There was what looked like a feeding tube running into one of his nostrils, an intravenous tube leading to a needle in the back of his right hand, and another tube, probably a drain, that disappeared beneath the white sheet midway up his still body.

Carver didn't like the way Henry looked. Not at all. He went back to the ICU waiting room and watched some daytime TV until a harried-looking man in white trudged in and asked for him. Dr. Montrose.

"Your friend's latest CAT scan and MRI revealed extreme trauma to the right temporal region of the brain," the doctor explained. He reeked of some chemical that made Carver dizzy.

"I didn't think he hit his head," Carver said.

"He wouldn't necessarily have had to. Hemorrhaging might have occurred due to extreme and sudden movement of the brain inside the cranium. An accident like Mr. Tiller's could cause that to happen. The impact would be that of the brain's outer membrane contacting the inside of the skull. It's similar to what happens to a boxer when he's punched hard enough."

"He seemed okay yesterday when I talked to him on the phone."

"He probably felt relatively well, too. It took time for the pressure and resultant impairment to develop. Early this morning his left side was partially paralyzed. Then he lost consciousness and hasn't yet regained it." Dr. Montrose raised his shoulders beneath his white jacket. "Someone his age, it's even possible this is a coincidental stroke and had nothing to do with the accident."

Carver knew what Henry would think of that possibility. "How likely is that?" he asked.

"Not very," the doctor admitted, "but I've seen it happen. Especially with patients Mr. Tiller's age."

"So what's the prognosis?"

"I'm afraid we're in a wait-and-see mode, Mr. Carver. But I have to be honest with you, he might never regain consciousness. Are you family? We might need you to sign some forms."

"Just a friend," Carver said. "I don't think he has any family left."

"I see." Dr. Montrose looked thoughtful. "Would you like us to call if anything else develops?"

Carver said he would. He thanked Dr. Montrose, then left his name and the phone number of Henry's cottage with Pru at the nurses' station.

Then he went downstairs, sat in the quiet coolness of the hospital cafeteria, and had a salad and a dry roast beef sandwich for lunch. He was sure Henry had been run down deliberately. To think otherwise would be stretching anyone's idea of the limits of coincidence.

The game might be about to change. If Henry died, Carver would be investigating a murder.

Of course, if Henry died, Carver would no longer have a client. Questions could be left unanswered. There'd be nothing compelling him to continue his investigation.

Like hell there wouldn't.

He left his sandwich half eaten and drove back to the Blue Flamingo, fighting the heat and frustration of sitting still every few blocks in the sluggish Miami traffic. Maybe Frank and Selma Everman had returned.

Maybe something about this Miami trip would go right.

14

THIS TIME Carver didn't phone upstairs first. He limped across the Blue Flamingo's lobby and stepped into an elevator waiting with open doors. The lobby had been deserted except for an ancient black man napping or dead in one of the armchairs. The desk clerk was facing the other way, apparently checking cubbyholes for room keys or messages while he talked on the phone.

Carver's luck was beginning to change. On the fourth floor the elevator stopped and a skinny little man with haunted dark eyes and thin black hair pasted severely sideways over a bald spot got in. Entering the elevator with him was the smell of perfumy cologne or deodorant and stale sweat, nauseating in such close quarters. The man was holding a gray plastic ice container with a blue flamingo decal on it. It was full of ice, which apparently was available on the hotel's even-numbered floors. The man glanced at the control panel, saw that the only glowing button said 5, and simply stood with his head tilted back, staring solemnly at a point above where the elevator doors met. He'd never acknowledged Carver's presence and might as well have been alone. Elevator etiquette.

On the fifth floor Carver hung back and let the man with the ice leave the elevator first. When the man turned left, Carver held the Open button in so the elevator would stay as it was, and waited a few seconds before stepping out into the hall. He stood leaning on his cane and bowed his head, as if trying to remember something, playing it casual.

The man with the ice bucket had paused and knocked on a door. Now he was shifting his weight from side to side, like a worn-down nervous boxer who has no punch left and is afraid of getting hurt. As the door opened and he edged inside, he looked back at Carver with the hostile hope of the poor and dispossessed.

Only when Carver approached the door and saw the room number was he sure it was 505; the man with the ice must be Frank Everman, and probably his wife, Selma, had let him into the room. There was music playing in 505.

Carver rapped firmly three times on the door with his cane. Everman had seen him and knew *he'd* been seen, so Carver wasn't going to go away. No use pretending the room was unoccupied; there was little choice for Everman but to open the door to nasty and persistent reality.

Which he did.

Everman was no longer holding the ice bucket, and was wiping his damp hands on his blue polyester pants. He was about fifty, but the deeply etched map of pain that was his face said it had been a tough half-century. The top two buttons of his white shirt were unfastened to reveal what appeared to be a rawhide necklace disappearing among his gray chest hairs. He was short as well as skinny, and he looked up at Carver as if he'd just done something wrong and been struck a blow in anger. There was little hope in his eyes now, and only a glimmer of hostility. He wasn't sure about Carver, despite the cane. He'd been around enough to recognize a certain dangerous kind of man.

Behind him, standing in the middle of the room and peering over his shoulder, was a tall but stooped woman with gray hair, badly fitted dentures, and a bewildered expression. She was wearing baggy green slacks and a yellow blouse with a stain on it that looked like coffee.

There was a robust polka playing in the room, a slightly cracked record, heavy on the tuba and accordion.

Carver said, "Mr. and Mrs. Everman?"

"Yeah?" said the man, making it a question.

"I'm from Key Montaigne," Carver said, raising his voice so he'd be understood over the music. "I'm here to talk about your son." *Oompah!* said the tuba, vibrating the floor.

A blank look came over the face of the man. Fear crept into the woman's woeful blue eyes.

"Our son's dead," Frank Everman said.

"I know. That's why I'm here. To ask you a few questions. I don't like it, but that's my job. Can I come in?" *Oompah! Oompah!*

Everman didn't know how to say no. Carver inserted his cane into the room first, as if it were part of him that was already inside, then limped through the door and past Everman, who made a sort of acquiescent grunt as he shuffled aside. The hall had been hotter than the lobby, and the room was hotter than the hall. It was actually a small suite. Carver could see beyond the overstuffed old sofa that matched the lobby furniture and into a room where the corner of an unmade bed was visible. Alongside the sofa was a fancy brass floor lamp with a bent yellow shade. A cheap reproduction of a Frederic Remington painting, a weary Indian on a wearier horse, hung on one wall. There was a bookshelf on another wall, but it held stacks of 33 rpm records instead of books, and a brown stereo turntable with lots of controls but only one knob, and that one cracked in half. The woman walked over and used the cracked knob to switch off the turntable, then lifted the stylus and carefully set it aside in its bracket. The room was astoundingly quiet in the absence of polka. It smelled of stale tobacco smoke and strong insecticide, now that Frank Everman was out of range with his cologne.

The woman must have seen Carver's nose twitch. "I just killed the biggest roach you ever seen," she said, and crooked her forefinger over her cupped hand as if depressing the button on an aerosol can.

"I'm glad you nailed him before I got here," Carver

said, smiling. Selma might be easier to deal with than the whipped loser Frank.

Frank tried to take charge, backpedaling quickly to the center of the room so he was standing next to his wife and facing Carver. "So whad'ya need to know about Lenny? I thought we told you guys everything possible."

"Probably you did," Carver said sympathetically, "but we need to hear it again to verify it." He looked over at Selma. "Losing your son as you have, you must understand we have to learn everything possible so we can try to prevent other kids from leaving home and ending up the same way. The streets are the worst kind of life for a minor."

"For anybody," Selma said.

"It was the drugs," Frank said. "Goddamn drugs and the scum that sells 'em is what killed our boy." He clenched his fists and looked fierce enough to tackle any drug dealer smaller than five feet tall.

Selma bowed her head. "Time to time, the way God works His will is hard to bear up under." She'd produced a wadded white Kleenex from somewhere and used it to dab at her eyes. Tiny pills of tissue appeared on her blouse to join the coffee stain.

"Did Leonard have a history of drug use?" Carver asked.

Frank looked puzzled, then said, "We told you fellas he did. His fuckin' peers got him using the stuff when he was no more'n eleven years old. Hell, we was surprised to find out. Exactly the kinda unsuspecting parents you read about. Lenny was hard to roust outa bed some mornings, but other'n that we seen no sign whatsoever he had a problem."

"What kinda drugs he use?" Carver asked.

"You name it and Lenny probably tried it in his young life. Toward the last he was smoking crack cocaine, is what I gather. But we don't know for sure except for what they found in his blood test after he . . . was gone. Once he got past twelve years old, Lenny never let us in on what was happening in his life. Lousy peers took over."

"That's not exactly true," Selma interjected, defending

her dead son and her competence as a mother. "It was just the drug part of his life he kept secret."

Frank snorted. "My feeling is drugs were his *whole* life. Him and the other poor fucked-up kids that caught a habit. Not to mention the bastards that deal the stuff. You lie down with them dogs, you're gonna get up with plenty of fleas. Then one day you don't get up at all."

"That's what usually happens," Carver agreed. "And Leonard had run away before, right?"

"Just temporarily," Selma said.

"Till the police brung him back," Frank told Carver, ignoring Selma. "Once when he was ten, and another time when he was eleven."

"How long was he gone those times?"

"When he was ten he was away less'n a week. Cops found him way the fuck up in Haines City. Time he was eleven, he was gone two months and some social worker found him right here in Miami, selling artificial flowers at a busy intersection."

Two months, Carver thought. That was a long time for an eleven-year-old boy to be on the streets and not fall prey to the perverts or the dope dealers. Time enough to become savvy and cynical and lost to yourself as well as the people who might be searching for you. It would be so easy for us to alleviate our social problems by making sure every kid in the country had education, medication, and some sort of basic physical and emotional nourishment. But Carver knew it wasn't going to happen. Fifteen or twenty years would have to pass in order to see the results, and political horizons extended only to the next election.

Selma said, "Looka here, Mister . . . ?"

"Carver."

"Mr. Carver. We're living in this hotel on welfare 'cause of Frank's disability."

"Got injured in an industrial accident," Frank said, with what sounded like pride.

"What I'm saying," Selma went on, "is that we don't wanna make no waves and bring the case worker down on us for neglecting Leonard—which we definitely did not do. But folks on the dole don't wanna call attention to themselves, you know?''

Carver said he understood. He looked hard at her. ''You really think it's plausible your runaway son went swimming in the ocean and drowned under the influence of cocaine?''

''Ain't that what happened?'' Frank asked.

Selma said, ''Leonard was a good swimmer.''

''Not juiced up on coke, he wasn't,'' Frank said bitterly. He screwed up his face and trained his injured eyes on Carver. ''To answer your question, yeah, it fits the way Lenny was, the way he was living at the time, that he mighta done something like that. Anyway, I guess the proof's in the pudding, ain't it?''

''Afraid it is,'' Carver said.

Selma moved her pale and flabby arm in a tired gesture toward the ice bucket. A bottle of bourbon and a plastic liter bottle of Coca-Cola Classic sat beside it on an old elliptical mahogany coffee table that looked like a surfboard on legs. ''You wanna drink, Mr. Carver?''

''No thanks,'' Carver said, ''I've taken up about enough of your time. One last thing, though, are you satisfied with the way the investigation into your son's death was handled?''

''Oh, hell, yeah!'' Frank blurted out. ''Them people down on Key Montaigne couldn't have been nicer, don't you think, Selma?''

''They was as comforting as anybody could be under the circumstances,'' Selma said.

''You acquainted with a man down there named Walter Rainer?''

''No,'' Frank said.

''Yes,'' Selma said. ''He was the nice fella give you a lift when the rental car got a flat.''

''Yeah, mighta been his name at that. Big fucker in a long gray car. Name Rainer sounds right.''

''So you don't have any doubts about the way Leonard died?''

''Doubts?'' Frank Everman stared at Carver. ''What kinda doubts?''

"Nothing, really," Carver said. "I just wanna make sure you're satisfied with the way everything was done. It's important we make it easy as possible for people who're gonna have similar experiences, because the sad thing is, there are plenty more kids out there living the way your Leonard did."

Selma said, "Often times—and I know it's a sin to think it—I do believe Lenny's better off now. I mean, the kinda discontent and mental suffering he was in. Whatever it was made him take to the streets. And the drugs and stuff. The horrible people he took up with. He was living a life of agony and might eventually have come to an even worse end. It's like the bible says about the wages of sin, and Lenny was led astray and into the wilderness early in life."

Carver wondered if she imagined her dead son in hell. How couldn't she, if she believed in an afterlife of reward and punishment?

Frank shook his head sadly. "Damned peers!"

Carver left the Evermans to their bourbon and their beer-hall music and rode the elevator down to the lobby. Their grief for their son didn't ring quite true, didn't seem to stab deep enough. On the other hand, it was possible they were so beaten down by poverty they'd become numbed to tragedy.

The explanation of the flat tire and the ride from Walter Rainer might well be fact, the one genuine coincidence that had tilted Henry's suspicion to conviction.

Carver had left the Olds parked in the lot alongside the Blue Flamingo, in the shade of the adjacent hotel that was deserted and under renovation. He limped over to it and was about to unlock the door when his cane was suddenly jerked from his grasp. He heard it clatter to the pavement as he twisted, stumbled, and fell back against the warm hood of the car, supporting himself with his elbows and with his stiff leg angled out in front of him like a brace.

He was looking at Davy Mathis, who was standing on the cane, smiling and holding a wood-handled steel cargo hook that had been honed to a gleaming point.

15

BEFORE CARVER could move, Davy suddenly stepped in close. Carver felt something sharp and painful digging into his crotch.

He tensed his body, looked down, and saw that Davy had the point of the cargo hook pressed into his scrotum. Davy patted him down skillfully with his free hand, making sure Carver didn't have a weapon. Carver thought of his gun back in Henry's cottage, still in Beth's suitcase. He hadn't figured he'd need it to talk to bereaved parents in Miami. It might not have helped anyway; it would probably belong to Davy now.

The length of the hook allowed Davy to move back slightly and still use his and Carver's bodies to shield what was happening from view. Anyone passing on the street might glance at them and see only two men having a casual conversation.

"You move a fuckin' millimeter," Davy said with a grin, "and I'm gonna gaff you and hoist you a foot off the ground. Give you a vasectomy while I'm goddamn doing it." He made a slight upward motion, an almost imperceptible shrug, and the hook moved. Sudden pain coursed through and nauseated Carver, making him dizzy. "You and I gonna have a talk," Davy said. He was wearing white pants and a sleeveless T-shirt; the sweat-coated hula dancer on his muscular forearm had wriggled when he made the move with the hook. He must have had fish for lunch; it was still on his breath.

"Where's your van?" Carver asked through clenched teeth.

"Parked down the street a ways. You don't know how lucky you are. I'm awful fond of my wheels. If you'da backed into the van the other day down in Key Montaigne, I'd have got out and gutted you asshole to belly button."

"Then you admit it was you who tried running me off the road?"

"Sure. You gonna fuckin' quote me?"

The point of the hook again rose a fraction of an inch, and Carver sucked in his breath. He couldn't answer, but that was okay with Davy, who probably asked a lot of rhetorical questions.

More fish breath. "If I'd have been trying to run you off the road, Carver, you'da fuckin' run off the road. What I was attempting was to get you to see plain reason, realize your future was someplace else."

"Or not at all."

"Ain't you per-fuckin'-ceptive?"

"Were you acting on Walter Rainer's orders?"

Davy sneered. "You're amazing. I got you by the balls directly, and you think you're the one doing the quizzing. Maybe I need a bigger hook. You talk when I ask you a question and not a word otherwise. Understand?"

"Yeah, I get the point." The words came out in a wheeze.

Davy laughed and spittle tattooed Carver's face. "Hey, maybe I really *do* need a bigger hook. What I come to tell you is, Henry Tiller's nothing but an old geek talking out his asshole. There's nothing to his fuckin' paranoid ideas. Now, you know what that means?"

"I got a feeling I'm about to find out," Carver said. His mind was whirling, trying to figure out a way for him to defend against the sharp cargo hook so he could go on the offensive. But there was no way. Any sudden motion would prompt Davy to hoist him like a live side of beef on the hook, and Davy would enjoy that.

The hula dancer jiggled her hips again and Carver felt the hook rotate. The twisting motion didn't add to his pain, but it carried a psychological horror that made his insides go cold and metallic-tasting saliva collect under his tongue. "Means you oughta seriously consider moving outa the Tiller place," Davy said, "and returning to whatever rock you live under on the mainland. You got that message loud and clear, fuckface?" Now the hook lifted another eighth of an inch and Carver heard his shrieking intake of breath as another shock of pain jolted through him. "Loud and clear?" Davy repeated.

"Loud and clear," Carver groaned. He swallowed. Nausea threatened to reverse the process.

Davy spat in his face and smiled like a man who'd just accomplished his mission. He lowered the hook and stepped back. "I really do enjoy dealing with assholes like you. Fuckin' small-time gimp, did you really think you were gonna cause somebody with some real grease any kinda trouble without bringing ten times more down on yourself?"

"I didn't know Rainer had that kinda grease."

"Well he does, and it's green, and you don't follow my advice, you're gonna get a special kinda lube job." Davy kicked Carver's cane under the car, then moved farther back and slid the cargo hook through a belt loop so it was concealed beneath his untucked shirt. "I tried to give you a hint the day before yesterday on Shoreline you wasn't wanted on Key Montaigne, but you insisted on ignoring it, so here we fuckin' are."

Davy paused as if expecting Carver to answer, but Carver remained silent. He still ached where the hook had gouged his testicles. Somewhere deep in his mind he tried to create a place the pain couldn't reach.

Davy gave a snorting kind of laugh, then said, "Miami's a great city. Got jai-alai, the races, nice beaches. What you wanna do now, Carver, is maybe enjoy yourself here, take in a few sights, find yourself some whore'll bed down with a gimp, catch some rays—being careful you don't get sunburned—then set a course to the north. Stay the fuck outa the Keys. That's my advice, and it's best if you got the sense to listen. Consider me a lighthouse warning you away from the rocks.''

The warning was plain enough. And if Carver had any reservations about Rainer being mixed up in something criminal, they were gone now. He must be a threat to Rainer, or Davy wouldn't have been sicced on him. Henry must have stumbled upon some vulnerability that scared Rainer.

''You the one ran over Henry Tiller?'' he asked, since Davy was in a gloating mood.

''That's another question you asked,'' Davy said, ''after I told you not to. You're lucky I don't feel like going to the trouble of getting the hook back out.''

''Gonna answer?''

''Let's just leave old Henry an ordinary hit-an'-run victim,'' Davy said. He gave Carver a little half salute, then turned and swaggered away.

Carver leaned against the car for a few minutes, perspiration rolling down his face. Then he worked his way down and crawled on the hot pavement to a point where he could lie flat and grope for his cane beneath the Olds.

As soon as his fingers closed on the hard walnut he felt better, less vulnerable, as if he'd recovered a flesh-and-blood missing limb. Part of him wanted Davy to return so he could smash the cane across his confident smile and then feed him his cargo hook. Wanted it badly.

Carver placed a hand on the chrome windshield molding and stood up straight. A dull pain throbbed in his groin, but he didn't think he'd been seriously injured. He'd been kicked there a few times, and he knew how that felt; this pain was similar but not as debilitating, though it made him dizzy and sick to his stomach with each cautious breath.

He brushed dirt off his clothes, then he lowered himself into the car and for a long time sat very still behind the steering wheel, waiting for the world to stop tilting and whirling. He was sweating coldly and trembling. From fear or pain or rage, he wasn't sure which. Probably a combination.

When he finally did start the car he drove north, exactly as Davy had instructed.

Not toward Del Moray and home, though. Toward a phone booth.

| 16 |

WHEN CARVER called the Municipal Justice Building in Orlando, he was told Desoto wasn't in his office but would return tomorrow. He was attending a conference on DNA identification in Fort Lauderdale. That worked out for Carver. Fort Lauderdale was only a few miles north of Miami.

Within the hour he was sitting in Desoto's room at the Pier 66 Resort on the Seventeenth Street Causeway. Desoto had been glad for an excuse to walk out on the conference's keynote speech by an FBI technician in the building's seventeenth-floor revolving restaurant. The view, he'd explained, was more interesting and comprehensible than the scientific jargon about genetics.

A woman was speaking Spanish from the clock radio on the nightstand by the bed. Desoto, dressed in a light beige suit, white shirt, and maroon tie, had sat on the room's small sofa, listening patiently to Carver describing his morning in Miami. His dark eyes were vague, as if his mind were elsewhere, but Carver knew he was concentrating. Desoto was deceptive in a lot of ways, a cop who looked and dressed like a tango dancer.

The radio began playing Latin music, the song the female DJ had introduced. "Eiiiyah!" a soulful voice cried from the speaker. Desoto made a steeple of his gold-adorned manicured fingers and said, "You could have Davy arrested down on Key Montaigne, *amigo,* but it wouldn't do any good. You said yourself, there were no witnesses when he threatened to make you a gelding."

Carver had thought that far ahead. "I'm not here because of Davy."

Desoto smiled handsomely, knowingly, the tanned flesh crinkling at the corners of his somber brown eyes, the kind of bastard women thought got even better-looking as he aged. "But you won't forget what he did, will you?"

"Would you?"

"Ah, no." The steepled hands parted in a palms-up, curiously humble gesture. A man began singing to the beat on the radio. He had a resonant tenor voice that haunted the air. Carver couldn't understand the lyrics, but the tone was tragic, a Latin lament.

Carver felt the breeze from an air-conditioning vent coolly evaporating a sheen of perspiration on his arms. He didn't like remembering this morning in Miami. "I need some information on the Evermans. And the Blue Flamingo Hotel in South Miami Beach."

"Such as?"

"Are Frank and Selma Everman really welfare recipients? Is the Blue Flamingo actually a welfare hotel? Do either of the Evermans have a record of child abuse or any other offense? How long have they really been in Miami?"

With a glitter of gold, Desoto held up a hand to stop Carver. "In short, were they telling you the truth, eh, *amigo?*"

"In short."

Desoto arched a dark eyebrow. "Your instincts tell you the Evermans were lying?"

"Instincts again, huh? You and Henry Tiller. I don't know if it was instinct or common sense. The Evermans sure weren't eager to talk to me."

"Not unusual, for people living their kind of life. You live on the dole, you get suspicious of authority. Not without good reason." Desoto idly twisted the gold ring on his left hand, sending shimmers of reflected light dancing

over his crossed legs. ''What else was there about the
Evermans that made you think they weren't leveling?''

''Maybe nothing,'' Carver admitted. ''I'm not sure myself what I'm fishing for, or even if there's anything to
catch.''

''What happened to Leonard Everman, my friend, it
happens hundreds of times a year or more, here and there
around the country. Runaways get mixed up with drugs
and the people involved in the drug trade, and it kills
them. One way or the other, sooner or later, it kills them,
even if it leaves them walking around and breathing.''

''I'd still like to verify the Evermans are on the up-and-
up.''

Desoto looked thoughtful. '' 'The up-and-up.' That
sounds like a line from a hundred old movies.'' He was a
classic film buff. ''I think Humphrey Bogart said it a lot.
Or maybe it was one of the Three Stooges. I'm not sure
which one.''

Carver said, ''Does it make a difference?''

''Only to the Stooges, I guess. I'll do what I can, *amigo*,
just like I promised. But in return, I want you to promise
something.''

''Oh?''

''Don't get involved in a personal vendetta with Davy
Mathis.''

''Sure, I promise.''

Too easy. Desoto looked dubious. ''Truth?''

''Truth.''

And it was the truth. Carver's vendetta wasn't with
Davy. That would be like blaming the guided missile instead of whoever had launched it at the target. In this case
it was Walter Rainer who'd pressed the red button. His
mistake was in not destroying the target.

''You going back to Key Montaigne today?'' Desoto
asked.

''Yeah, I left Beth down there.''

''How is she these days?'' Desoto's voice was mechanical. He still wasn't quite sure about Beth. Her years with
Roberto Gomez might have corrupted her beyond redemp-

tion. Only a few people, maybe only Carver, knew how strong she really was. Maybe as strong as he was.

"She's doing okay," he said.

Desoto stared at him, his handsome head bobbing ever so slightly in time with the music, a morose guitar solo now.

"Better than okay," Carver said for emphasis.

"Hear anything from Edwina?" Desoto asked.

"No, but I hear about her. She's still in Hawaii selling condos." Carver didn't often think about Edwina anymore, about the time they'd so tentatively yet so intimately shared their lives. He'd assumed he'd never reach that point, but he had, and sooner than he would have guessed. The tragedy of life wasn't so much that we missed people, but that we stopped missing them. Days, weeks, months, years passed, and lost faces became indistinct in the fog of memory. Endearing gestures could no longer be recalled. Emotions dulled.

Desoto stood up and buttoned his suitcoat, a tall man dressed for his luxurious surroundings. "I need to get down to one of the conference rooms. Gonna be on a panel on DNA and sex crimes. You should stick around and sit in, maybe learn something."

"In case I wanna be a sex criminal?"

"You'd decide against it, once you learned how this DNA identification works."

"It isn't that I'm not interested, but I better get back."

"Tell Beth I said hello," Desoto told Carver. He tried; Carver appreciated that.

He said he'd convey the message, then thanked Desoto for his help and stood up.

Desoto said, "I'll phone you soon as I get any information. Part of the reason I'm doing this is for Henry Tiller. You understand what I mean?"

"I understand," Carver said. "Henry comes around, he'll appreciate it, too."

He limped over to the door. Behind him the vocalist with the haunting voice had joined the guitar in a melancholy but beautiful melody. Carver wondered if all of human experience was embodied in Latin music. Desoto thought so. Maybe he was right. For all of us the tragic and joyous music played while we lived and danced, and then it stopped. The only question was how soon.

Desoto switched off the radio and walked with him to the elevator.

AFTER LEAVING Pier 66, Carver drove south toward Key Montaigne. The convertible's top was up and all the windows were cranked down, and the wind beat like a pulse through the steel struts and taut canvas. Occasionally he checked his rearview mirror, but Davy's black van was nowhere in sight on the heat-wavering highway.

It didn't really matter. Carver's presence on Key Montaigne would be common knowledge within hours after his return. Davy wouldn't like that. Walter Rainer wouldn't like it.

Carver smiled and pushed the Olds's speed over the limit.

| 17 |

BETH WAS sitting at the kitchen table, eating a sandwich and drinking a beer, when Carver entered Henry's cottage. There was a lot of daylight left, and plenty of residual heat from the scorching afternoon. The ocean breeze that stirred the palm fronds was a warm one and brought no relief. But Beth had the air conditioner off; she wasn't bothered by heat as much as most people. Growing up in a theft-gutted housing project in Chicago, living in an upper-floor unit where a safely opened window was a luxury, might have something to do with that.

As soon as he dropped his scuffed leather suitcase on the floor, he went to the living room window and switched on the air conditioner, set its thermostat on Coldest and its fan speed on High. Then he turned on the box fan sitting on the floor and aimed it so it blew a stream of the cool air into the kitchen.

"How'd it go in Miami?" Beth asked around a bite of sandwich.

Carver didn't answer. Instead he limped into the bathroom and splashed cold water on his face and wrists. When he went into the kitchen, it was still too hot in there. Florida could be a beast.

"See Henry Tiller?" Beth asked. She was wearing a black T-shirt with a blue marlin on the chest, Levi's faded

105

almost white, no shoes. Her brown leather sandals were lying on the floor near the chair. Her body glistened with sweat but she didn't seem to mind.

"Saw him," Carver said. He got a can of Bud from the refrigerator and popped the tab. "He didn't see me, though." He took a long swig of beer and explained to Beth what had happened to Henry.

Beth finished her sandwich and licked her fingers. She said, "He doesn't come outa that coma, we're talking murder."

"Uh-huh."

"Serious shit," Beth said. Now she finished her beer, leaving only a sudsy residue in the bottom of the tall, tapered glass she'd rummaged from Henry's cabinet. "You gonna ask the girl spy if she saw anything interesting last night over at the Rainer place?"

"I'm asking."

"Answer's no. There was movement over there about three o'clock, but even with the night binoculars I couldn't tell what was happening. So today I drove around to a couple of points on shore I noticed from the surveillance spot. An area around the research center or aquarium or whatever it is provides a clear view of the Rainer dock. So does a short section of coast you can't see from this side with the boat docked where it is, down Shoreline where it turns before leading toward the major metropolis of Fishback. Nothing can go on in Rainer's backyard that can't be seen from those two parts of the island, so he's got no choice but to move by night if he suspects he's being watched. A wiry Latin guy was there with Rainer, Hector Villanova, I s'pose. And there was a tall blond woman, probably the missus, Lilly. What with the darkness and all the foliage and such, there was no way to know what all the bustling around on the dock was. I'm sure of one thing, though: that guy Davy wasn't around last night."

Carver told her he knew that, then told her how he knew. She seemed unimpressed by Davy's theatrics with the sharpened cargo hook, but then she wasn't the one who'd felt its point and almost became shish kebab.

She gnawed her lower lip for a few seconds and looked thoughtful. "If they're trying that hard to scare you off the case, leaving no doubt that's exactly *what* they're doing and practically admitting they've got plenty to hide, you must be probing a mighty sensitive nerve."

"Henry must have probed the same nerve."

Beth toyed with her empty glass, rotating it on the table, running a long, lean finger down the tapered curve of its damp side. "You gonna?"

"Gonna what?"

"Do what Davy said, give this up and head back north?"

He smiled. "That what you plan on doing?"

She smiled back. "While it's still light out, I can drive you over and show you the view of the Rainer estate from farther down the shore."

Carver said he thought that was a good idea. She buckled on her sandals and stood up, then placed the empty glass in the sink and hook-shot her beer can into the wastebasket. She didn't look as if she belonged in a kitchen.

He took his beer with him, letting her drive the LeBaron. The top was down and the sea breeze was just beginning to cool as it roiled around the car's exposed interior, pressing on the back of Carver's neck and flipping his shirt collar. If there was any doubt he'd returned to Key Montaigne, this ride in Beth's open convertible would confirm his presence, and word would certainly get back to Walter Rainer. That was okay with Carver. He thought about Davy in Miami, felt himself getting mad, then very mad, and took a sip of beer.

Beth was looking over at him, grinning, a woman who'd been in hell and had the determination and character to escape the ruins of her dreams and delusions. After a certain point—the point she'd passed—that was impossible for most people, but not for her. She was something rare, all right. And still grinning. He wondered if she could read his mind.

Probably.

On the curve of Shoreline Road she'd described, it was possible to pull to the side and park on the gravel shoulder.

She aimed the car's sloping white hood toward the sea, sliding the shift lever into Park and letting the engine idle almost silently. A gull swooped low to examine them, then screeched in apparent anger and glided back toward the sea. They sat there in the breeze, looking along the stretch of shore to where it angled in the sun and provided a distant but comprehensive view of the ocean side of the Rainer estate. The white hull of the docked *Miss Behavin'* looked smaller from here.

"Some regular binoculars in the glove compartment," Beth said.

Carver got them out, a compact pair of 10×50 Bausch & Lombs with rubber eyepieces. He fit the binoculars to his eyes, trained them through the windshield, and brought the Rainer estate into focus.

The house was a massive layer cake of white clapboard and stucco with a red roof. Beside it the rectangular swimming pool glittered silver as tinfoil in the angled sunlight. For a second Carver thought he saw a blond woman in a swimming suit strolling from the pool into the house, but he couldn't be sure from this distance even with the binoculars. There were palm trees and flowering tropical shrubs of every size on the ground sloping up from the dock. What appeared to be a stone path led through the foliage, from the house to where the boat was moored. The doors were raised on an attached four-car garage. Carver could see the trunk of what looked like a big gray Lincoln. A blue minivan was parked facing out of the deep shade of the garage.

He felt Beth's fingers on his shoulder. "To your right," she whispered, as if they might be overheard.

Carver ranged that way with the binoculars and saw Davy's black van creeping like a distant dark beetle along the tree-lined driveway. It disappeared beyond the house for a while, then emerged on the side nearest Carver and stopped in front of the garage. After a brisk but smooth maneuver, it backed into the shadows of the garage. So dark was the garage's interior that Carver couldn't see anything going on inside it. A minute or so passed, then all four overhead doors slowly descended simultaneously.

They were painted the same wedding-cake white as the house and had no windows.

"Think we oughta set up an observation point someplace over here?" Beth asked, sounding like a military strategist.

Now that the car was sitting still, the sun felt hot on Carver's bald pate and the back of his neck. He lowered the binoculars and shook his head no. "Better to stay where you were last night." The hunter's blind he'd constructed by bending branches and fronds and tying them together with twine ensured that no one would see Beth or him even in daylight unless they were only a few feet away. "The view's not as clear there, but we're closer."

He raised the binoculars to his eyes again. Near the side of the house he saw a brief glimmer of light, like the setting sun glancing off a lens. Were Carver and Beth themselves being observed?

"Ready to go back?" Beth asked.

He said he was and slid the binoculars back into the glove compartment.

When they drove up to the cottage it was dusk. Carver saw Effie's rusty Schwinn bike leaning against the porch.

"What's the deal?" Beth asked, spotting the bike.

"Effie's," he told her.

Beth looked sideways at him and pursed her lips.

"She's a fourteen-year-old kid who comes in a couple of times a week and cleans for Henry Tiller. Lives down Shoreline and pedals back and forth on her bicycle."

Beth parked the LeBaron and got out. As Carver set the tip of his cane and straightened up from the car, the porch's screen door opened and Effie stepped out. She jumped down the three wooden steps to the ground, letting the door slam and reverberate behind her.

"Mr. Carver!" she said, sounding relieved. "I saw your car and figured you was home, but when I went inside and called, you didn't answer. I was afraid maybe something'd happened to you."

"Like what?" Carver asked.

"Well, like what happened to Mr. Tiller." She was wearing black shorts and a tan knit pullover shirt with a collar. Her oversized jogging shoes made her skinny legs look as if they belonged on a newborn colt. When Carver didn't answer right away, she stared curiously at Beth, who smiled at her.

"This is Beth Jackson," Carver said simply. "She's staying with me."

Effie's green eyes widened, then she put on a blasé expression and said, "Okay," as if Carver had sought her approval. "She gonna clean, too?"

Beth said, *"Too?"*

Carver laughed. "You still got a job, Effie. Beth's my assistant as well as my significant other, but detergent is no friend of hers."

"I don't deny it," Beth said.

"Hey, neat!" Effie was grinning at Beth. It was a grin meant for orthodontic braces, though her teeth were straight. She might outgrow it by the time she was thirty. "This mean you're a detective, too?"

"Sort of," Beth said, "whenever Carver bothers to deputize me."

Effie looked puzzled, not quite sure if she was being put on. "I thought I'd ride my bike here and see if you heard anything about Mr. Tiller," she said.

Carver told her about Henry's brain injury and coma. For an uncomfortable moment he thought she might dissolve into sobs. Beth moved close to her and rested a hand on her skinny shoulder.

"But he's maybe gonna be okay?" Effie said.

"The doctors think he might be," Carver told her. "Right now they don't know too much about what's actually wrong with him. They're gonna do some more tests."

"You find out anything about what he thought might be going on here?" she asked.

"Not much. But I'm sure something *is* going on, Effie, so I think you better be careful about who you talk to and what you say."

"I promised Mr. Tiller I'd be quiet about this," she said, "and I will."

Beth backed away and looked down at her. "You seem the sort who keeps promises," she said.

"You ever been a model?" Effie asked her.

Beth chuckled. "No, not me. Not even a model citizen." She looked at Carver. "I like this girl, Fred."

"Another reason I came here tonight," Effie said, gaining confidence, "is to offer to help you find out what's going on with Walter Rainer and those creeps he's got working for him. I mean, nobody pays any attention to a kid with a bike. I can hang around in Fishback, watch and listen and report to you."

"Yeah, your mom and dad would love that."

"My dad's at the station all day. My mom . . ." She stared hard at the ground and made a face by scrunching up her lips. "My mom stays around the house. She drinks some."

Carver and Beth glanced at each other.

Carver said, "Effie, I appreciate the offer, but this might be plenty serious, and I can't take the responsibility of putting you in any kinda danger. You come here and clean on your regular days, and I'll tell you anything you wanna know about Mr. Tiller, but that's about as involved as I can let you get."

"But living here on Key Montaigne, I know I can help!"

"Damnit no, Effie! I mean it."

"But—"

Beth raised a long forefinger to her lips and shook her head. "Best listen to him, honey. He gets in these uncompromising moods."

Effie nodded. Gulped. She looked as if she wanted to speak but didn't trust her voice. Jesus! What was the big deal here? Uncompromising mood? Like Charles Manson? Carver felt as if he'd just shot her dog.

She spun away angrily and stalked to her bike. Threw a freckled leg over it without looking at him.

"Why don't you hang around awhile?" Carver asked. "Have a soda?" He shifted his weight awkwardly over his cane and didn't know what else to say to her.

She shook her head violently, still facing away from him. Her red hair bounced and what appeared to be a bobby pin flew out, catching sunlight.

"Listen, Effie—"

But she didn't listen. Instead she gripped the handlebars as if trying to throttle necks of geese, stood high on the pedals and rode away fast.

Beth watched the dust behind the bike settle in the dying light and said, "Don't worry, she'll forgive you by tomorrow."

"I didn't know what else to tell her," Carver said, still feeling small enough to get lost in one of his shoes. He wondered if he'd have similar conversations with his own daughter, Ann, who was only eight now and lived with his former wife, Laura, in St. Louis. Probably not; it was Laura who'd have to deal with a teenage Ann on a daily basis. Carver wasn't sure how he felt about that.

"Nothing else you coulda told her," Beth said. "You did right, Fred."

"Then why's it feel so wrong?"

"C'mon into the cabin or cottage or whatever the fuck it is, and I'll change that."

And she did.

LATER THEY microwaved and ate two of the frozen macaroni-and-cheese dinners he'd picked up at the Food Emporium, then watched the national and local news on television. The world was in a hell of a shape, but Key Montaigne seemed to be faring okay.

Except for whatever it was the fat and rich and influential Walter Rainer was doing that required somebody like Davy to run interference for him.

Roberto Gomez's widow was sitting up in bed reading Kafka when Carver left to take his position in the blind and watch the Rainer estate.

Kafka! he thought, loving her a lot just then. Amazing! And in that instant he understood with striking clarity what it was a savvy old cop like Henry Tiller knew that escaped those younger and less seasoned. In this world, why should anyone on Key Montaigne be surprised at anything Walter Rainer or anyone else might be doing?

Anything!

18

THE NIGHT view across the water to the Rainer estate was obscured by a low haze along the shore. The infrared binoculars enabled Carver to see little other than the vague and surreal shapes of shrubbery or palm trees.

He settled deeper into a sitting position, his stiff leg extended before him, his cane lying across his lap. Crickets screamed in the surrounding darkness, and he was sweating heavily. The temperature was sure to drop a few degrees now that the sun was down. He was all for that.

But the night stayed warm, and Carver continued to perspire. He wished he'd brought something cold in the thermos bottle instead of coffee, though he needed the caffeine to stay alert. Otherwise he might fall into a pattern of drowsiness alternating with bouts of unease at the unidentifiable sounds around him. The secluded blind could be eerie.

At a few minutes past three a wavering yellow beam on the Rainer grounds attracted his attention, a man walking with a flashlight.

Carver put down his thermos cap full of black coffee and strained forward to peer through the fog. The ghostly flashlight beam moved down to the dock area, but he couldn't make out the form behind it. The light disappeared for a while, then reappeared like a disembodied point of energy and moved back toward the house. Some-one making the rounds, checking on the dock and boat; Rainer probably seldom slept easily, even with his minions on guard.

Carver thought maybe he should have armed himself. He'd originally figured it would be better not to be carrying a gun if someone saw him and called the law. Hiding and spying on a neighbor was bad enough, even without firepower. However, it might be a good idea to see that Beth was armed during her shift on the stakeout. Things had changed with Henry's coma and after the run-in with Davy in Miami, gotten decidedly more dangerous. Better to have conflict with Chief Wicke than to leave Beth alone and unarmed in the dark to face Davy or Hector. She wouldn't see it that way; she'd say she was as capable of handling trouble as he was, and if she needed to be armed, so did he. Possibly she was right.

The coffee ran out around four o'clock, but Carver could still taste its bitterness along with the bologna sandwich he'd eaten a few hours before. Mosquitoes had discovered him and spread the word. He slapped at one that was enthusiastically sampling blood from his forearm and couldn't be sure if he'd struck it or not. He wished he'd brought Beth's insect repellent. Spray the bastards! Fog of death! He lowered the binoculars and dragged the back of his hand across his forehead. Definitely he'd been too long on surveillance.

He found himself staring at the dark water and measuring the distance from where he was to the Rainer estate. For Carver, who'd become part fish during his therapeutic swims, the swim across the cove posed no challenge.

Deciding that anything might be better than sitting here being devoured by night insects, he stripped down to only his pants and rolled the legs up tight just below his knees. Then he left the cover of the blind and used his cane to make his way down to the narrow rocky beach.

It wasn't easy to maneuver himself over the slippery sharp stones and into the water, but finally he managed and left his cane jutting from the sand so he could find it when he returned.

The water was a cool comfort as he extended his powerful arms and struck out across the dark cove.

By the time he reached the hull of the *Miss Behavin'* he was breathing hard, but he knew he had plenty of stamina left to draw on. The boat seemed much larger up close, an oversized rich man's oversized toy.

Carver dragged himself onto land where the dock met the shore. He could see most of the house from where he lay; it was dark except for a dim glow in two of the upper windows. A breeze danced in from the sea, playing over his soaked pants.

His body tensed and he was quiet and still. Listening.

He heard clearly now a soft scuffing noise, like that of a small animal scampering over the dock.

He remained still, then saw whatever it was skipping and rolling across the rough wood.

Not an animal. Nothing alive.

With relief he reached out a hand and snatched it from the breeze.

A New York Yankees baseball cap being propelled by the wind. It was a very small size; possibly it belonged to Lilly Rainer. He tossed it aside, nothing to worry about, but his heart was still pumping fast. He felt vulnerable. Here he was, barefoot and without his cane, in enemy territory.

Forcing himself to move forward, he stayed low and inched alongside the splintery dock and onto the lawn. Time for tactics. He wanted to work in closer to the house, maybe even peer into a window. He was no longer breathing hard from his swim. Behind him the *Miss Behavin'* bumped softly against the dock buffers, and he could hear water lapping at its hull.

About ten feet from the dock was what looked like a small shed that probably contained tools and the nautical supplies necessary to service the yacht. And possibly something he could use as a makeshift cane. Carver reached it and found the door secured with a padlock the size of his fist. But there was something leaning against the side of the shed, in shadow. Tools, maybe.

No, not tools. What he'd seen was only a collapsed

folding stool, canvas and metal. Something portable to sit on for lengthy jobs during boat maintenance.

He ripped the canvas away and bent one of the metal legs back and forth until it broke, leaving him with a two-foot length of hollow steel tubing with a sharp point on one end. Not much of a cane, but at least it would serve as a weapon if he couldn't hobble fast enough to escape danger. He hefted it in his hand, feeling better, looking around.

After fifty feet away lay some dense shrubbery. He decided to use it for cover, then figure where he might go from there. Setting the pointed tip of the metal tube in the ground, he moved in an awkward crablike gait toward the bushes.

He had no sensation of tripping the alarm.

A horn blared from the direction of the house. Carver swallowed his heart. Half a dozen windows suddenly glowed, even as he was hurriedly backing away toward the sanctuary of the water.

Floodlights bathed the grounds in white brilliance as he crossed the dock and scooted backward out of sight, found the coolness of the water. He'd been exposed for only a few seconds. Maybe he hadn't been seen. Maybe he had a chance here. The horn screamed no, he didn't.

He surface dived and swam underwater until his lungs ached. When finally he came up for air, he began a crawl stroke away from the light and noise behind him.

Then the horn abruptly ceased its frantic wailing and the only sounds were Carver's ragged breathing and the splashing of his strokes. Glancing behind him, he saw that the floodlights had been extinguished.

He swam another hundred yards before easing back on his effort. His adventure had almost proved a fatal mistake. He should have realized Rainer might have an alarm system that extended beyond the house.

No real harm done, he assured himself. He'd tried to snoop in close, activated an alarm, and made his escape. Disaster averted.

Thought he'd made his escape.

He heard the boat roaring toward him before he saw it.

* * *

IT WAS a small, open speedboat with what looked like only
one man in it. He was standing up so he could see over
the low windscreen, a dark form in the bucking little boat.
Hector, Carver thought, but he couldn't be sure.

He treaded water slowly, with only his head above the
surface, praying he wouldn't be seen on the glimmering
dark plain of the sea.

The speedboat, he saw now, was a fourteen-foot runabout, the kind that could go like crazy if powered by a
large enough motor. It slowed and settled lower in the
water, cruising in a wide circle as the figure behind the
windscreen leaned forward, scanning open water.

The man suddenly straightened, and the bow of the boat
swung around to aim at Carver. The motor snarled and
the bow rose to cut through the low waves, picking up
speed as it closed on him.

It was difficult to judge speed and distance in the dark,
to reject panic and think calmly through his fear. Carver
waited until the boat was close, then dove underwater and
stroked straight down.

He was buffeted about by the boat passing just a few
feet above him. He surfaced in its churning wake, spitting
seawater, peering in all directions. No danger of panic
now; he was angry enough to hold fear at a distance.

The boat was turning around for another pass.

As Carver treaded water something jabbed him in the
thigh. He realized he was still gripping the metal stool
leg. Then he heard the snarling engine, and the runabout
was after him again.

This time he didn't wait so long. He ducked underwater
and swam at a right angle to the boat's line of attack. Hung
suspended below the surface and watched the tumultuous
passing of the boat's hull twenty feet to his right.

When he poked his head above water, the boat was
drifting with its motor idling, not fifty feet from him. He
heard the roar and saw the cleaverlike bow come around
as he ducked down again. The boat's pattern was narrow-
ing. His death was going to be the result of close up work,

each pass leaving him less and less time to take evasive action.

He knew, and the man in the boat knew, that soon he'd tire himself out and fall victim to the speeding, slashing hull or the whirling prop.

Carver jabbed himself in the leg again. *Damn!* He dropped the metal tube so he could swim better, then on second thought groped for it, and caught it before it sank out of reach. An objective kind of desperation had come over him, his mind darting like a bottled insect seeking escape and survival.

He surfaced gradually, studying the boat that was waiting for him. It looked, and had sounded slapping the waves, as if it had a fiberglass hull. The man in the boat had something in his hand now. As he spotted Carver and raised his arm, Carver realized the something was a handgun with a long silencer fitted to the barrel. His assailant had decided it would be easier and faster to use firepower. He gulped air and went underwater, sensing or feeling the passage of a bullet spiraling past him.

Christ! This was getting out of hand!

When in doubt, do the unexpected.

Remaining submerged, he swam toward the boat.

It was now almost motionless in the water, its motor idling, so it provided a stable platform and enabled the man with the gun to take accurate aim when Carver surfaced.

But Carver wasn't ready to surface. He stroked lower, then arced straight up at the bottom of the fiberglass hull, jabbing the sharp-tipped metal stool leg at it with all his strength. He jabbed again! Again! Focusing the might of his powerful upper body. Kicking from the hip with both legs for maximum force. Wishing he had swim fins to gather even more power for his frantic upward lunges.

There! He thought the metal tip penetrated, but he couldn't be sure. His lungs were burning and crying for oxygen.

Fifty-fifty, he thought, and surfaced on the boat's starboard side. Gasped for air. There was noisy scrambling in the boat and a man very calmly said, ''Here's something for you.'' Carver heard the nasty spitting sound of the silencer as he ducked down again beneath the water.

He thought he saw damage on the bottom of the hull, and he attacked the same spot with his spear of steel. But it was impossible to break through the thick fiberglass.

As he was preparing to strike again, the prop churned and the boat shot forward. Instinctively he jabbed upward as the hull passed over him. The length of sharpened steel was wrenched violently from his hand and sank.

He came to the surface for air and saw that the boat was slowly turning.

But its motor didn't sound right. It was laboring, its pitch rising and falling. It began a sickly, muted clanking. Carver realized he must have snagged the prop as he'd jabbed upward with the sharp metal.

He swam away from the boat slowly, watching the man standing up in it and peering around, looking for him. As the man's head turned toward him, Carver let himself sink gently beneath the surface and swam a few strokes. Surfaced again and saw that the man was now facing away from him. He edged farther away from the boat, making hardly a ripple in the dark water.

Using a lazy sidestroke, he continued to put distance between himself and the crippled boat. Soon he'd be out of accurate range of the silenced handgun.

He kept watching as the man gave up the hunt and the boat putted slowly and laboriously toward shore with its damaged prop.

Carver floated on his back for a few minutes, staring up at the night sky and regaining strength and wind. He offered a brief prayer of thanks, to whom or what he wasn't sure.

Then he got his bearings and stroked for land.

19

It was a little after five when Carver struggled back into his clothes. He turned his back on a majestic sunrise and through fading shadows made his way the three hundred yards to the cottage. Serious tropical heat was building already, and sweat was rolling down his face as he pushed through the screen door and used his key on the main door. He tried not to let his cane thump on the wooden floor, didn't want to wake Beth.

The cottage's interior was dim, but he could see well enough to move cautiously to the bathroom. There was a long scrape on the heel of his hand from when the boat's propellor had yanked the length of steel from his grasp. He peeled off his clothes, soaked for perspiration and the sea, and let them lie in a pile on the floor. Tidiness could wait until he woke.

After a quick shower, he toweled dry, retrieved his cane from where he'd leaned it on the washbasin, then made his way into the bedroom.

It was hot enough outside even for Beth. The air conditioner was toiling away and she was sprawled nude on top of the sheets. She opened one eye halfway, as if merely to register his presence and identity, then closed it and appeared to go back to sleep.

Still damp from the shower, he lay on his back beside

her, feeling his sore hand throb and currents of cool air play over his body. She moved one of her feet slightly so her toes barely touched his ankle, continued reassurance that he was there beside her. Beneath the hum of the air conditioner he could hear her deep, even breathing. He stared for a while at the shadows fading on the ceiling, then closed his eyes. Dreamed he was being pursued by a gigantic buzzing mosquito. Or was it an airborne speedboat?

WHEN HE opened his eyes Beth was gently shaking his shoulder, telling him it was ten o'clock, when he'd said he wanted to get up. She was wearing a white blouse with a black triangle pattern. The warm denim roughness of her Levi's lay against his bare arm.

Grabbing her wrist, he pretended he was going to pull her down into bed with him. A bluff, not like when he was a younger man. Didn't fool her.

"I'm fully dressed, Fred. You wanna do that kinda stuff, you shoulda woke me last night."

"You mean morning," he said. "Five o'clock's when I got back."

"Hmm. Shouldn'ta woke me after all."

He ran his tongue around the insides of his cheeks. Terrible taste. Coffee and bologna and seawater. Yuk! She was watching him with her fists on her hips as he rolled over, grabbed his cane and struggled to sit on the edge of the mattress. His feet made contact with the floor. Henry's bedsprings squealed with his effort.

"You all the way awake, Fred?"

"Sorta. Had breakfast?"

"Nope. I read until late and just woke up about an hour ago myself. I figure tonight's my turn to squat out there behind branches in that spooky blind and spy with binoculars, I better get all the sleep I can this morning."

"Lemme get dressed," Carver said, "and we'll drive into Fishback for some breakfast."

"We could eat here," Beth said. "I can fix us some bacon and eggs while you're getting yourself together."

He stood up and waited for dizziness to pass, a lithe,

muscle-ridged man leaning nude on a cane. "Let's eat in town," he said. "I got my reasons."

"Such as you wanna be seen. Wanna let those dickheads across the way know you weren't scared away."

"I guess it's something like that."

"That exactly. Go splash some water on yourself and get into some clothes so we can eat. I'm hungry." She sounded angry, too. Ah, well.

Angry or not, as he limped toward the bathroom, she leaned over and kissed him on the cheek. "Want me to get your gun outa the suitcase?"

He said, "It wouldn't be a bad idea, in case Fern tries to overcharge us."

On the drive into town, Carver told Beth about what had happened last night.

"First they were going to make it look like you mighta died accidentally," she said thoughtfully. "Then they decided to shoot you and probably hide your body. Wanted your ass real bad. Something to think about, isn't it?"

He said, "I've thought about it."

"You get the idea they knew it was you they were after?"

"They can't be sure who it was," Carver said, "I think."

"Wanted you real bad," Beth repeated softly.

She didn't speak the rest of the way into town. He figured that was probably for the best.

FERN WAS indeed on duty this morning. Order pad in hand, she trudged across the tile floor of the Key Lime Pie and smiled down at Carver and Beth. There were a dozen other customers in the restaurant, all of them in booths where they could stare out the window at the cosmopolitan bustle of Fishback. The ceiling fans were ticking away at a fairly brisk speed and it was cool in there, a slight breeze from above. Smoke or steam was drifting from the kitchen, over the serving counter, but the body of air from the fans held it at bay and let only the scent of frying bacon waft out into the restaurant.

Carver glanced at the grease-spotted menu and said, "What's good, Fern?"

"Not your chances of a long and prosperous life."

He looked up at her. "What's that mean?"

"Means Key Montaigne's a small place, an' word gets around."

"Which word?"

"That you're meddlin' where you shouldn't be, that you been warned."

"And ignored the warning?"

"Well, you're here, ain't you?"

Sometimes Carver had his doubts about that, but he didn't want to get metaphysical with Fern.

"What was that crack about long life?" Beth asked.

Fern stood solidly with pencil poised and eyes averted as she said, "This island's kinda deceptive in some ways. Beautiful to look at, with all the green an' the colorful flowers, the tourists walkin' around town or goin' out to sea in charter boats. Like paradise under a blue sky. But there's some awful rough people here. *Awful* rough. An' as a Christian woman I feel compelled to let you two know that. Now I done let you know, so that's that."

"Are these rough people into drugs?" Beth asked.

"I honestly ain't sure what's goin' on, but maybe it's drugs. An' you didn't hear it from me."

"Okay," Carver said.

"Two coffees, was it?"

"Right. With cream."

When Fern returned with the coffee, Beth and Carver both ordered the scrambled egg special.

It arrived at the table within a few minutes with toast, strawberry preserves, and Canadian bacon. Fern commanded them to "Enjoy" and plodded back behind the counter.

Carver decided the Key Lime's breakfast was its best meal. Whoever was in the kitchen was an expert fry cook.

When they'd finished eating, they each had a second cup of coffee. Then Beth went into the rest room while Carver paid the check and limped outside to smoke a Swisher Sweet cigar. He was leaning back against the front right fender of the Olds, squinting into the sun and touching flame to tobacco, when a shadow drifted across the ground in front of him.

Immediately he flicked the match away and turned, keeping a firm grip on his cane, aware of the bulk and deadlines of the Colt automatic in its holster beneath his shirt. Davy wouldn't get the chance to move in close with the cargo hook again.

But it wasn't Davy standing five feet away and smiling at him.

It was Walter Rainer.

20

RAINER WAS wearing what looked like the same white sport jacket today, only it was more wrinkled. He had on a money-green shirt, open wide at the collar so his thick gold chain showed against the glistening expanse of his chest. Up close his face appeared puffier, yet there was an added sharpness to the features set in that doughy expanse of flesh, an almost startling shrewdness and vitality in his tiny blue eyes. He was a fat man suffering in the heat, reeking of sweat and deodorant.

He said, "Thought we ought to talk, Mr. Carver." Beyond him, on the other side of Main, the long gray Lincoln was parked. A tall Latino dressed in jeans and a black muscle shirt that revealed a wiry and powerful physique was standing near the car with his arms crossed, looking cool and controlled. Hector Villanova, no doubt. Carver recognized him from last night in the boat. About thirty and lean and tough-looking; if people could become panthers, Hector was halfway there. He caught Carver's eye, smiled and nodded. He could be friendly and slash you up with a boat prop.

"I see Hector's keeping an eye out for your safety," Carver said. He drew deeply on the cigar and exhaled a white stream of smoke that the breeze spirited away.

"Ah, that's right, you more or less know Hector," Rai-

ner said. He had a reedy voice that didn't match his huge
body and would soon get annoying. "Know him from a
distance, that is."

Did he mean last night? No, he'd be playing dumb about
that. Carver recalled the glint of sunlight off a lens yesterday. That was okay; Rainer still probably didn't know
where the blind was, or when or how often he was being
observed. Carver hoped. "Were you going to ask me how
Henry Tiller is?" he asked.

Rainer shrugged. "No, no, my information is that the
poor man's slipped into a coma. That's how it happens
sometimes with our senior citizens. The slightest illness
can escalate unexpectedly." He screwed up his fat face in
the heat and dragged a hand slowly across his glistening
chin to wipe away perspiration, as if he'd drooled. Wiped
the hand dry on his pants. "What I actually wanted, Mr.
Carver, was to apologize for the unfortunate and painful
incident in Miami. I honestly vow to you that Davy wasn't
acting on my instructions. He has a troubled past, is indeed a troubled young man, and at times his emotions
propel him into mistaken assumptions and unwise actions."

"He didn't seem out of control to me," Carver said.
"He seemed like a man going about his job and enjoying
it immensely."

"Well, Davy does make the most of the moment, in his
swashbuckling way. He's rather like a buccaneer born too
late." Rainer shuffled closer. He was so heavy his legs
seemed barely able to support and move him simultaneously.
"Listen, Mr. Carver, despite poor Henry Tiller's mis-
guided suspicions and Davy's independent and unforgiv-
able behavior in Miami, there's really no reason to badger
me, to pry into my affairs as you're doing." He shot a
sweaty smile Carver's way, though his eyes remained di-
amond chips. "I can say sincerely there is no basis in fact
for suspicions about the way I conduct my affairs. I'm
simply a retired businessman who got lucky in commerce
and is trying to live out a life of harmless leisure. It's
possible there's a tinge of envy in some people, and they
want me to suffer rather than live what to them must seem

an idyllic existence. I don't know, or pretend to know, what motivates certain people. The complexities of the human mind are a mystery to us all. I do know that your being here at Henry Tiller's request is a waste of his money, your time and effort, and is making life difficult for me.''

''Difficult how?''

''It isn't pleasant to know your affairs are under professional scrutiny, Mr. Carver. That everything your employees do reflects on you unfavorably in someone's tilted perspective. In short, I don't think I've done anything to warrant this kind of persecution. I could speak to Chief Wicke about it, get it stopped through legal measures.''

''Bringing the law into your affairs could cut both ways,'' Carver said.

''Only if I have something to hide.''

''And here you are talking to me instead of to Chief Wicke or the Drug Enforcement Administration.''

Rainer raised his eyebrows, furrowing his wide forehead. ''The DEA? What have they to do with this?''

''Maybe nothing,'' Carver said. ''Maybe something.''

''Schoolyard talk, Mr. Carver.'' Rainer's thin voice deepened an octave with disdain.

Carver said, ''Schoolyard's an educational place.''

Rainer's hand moved to an inside pocket of the white jacket, and Carver's hand edged toward the holstered Colt beneath his shirt. Across the street Hector stood straighter in the sunlight and uncrossed his arms.

It was a thick white envelope that Rainer withdrew from the jacket. Smiling sweatily, he raised the unsealed flap with his thumb so Carver could glimpse the green of the bills inside. ''There are fifty one-thousand-dollar bills here, Mr. Carver. Clean money, believe me. Money I'm willing to pay in order to purchase my wife's well-being.''

Huh? ''Your wife?''

''Lilly's a woman of delicate composure, has in fact suffered clinical depression in the past and had to be confined and observed for her own safety. The suspicions of Henry Tiller, and now your constant if sometimes indirect intrusion into our lives, have been a strain on her. I'm a very rich man, and I'd consider it money well spent if you'd take it and leave her—us—alone.''

"And if I don't accept the money?''

"I've spoken with my attorneys, Mr. Carver. If you refuse my offer, I can go to the Key Montaigne police and have you charged with harassment.''

Carver looked at his half-smoked cigar, remembering Davy in Miami. Davy, doing muscle work for Rainer, despite what Rainer claimed. Anger rose and blazed in him like a flare. He said, "I don't think you'll do that.'' He flicked the cigar in the direction of Hector and watched it bounce sparking in the street. Hector, standing motionless again with his arms crossed, didn't change expression. Obviously he wasn't afraid of cigars.

"Why wouldn't I do that, Mr. Carver?'' Rainer sounded genuinely dumbfounded.

"Because you don't know how much Henry knows, or knew. That's why he was run down. And you don't know how much I know. You don't know how far it would spread.'' He nodded toward the envelope. "Maybe that money isn't clean. Maybe it tracks all the way back to someplace in Mexico or South America.''

Rainer widened his eyes in bewilderment. "Please stop fantasizing, Mr. Carver. Take the money.''

"That'd be extortion on my part,'' Carver said.

"Not at all. *I'm* the one who approached *you*. Party of the first part, as the attorneys say. If you'd like, I can even sign a statement to that effect.''

"Thanks, anyway.''

"Then I haven't convinced you?''

"No.''

Rainer looked as if his feelings had been stepped on. He lowered his massive head into the folds of his thick neck, appearing for an instant like a huge crestfallen infant in adult clothes. Then he seemed to brighten, and he slipped the envelope slowly back into his pocket. "There's no necessity for haste,'' he said. "Do think about it. Consider it in the manner someone in your relatively modest position should mull over fifty thousand dollars. So very much money.'' He smiled with the old, old knowledge.

"You'll do that, I'm sure." His eyes fixed on something off to the side, and his smile gained wattage as Beth walked up to stand next to Carver. "Perhaps the young lady might influence you."

"Regarding what?" Beth asked.

"I've just offered to hire Mr. Carver away from his present employer for fifty thousand dollars. A boy and girl don't need Manhattan to enjoy that much money."

Beth laughed. Roberto Gomez, whom she'd once described as an island in a river of money, had kept rolls of hundreds of thousands of dollars lying about their luxury condo. "I used that much money for coasters," she said.

Rainer looked at her curiously. She was obviously an element he didn't understand, and that bothered him.

"Do think about the offer," he said, and turned and waddled slowly across the street to the gleaming gray Lincoln. Hector opened a rear door for him and stood by dutifully while Rainer worked his bulk into the car.

Without a glance at Carver and Beth, Hector shut the door softly, then stalked around and got in behind the steering wheel. Behind the tinted rear side window, Walter Rainer's profile remained fixed straight ahead as the car glided away from the curb and down Main Street. It rode low in back and listed toward the side where Rainer sat, the hot vapor of its exhaust shimmering behind it.

"Fat man thinks he can buy a lot for a measly fifty thousand," Beth remarked.

Carver didn't answer. Beth had become inured to the lure and curse of big money, knew what it had done to her and no longer craved it. But a part of Carver was aware that Rainer's offer had been perilously close to his price.

Maybe Beth knew what he was thinking. "Go for those fifty big ones, Fred, and you can afford a toupee."

Carver said, "Get in the car."

21

AFTER DROPPING off Beth at Henry's cottage, Carver drove along Shoreline to the Oceanography Research Center.

The *Fair Wind* was now at the dock, a stubby, functional-looking gray-hulled boat with raked navigational antennae jutting from its faded green bridge. A green stripe was painted just above its waterline, and there was machinery, what looked like compressors, mounted on the cluttered deck. It was nothing like the sleek and fun-loving *Miss Behavin'*, visible in the same sunny, panoramic view of Key Montaigne's curved and sandless coast. Scrubwoman and socialite.

Suddenly aware of the sun's bludgeoning heat, Carver limped toward the main building.

This time Katia Marsh was in the outer room, explaining to a group of six primary-school-age children about the meaning of bright colors on tropical fish. She smiled at Carver, and he mouthed the words "Doctor Sam" and raised his eyebrows inquisitvely. She pointed to the door to the hands-on Tide Pool Room. All of the children and the teenage girl with them looked at the door to the lower level, then back at the four-color poster Katia was showing them, as she began to speak again. Something about the lifespan of eels.

Carver pulled open the heavy door, stepped onto the

steel landing, then descended the short flight of metal steps. Dr. Sam was standing at the far end of the room, jotting something on a clipboard tucked into his hip as he glanced back and forth between it and whatever was displayed in the shallow tray before him. Even after he heard Carver's cane bonking down the steel stairs, he methodically finished what he was writing before looking up.

Dr. Sam Bing was a somewhat short man and bald, with only a fringe of gray hair around his ears, like Carver's hair, only straight and much shorter. His narrow eyes were magnified by round tortoiseshell spectacles. He had the face of a German bureaucrat, fine, even features, a slash of a mouth above a strong jaw, and a wide forehead that shone like a light bulb as it reflected the fluorescent brilliance glaring down from the ceiling. The light in the room was made wavering by the play of water behind the glass observation wall of the aqua tank. Victor, the huge gray shark, was still gliding in effortless circles, barely missing the glass on each pass, as if trying to make the most of the limited space fate had allotted.

Carver limped toward the waiting researcher and introduced himself.

Dr. Sam shook hands deliberately and with seeming reluctance, letting the clipboard dangle at his side. He'd been making notes about what looked to Carver to be slugs and starfish in the watery display tray. Some profession.

"How was Mexico?" Carver asked.

Dr. Sam semed to expect the question; Katia or Millicent or both had mentioned Carver's earlier visits. "They speak a different language there," he said.

"Did you buy any bargain specimens?"

The doctor's thin lips twitched in a smile. "There's no lack of communication when it comes to talking price. Bargains are hard to find among suppliers south of the border." He stole a glance at the display tray, maybe at a just-acquired critter. "My wife told me you questioned her," Dr. Sam said in a modulated, precise voice. "I don't know if I can add anything to what she told you."

"You spend more time here than she does," Carver

explained, "so I thought it more likely you might have noticed something across the water at the Rainer estate."

"Something of what nature?"

"Anything unusual."

Dr. Sam shook his head. "No, but then I'm not watching for anything unusual. I have no reason to be concerned with what's happening in that direction. I don't really know Walter Rainer."

"What about Henry Tiller?"

"I've met him." Water trickled softly in the display tray. Something had moved. "By the way, how is he?"

Carver told him.

Dr. Sam looked angry. "Damned shame, that accident. A man can live so long in a dangerous occupation and retire uninjured, then something comes out of left field and gets him." He smiled sadly. "But that's the story of life, I suppose."

"Seems to be," Carver said. "I noticed the *Fair Wind* moored at the dock. It used to be a deep sea fishing boat, right?"

"Yes, it did. The research center bought it about three years ago, and I had it converted to serve primarily as a diving platform." Dr. Sam paced over and stood before the glass. The shark circled behind him. It was striking, this spare little man in a white smock, holding a clipboard and standing so unconcernedly while a thousand pounds of devouring carnivore regularly passed inches away from his back. The shark, however, didn't seem to appreciate the irony; it appeared to pay no attention to Dr. Sam, as if there weren't enough scientist there to make a decent snack. "From what I've seen of Walter Rainer," Dr. Sam told Carver, "he's simply another wealthy snowbird who settled here in the Keys to take in the sun and enjoy what he considers to be the fruits of his labor."

"You sound slightly cynical, Doctor."

Dr. Sam made a face and then forced a smile, as if he couldn't make up his mind what sort of mood he was in. "Oh, I suppose I am. It gets to me sometimes, the way I have to grovel for funds, apply for research grants, and accommodate tourists in order to finance the useful work we do here, while all around me I see the rich and selfish leading useless, hedonistic lives.''

"Would you describe Walter Rainer as hedonistic?''

"Not necessarily. I wasn't being specific. As I told you, I hardly know him. But as far as I can tell, all he does after whatever work he performs to make vast sums of money is play with rich men's toys. Big house, luxury cars, a yacht, a—''

"Beautiful wife?'' Carver had only glimpsed Lilly Rainer.

"I wouldn't call Mrs. Rainer beautiful,'' Dr. Sam said. He smiled. "And it seems to be common knowledge that it's plastic surgery enabling her to look like a thirty-year-old. But that's okay. If Rainer wants to buy beauty with some of his fortune, fine. I only wish he and the people like him on Key Montaigne would realize we're trying to do important work here, and often we have inadequate funding.''

Dr. Sam seemed obsessed with funding for his research. Carver wondered if he was going to hear a pitch for a donation. "Why the interest in sharks?'' he asked.

The doctor glared at him as if Carver should have worked out the answer to that question long ago. "Not only will a greater understanding of their habits save lives,'' he said, "but there's no way to know in which direction and how far a larger body of knowledge will take us. Sharks are creatures so suited to their environment that they haven't evolved to speak of for ages. They're primitive and close to man on the lower end of the evolutionary scale, a living window on the dawn of our existence.'' Was this the spiel the doctor laid on tourists? The torpedo shape of the shark glided near again, momentarily changing the arrangement of light and shadow in the room.

"Can you tell me anything about Leonard Everman?'' Carver asked.

Dr. Sam cocked his head to the side and looked thoughtful. "I don't think I know anyone by that name.''

"He was the boy who drowned recently off Key Montaigne. He had traces of cocaine in his blood.''

"Ah, yes. I recall the name now. All I know is what
was in the news. The boy was a runaway, correct?"

"He was," Carver confirmed.

Dr. Sam shook his head. "Sad, what's happening to
kids today, the way drugs get a hold on them. Maybe it
has to do with the disintegration of the American family.
I admit I'm influenced by a middle-American Baptist morality; we never quite shake that once it's put in place
during childhood. But I'm not talking about morality so
much as family and social unity." He glanced at the sea
life in the displays lining three walls. "Social structure, if
you could call it that, is at least fairly constant in the realm
of nature. In our society it's lack of predictability that's
causing many of today's problems and making people want
to opt out of reality."

"You're probably right," Carver said.

"None of us is as far from nature as we'd like to think.
Some of our needs are primitive and unchanged from millions of years ago, still burning but in different guises."
The shark glided close and seemed to gaze out at him,
then wheeled into murky water and misshapen image at the
other side of the tank. "Anyway, Mr. Carver, I'd like to
help you, but I can't. As far as I know, Walter Rainer's
just another rich and parasitic Key Montaigne semi-retiree.
At least that's how I think of them, those people who
hardly have to work for a living and don't seem compelled
to accomplish or create anything other than wealth."

There went Dr. Sam sounding bitter again. Hadn't he
known from the beginning that few shark researchers got
rich?

A peal of childish laughter found its way through the
thick door.

"If you don't mind, Mr. Carver, I'd like to finish my
notes in here before the summer school tour comes down
those stairs."

Carver said sure, he understood, and thanked Dr. Sam
for his time.

Unfortunately he seemed to have taken up too much of
it. As he limped toward the exit, the door burst open and
kids streamed clomping down the steel steps, trailed by

their teenage escort and Katia Marsh. Katia glanced at Dr. Sam and made a helpless motion with her head. He nodded to her, then stared strangely—perhaps with genuine hatred—at a slight blond boy about eight years old. He seemed unable to avert his gaze until the boy looked back at him, puzzled and without recognition. Then Dr. Sam smiled thinly, jotted down a few more notes on his clipboard, and seemed to escape into himself and not notice the shrill young voices and unchecked energy around him.

Carver waited until the steps were clear, then he hobbled up them with his cane and shoved open the door. "Children, this is Victor," he heard Katia loudly proclaim as the door swung closed behind him. He limped toward the sun held at bay by the tinted glass doors leading outside.

The breeze off the sea had picked up. The *Fair Wind* was bobbing at the research center dock. Beyond it the smooth white hull of the larger and luxurious *Miss Behavin'* appeared motionless at its mooring across the sunshot water. A pelican went into a wobbly, awkward glide to settle on the guardrail of the parking lot and stare with mild interest at Carver.

Limping across the lot, Carver tried to fit his conversation with Dr. Sam together with that of his reclusive wife Millicent. The wife seemed to be hiding something, while Dr. Sam came across as candid and cooperative. It didn't figure. After all, they lived together, slept together, should know all about each other and share the same secrets.

Unless Millicent Bing was keeping something from her husband as well as from the outside world.

That wouldn't be all that unusual in a wife. And it was no business of Carver's.

Unless the something concerned drugs and Walter Rainer.

22

"YOU FIGURE the good doctor's being less than candid?"
Beth asked, when Carver had returned to the cottage and
told her about his talk with Dr. Sam. She was wearing
shorts now, and a white T-shirt with JUST DO IT lettered
on it. Sitting relaxed yet with an odd regality in the porch
glider, she was reading by the sunlight filtering in through
the trees and the screen. She'd finished Kafka and had tied
into something now by Robert Parker. Hmm.

"I'm not sure," Carver said. "It's hard for me to know
what academic types are thinking. Dr. Sam might be lying
like a politician, bending over backward to make me think
there's no connection between him and Rainer."

"Like the hot-to-trot damsel who doth protest too vig-
orously?"

"Something on that order. And Katia acts as if everything at the research center's up-front and honest scientific
toil, tainted only by the evils of tourism to help turn a
dollar. A dewy-eyed idealist."

"Still," Beth mused, laying aside Parker, "she's interested
in sharks."

"Even obsessed by them," Carver said.

Beth stretched languidly, long arms, hands, fingers, fin-
gernails, attaining incredible and graceful reach. "If anything *is* going on at the Rainer place," she said, "it's hard

136

to believe somebody at the research center didn't at least get a whiff of it. *Everything* can't be occurring at night, and the view's too good not to notice what's happening over there.''

Carver hobbled across the porch with his cane and lowered himself into the nylon-webbed lawn chair. Flicking a tiny spider off his forearm, he remembered the sun-hazed view across the water from the research center, the clean white hull and gleaming brightwork of the *Miss Behavin'* lying beyond the gray and functional *Fair Wind*. Wealth and leisure contrasting with selflessness and labor. Would workaholics like the Bings and Katia Marsh notice anything outside their immediate range of vision and interest? Did they really care about anything other than their work?

''What about this Katia and Dr. Sam?'' Beth asked.

Carver knew what she meant. ''Neither of them's the type.''

''Hah!''

Well, maybe she was right; she'd been reading Kafka and Parker.

''Live with a woman who's the way you describe Millicent Bing,'' Beth said, ''and a young beauty interested in sharks might seem mighty appealing.''

Carver said, ''She wouldn't have to be interested in sharks.''

Beth glared at him and raised an eyebrow. Jokingly, though. He thought. She crossed her bare and beautiful brown legs and leaned back in the glider, not only unconcerned with romantic rivals, but arrogantly confident. He figured she might gibe him with a mock warning not to stray, but she said, ''That the phone ringing?''

He tilted his head to the side and listened, heard faint electronic chirping from inside the cottage. ''Phone,'' he said, reaching for his cane.

She knew she could make it inside faster than Carver, so she jumped up and breezed into the cottage. The swinging empty glider lapsed into a paroxysm of descending squeaks behind her, as if objecting that she'd risen.

He was standing, poised over his cane, when she returned seconds later and told him it was Desoto on the line. Not much small talk between Desoto and Beth.

"Amigo," Desoto said, when Carver had come to the phone. "I got some information for you, compliments of contacts in Miami."

It was hotter inside the cottage. Carver started to sweat. "Something about the Evermans?"

"And more. We'll start with the Blue Flamingo Hotel. It might be a breeding farm for fleas now, but it's considered to be valuable property because of its potential. That part of South Miami Beach figures to be a major tourist spot when it develops over the next ten years or so."

"They say it'll be like the French Riviera," Carver said. "Croissants and everything."

"Mustn't be so cynical, *amigo.*"

"I've heard that before." And noted the cynicism in Dr. Sam. Maybe it was a communicable disease.

"I had a title search done in Miami," Desoto said, "and it seems the ownership of the Blue Flamingo's a hazy maze of paperwork. Owner of record's something called B.F. Holding and Investment Company, but try to find out who owns *that.* Thing is, there's a possibility the hotel's actually owned by organized crime, but not necessarily the good old-fashioned mafia. More likely one of the South American drug cartels."

"And you told me not to be cynical. Is there any way to be positive about ownership?"

"Oh, sure. Enough lawyers, enough time, we could follow the paper trail and find out. I don't know what it'd exactly mean one way or the other, though. All that drug money's gonna be invested somewhere. It buys hotels, food franchises, politicians, stock in major corporations. The money gets cleaner the farther away it gets from the source. Lots of drug money gets dropped into collection plates at church. Ask your friend Beth."

Carver let the remark about Beth pass without comment. "I don't have lawyers and time," he said.

"The Blue Flamingo's a low-cost hotel that's used now and then to temporarily house welfare recipients," Desoto told him. "Which brings us to the Evermans, *amigo.* State welfare's got no record of them on their rolls. 'Course, it's not unusual for some of the poor or homeless to become confused or to lie about their status after they've been dropped from the system. And it's also possible the Evermans are running a scam and collecting welfare checks under other identities. The kinda entrepreneur couple Republicans love.''

"Can't we find out?"

"It'd be up to Welfare to investigate, and as usual they're underfinanced and understaffed. We got a zillion billion poor, and Welfare's only a single point of light.''

"Any kinda arrest sheet on either of the Evermans?" Carver asked.

"Nothing kicked out by computers here or in Washington. But then, I only had their names to work with, and those're probably false. Get me some fingerprints, and I'll bet the computers'll go wild printing out priors on the Evermans.''

"Maybe I'll have to do that," Carver said. "Or maybe I'll talk to them again." His palms were wet; he switched hands on the phone.

"However you play it, *amigo,* be extra careful. All that anonymity's kinda scary.''

"Isn't it, though?" Carver said.

"I'm sorry I couldn't tell you more my friend. Or at least something heartening and more definite. The hotel's possible link to big drug money can't be good. Might even be dangerous. Anyway, I regret bearing bad news.''

"Don't," Carver told him. "If I know all the news possible, it's less likely to jump up and surprise me." He thanked Desoto and hung up.

"So what's the deal?" Beth asked. She'd come in from the porch and was standing just inside the door, her book at her side with a finger inserted between the pages to keep her place.

Carver told her.

"Some days it doesn't pay to pick up the phone," Beth said, just as the phone rang again.

Carver lifted the warm plastic receiver and pressed it to his ear.

A voice from Faith United Hospital in Miami informed him that Henry Tiller was dead.

23

"WE GOT murder now," Beth said, when Carver had hung up and told her about Henry Tiller. She might have been informing him they had mice. Her deep dark eyes were fixed on him, but there was nothing in them to indicate what she was thinking. Death was something she'd seen from a lot of angles.

He told her then about the Blue Flamingo Hotel and there being no welfare records on the Evermans.

"Shouldn't surprise you, people like that'd lie to you," Beth told him. "The system fucks them over enough for telling the truth, lying seems the wise thing to do even if the truth's just as harmless."

"Question is, what else might they've been lying about?"

She shrugged. "That's a question you'd have to put to them." A smile. "Not that they mightn't lie." She strode over to the sofa and sat down, crossed her legs. "Going back to Miami?"

"Gonna have to, don't you think?"

"Yeah, not much choice." She didn't seem pleased. "I guess that means I spend time in the brush again tonight with my thermos of coffee and my Captain Midnight binoculars."

" 'Fraid so."

"When you leaving?"

"Now."

She smiled very faintly. "That's what I like about you, Fred, you're direct."

He remembered Roberto Gomez had been the direct type, too. In his business, that often involved someone's untimely death. There must be a lot Beth hadn't told him. The thought made him uncomfortable. Made him perspire even more. The cottage's window units weren't keeping up with the heat and humidity today.

"You don't seem awed by the fact we're dealing now with a homicide," he said.

"I'm not. I always thought the object of running over Henry Tiller was to take him out of the game."

"Still," Carver said, "this raises the stakes, increases the danger."

"I suppose."

"I can't read you sometimes," Carver told her.

She said, "You like that about me."

"Now and then you sound like Desoto."

"Oh?"

"He's always psychoanalyzing me, calling me obsessive, seeing ulterior motives and subconscious drives, making it all more complicated than it really is."

"I like Desoto. I know he doesn't approve of me, but I like him."

"He'd approve of you if he knew you the way I do," Carver said.

"I'm sure he would." There was no mistaking the lascivious look in her eye.

"That's not what I meant."

"Uh-huh. Maybe that subconscious thing."

Well, maybe. If it was subconscious, how would he know? He was amusing her and didn't care for that; he'd had enough of this game. "When you go to the blind tonight and take up surveillance," he said firmly, the dominant male in command, "you be extra careful."

She said, "You watch out for your balls in Miami."

* * *

IT WAS late afternoon when Carver entered the sweltering dimness of the Blue Flamingo's lobby. Hell of a place to have to live, he thought. To play out the last days of a dwindling life in what advertisers called the golden years. No fun to be stuck here as a welfare transient, either.

He took the elevator to the fifth floor and knocked on the cracked enameled door of Room 505, listening for some sound from inside. He could hear something, not polka music, a soft and wavering whirring. When he knocked again, louder, the sound stopped abruptly.

The woman who opened the door wasn't Selma Everman. She was Latin, in her forties, with an emaciated figure and flecks of gray in her long black hair. She had wide-set brown eyes that seemed immense in her creased and narrow face. Her left check was hollowed unnaturally, as if most of her molars were missing on that side. She slipped her hands into the back pockets of her jeans and smiled at Carver, the hollow in her cheek deepening.

He said, "I'm looking for Mr. and Mrs. Everman."

The woman's smile became puzzled and she shook her head, made a helpless gesture with her hands. *"Español,"* she said.

Great, she didn't speak English. Beyond her Carver saw an old Hoover canister vacuum cleaner on wheels and remembered the whirring noise he'd heard. He stepped into the room and saw that it was orderly, not cluttered as it had been when he'd visited the Evermans. The bed was made with military fastidiousness. There were wide tracks on the worn carpet from the Hoover.

"You're the maid?" he asked, starting with the obvious, as if he or the woman were an idiot. Language barriers caused that kind of behavior.

Her smile widened and she nodded.

"Are the Evermans gone?" He lifted his cane for a moment and used it to make a gesture that took in the room and ended in a wave at the door.

"They check out," she said, nodding.

"When?"

She lifted her shoulders and shook her head.

"Hoy?" he asked.

"Sí."

Which could mean this morning or this afternoon, not last night. He wasn't really getting anywhere. He limped farther into the room and looked around. The maid didn't attempt to stop him, only stood looking at him with amiable curiosity.

If the Evermans had cut and run, they would have done everything possible to remove any sign of themselves. And what details of fingerprints they might have missed, the industrious maid would have cleaned away.

"Have you done the bathroom?" Carver asked.

She nodded. He wasn't sure if she'd understood.

He went to the door and looked in at the sparkling white porcelain. There was a yellow rubber bucket full of cleaning supplies on the floor near the toilet bowl, which had a paper sanitary strip across its rough wooden seat.

"You do good work," he said despondently, and limped around her and back out into the hall. She grinned at him as if unsure she'd been complimented. Leaving the door open, he started toward the elevators. Behind him the vacuum cleaner began to whine again.

The paunchy desk clerk with the dyed black hair and the ugly mole beneath his eye was on duty again today. Though he was wearing a tightly knotted wide blue tie, his white shirt was untucked, as if he'd settled on a compromise over whether to dress businesslike or casual this morning. He was standing at the end of the desk, drinking coffee and eating a jelly doughnut. When Carver had stood at the desk for several seconds, the clerk looked at him, washed down a bite of doughnut with a slug of coffee, and made a face as if he'd burned his tongue. Said nothing.

"I'd like to know when the Evermans checked out of five-oh-five," Carver said.

Still without talking, the man took a huge bite of doughnut, getting jelly on his fingers, and walked down to where Carver was standing on the other side of the desk. He reached low and carefully fished up a blue clothbound book and leafed through it, getting sugar and jelly on the pages even while handling it with a gentle reverence; the record of his days and nights as well as the names of guests and the dates and times of their arrivals and departures. The Book of His World.

Carver waited until he finished chewing and swallowing the bite of doughnut. It took a while, but then what was time at the Blue Flamingo? Not money, that was for sure.

"Early this morning," the man finally said. He ran his tongue quickly over his molars; it moved beneath his cheek like a mouse under a carpet. He stared at the book again. "Was five after eight, to be precisely exact."

"Welfare pay for the room?" Carver asked.

The desk clerk looked at him oddly. "Uh-uh, not that one."

"Who paid?"

"The . . ." He consulted The Book yet again; it held all the answers he'd need in life. ". . . Evermans themselves."

"Check or credit card?"

The desk clerk laughed. There was doughnut stuck between his yellowed front teeth. "You kidding? We don't get a lotta American Express types here. And I don't see many checks other'n Social Security. People was in five-oh-five paid cash. They took the room on June seventh."

"How'd they act? I mean, did they spend a lotta time here in the hotel? Did they disappear for weeks at a time? Did they have a pet lion?"

"Listen, mister, I don't pay attention to what any of the guests here does." He squared his shoulders and tried for an imperious attitude but didn't come close. "The place ain't the Holiday Inn, but one thing the money buys is privacy."

"What if I told you I was police?" Carver said.

"You're not."

"How do you know?"

"You'da already told me. Wouldn't make any difference anyway. I got no reason to lie. I'm telling you how it is, and if you don't like it, tough shit."

Carver didn't like it. The Evermans had come and gone like ghosts, and no one knew why or even who they were, and he'd been standing in the same room with them and now they were lost to him. Maybe they'd sensed trouble after his visit and simply disappeared, as they'd often done in life. Or maybe there was something they weren't telling him about their son's death.

As he planted the tip of his cane and turned to leave, the desk clerk ambled back to where his coffee and the rest of his jelly doughnut were and took another greedy bite of doughnut. This time jelly squirted down his tie and the front of his white shirt. He seemed unaware of it and Carver didn't tell him.

It felt good to leave the Blue Flamingo, as if the bright heat outside could purge whatever poverty and despair might have clung to him. Carver registered up the street at a Howard Johnson's, then spent most of that evening wandering up and down Collins like a tourist and watching for Frank and Selma Everman.

He never saw them, but he saw plenty of people like them. Middle-aged or older, and poor, in a neighborhood that was moving upscale and gradually cutting them adrift.

After nursing a beer for a while in the Howard Johnson's lounge and watching a Yankees game on television, he went upstairs and slept straight through until nine in the morning.

It was past one o'clock when he got back to Henry's cottage. Beth was still asleep after being up all night watching the Rainer estate. The air conditioner had been on a long time and the bedroom was cool as well as dim. Carver looked at the contours of her body beneath the light sheet. One of her legs had worked its way out and appeared remarkably lithe and tan against the white linen.

He felt like holding her to him, kissing her, but he decided to let her rest. He'd stretch out quietly beside her and catch some sleep himself.

Then he noticed the bruise on her cheek and the deep cut on the side of her forehead.

He nudged her awake, scaring her until she recognized him, angering her in her grogginess. Her lean body had jerked spasmodically. Now it relaxed somewhat, but she still looked startled and angry.

"What the hell's the deal, Fred?"

He told her that's what he wanted to know.

You pulled thousand wave work wrap and retina
on the right
'What about your name?'
the stronger she was one of retina muscle with she had

24

CARVER SWITCHED on the lamp by the bed, and Beth frowned and sat up. She leaned her back against the headboard and raised both hands to cover her eyes and face. The perfumed, perspiration scent of her body rose to him; he liked its familiarity, its intimacy, what it triggered in his memory.

He gently pulled her hands away from her face. The bruise beneath her eye was an ugly purple stain, but the cut on her forehead, though deep, was only about an inch long. It would leave a light scar.

"You need stitches," he said.

"I don't want them. If I mark up, I know a plastic surgeon who can fix it." The wife of Roberto Gomez speaking; money could fix anything.

His gaze took in the rest of her that was visible above the wrinkled sheet. No apparent bruises or other injuries on her body.

"You hurt anyplace else?"

"Not so's you'd notice."

Her guarded independence, keeping him fenced out, was beginning to annoy him. "That mean no?"

"Means no, Fred."

"What happened to you?" he asked.

''You barged your ass in here, woke me up, and turned on the light.''

''What about your face?''

She sighed and seemed to relax, maybe with the realization she wasn't being entirely reasonable about his concern. Settling down in the bed with her head propped on her pillow, she patted the mattress beside her. Carver supported himself with the cane, leaned over, then lay down next to her on his back. He was on top of the sheet, her lower body was beneath it, but he could feel the radiating warmth of her hip and thigh. His sun.

''Late yesterday afternoon I happened to look over and saw smoke floating above the Rainer place,'' she said. ''I got the binoculars and went to the blind, thinking maybe the house was on fire. It wasn't, though. The only fire was in a big stone barbecue pit. The Spanish guy, Hector, was standing in front of it with a long fork or something, every once in a while prodding or turning whatever was on the grill. Then Rainer waddled outside, along with a blond woman in a swimming suit and sandals.''

''Young, well-built woman? Attractive?''

''In an aerobics class kinda way.''

''His wife Lilly.''

''I figured. She and Rainer stood around talking to Hector, then after a while Hector took whatever he was cooking off the grill and put it on a big platter. Then they went into the house or around by the pool out of sight. After about an hour Hector came back into view carrying something in a bag and walked down to the dock. He took the bag onto the boat, then came back and burned some more meat on the barbecue pit. When that was done grilling, he put it in a big plastic container and carried it on board, too.''

A bird began a desperate, high-pitched chattering outside. It was joined by another, maybe its mate in a domestic tiff, then they were both silent. ''So maybe they were laying in some food because the boat was due to put to sea last night,'' Carver said.

''That's what I figured. But it didn't leave the dock. I

stayed there till sunset, and I noticed exhaust fumes around the boat.''

''Generators running.''

''Uh-huh. Keeping air-conditioning and appliances and what have you going.''

''Keeping the barbecued meat refrigerated for a certain fat man.''

''Could be.''

The two feisty birds were at it again outside, starting to get on Carver's nerves now. ''Still doesn't explain your face,'' he said.

''Patience was never your long suit, Fred.'' She pressed her thigh tighter against his. ''After a little while I went back to the blind with the night glasses and took up the regular surveillance.''

''Wait a minute,'' Carver said, being impatient again. ''You never mentioned Davy. Was he around yesterday?''

''I didn't see him and I wondered about that, with you in Miami. You know, after what happened last time.''

She didn't have to remind Carver of last time.

''I didn't notice him in Miami,'' he said, ''but it's a lot larger than Fishback.''

''About midnight, though,'' Beth went on, ignoring Carver's sarcasm, ''his black van drove up to the house and turned toward the garage. No lights coming from the area of the garage, and the van had its lights off. I almost didn't see it even with the night glasses.''

''I don't suppose you could tell if Davy was driving?''

''Nope. Damned thing mighta been driven by remote control, for all I know. Looks like some kinda cartoon vehicle anyway.''

''Not a funny cartoon, though.''

''Except maybe for the Davy part, which is his problem and doesn't make him less dangerous.''

Carver knew he shouldn't be surprised that she understood men like Davy. He nodded, but he doubted if she saw him. She was still staring at a point where the ceiling met the wall. He wondered if the *Miss Behavin'* had been waiting for Davy's arrival before embarking. ''Those goddamn birds!'' he said.

"They're only being what they are," Beth told him, and just then the birds ceased their nattering.

"So what happened after the van arrived?" Carter asked.

"Nothing," Beth said. "Then about one in the morning something happened where I was. Some guy dressed in black and wearing a stocking over his head jumped outa the bushes at me."

Carver propped himself up on one elbow and stared over at her. She still didn't look in his direction.

"He had some kinda weighted leather sap," he said, "and he took me by surprise, so when he swung at me the first time, I didn't quite get outa the way and he barely caught me on the cheek. Then he shoved me up against a tree, grabbed me and tried to get me on the ground, took another poke at me, but this time with his fist. Wearing a ring, I guess." The cut on her forehead.

"He say anything while this was going on?"

"No, only grunted like a hog each time he swung or expended effort on me."

She was quiet for a while, her dark features fixed and impassive. Carver knew she was proficient in martial arts, but he wasn't sure how good she was. He felt himself getting angry, mostly at Rainer and whomever he'd sent after Beth, but partly at himself for exposing her to being assaulted.

"Then what?" he asked.

"Then his ass was mine. The surprise wore off. He swung again and I chopped his arm. I'm pretty sure I busted his wrist. I can tell. I heard bone crack."

"You've heard that before?"

"Yes."

"The man who went at you, how was he built?"

"It was too dark and it all happened too fast to tell for sure. I remember the smooth material of his shirt, muscle underneath, and the feel of his stocking mask against the side of my neck when he tried wrestling me to the ground. It mighta been Davy. Coulda been Hector, for that matter. Not Rainer, though."

''No, it wouldn't have been Rainer. That's the kinda work he hires done.''

Carver felt his rage spread hotly, almost as if he were being immersed in scalding water. Unbearable. He swiveled around on the bed, found his cane where it was lying on the floor, and stood up. The bedsprings squealed. The birds started in again outside, loud even over the hum of the air conditioner. What the hell kind of bird made a nerve-grating sound like that?

Beth still wasn't looking at him. ''Where you going, Fred? Out to shoot those birds?''

''No. To talk to Walter Rainer.''

''I was afraid of that. Is it a smart thing to do?''

He didn't answer. Didn't know the answer. It didn't matter anyway.

It was time to forge ahead without worrying about smart or dumb.

25

CARVER NOSED the Olds up to the chain-link gates blocking access to the Rainer driveway. The gates were eight feet high, as was the fence that disappeared into the foliage on either side of the drive. Heavy vines bearing lush red and purple blossoms covered most of the fence that was visible beyond the gates. A sweetly sickening fragrance drifted to Carver through the open car windows, like the scent of corruption.

Trying not to breathe too deeply, he climbed from the Olds and limped to a call box mounted on a red wooden post near the gates. He opened the box, picked up a gray receiver and after about half a minute a man's voice said, "Yes?"

"Fred Carver to see Walter Rainer," Carver said.

"You got an appointment?" There might have been amusement in the tone.

"No. But I wouldn't be surprised if he was expecting me. Tell him I'm here."

There was a long stretch of silence. Carver stood in the hot sun, looking at the drive curving out of sight beyond a grouping of date palms, listening to the drone of bees working at the blossoms. The driveway was paved with chatahoochie, small, smooth black and brown stones set in concrete and glazed over. It was used often in wealthy areas of Florida.

Finally a voice in the receiver said, "Mr. Rainer'll see you. The gate'll open automatically. Drive up to the house, then walk around back to the pool."

Even before Carver had gotten back to the car, there was a soft humming and the double gates swung smoothly open. After driving through, he glanced in the rearview mirror and saw them easing shut. They reminded him of the jaws of a trap, viewed from the unfortunate side.

There was a tall portico in front of the house. The entrance was also tall, a massive carved oak door behind fancy black ironwork. The desired effect apparently was to make visitors feel small and insignificant even before they rang the doorbell. Carver drove beyond the portico and parked near the end of the semicircular driveway's loop.

There seemed to be no one around, no one waiting to escort him to the great man. That was okay; he didn't need hospitality or the hypocrisy that he was welcome. The breeze was blowing steadily in from the sea here, and beyond the corner of the large house he could see emerald-green water shimmering in the sun. A flagstone walk led around the corner. He set his cane on one of the slanted stones and started walking. He heard a splash, probably someone diving, and knew he was moving in the right direction.

The pool was even larger than Olympic-size; it was to other pools what Walter Rainer was to other people. Rainer sat in an oversized padded lounge chair alongside a pale blue metal table with a dark blue fringed umbrella sprouting from it. He was wearing gigantic blue swimming trunks with a red flower design, white rubber thongs on his bloated feet. Though his mammoth flabby body was coated with sweat and suntan lotion, his hair was dry; he hadn't been in the water. And he was pale as the slugs in the research center tanks; probably he got very little sun. In front of him on the table was a heavy crystal glass with a hobnail bottom. When Carver got closer he noticed grains of salt on the glass's rim.

In the stark shade of the umbrella, Rainer smiled at him. "Sit down, Mr. Carver." He motioned with a flabby arm. "Can I have Hector bring you a margarita? He mixes the best in the Keys."

"No, thanks." Carver ducked beneath umbrella fringe and lowered himself into a padded chair like Rainer's, only normal size. "I didn't see Hector around. Or Davy."

"One or the other is always nearby," Rainer said confidently.

"I'll bet."

There was more splashing from the pool. The blond woman, Lilly Rainer, climbed out of the water by way of a shiny chrome ladder. She was deeply tanned and her muscles rippled beneath smooth flesh. Her suit was red but there was so little of it that color hardly mattered. She had practically nonexistent breasts. Broad, muscular shoulders. Trim hips and buttocks. Probably in her forties, but younger at a glance and still an athlete. Without looking at Carver or her husband, she walked with perfect balance toward the diving board, dripping a fresh trail of water on the pale concrete apron. Her wet footprints described a perfectly straight line.

Rainer's gaze touched on her lightly, as if he'd just noticed her and wasn't much interested. "My wife, Lilly," he said. "But then you know that, even though you two have never met."

"It's my business to find out things," Carver said. On the far side of bushes, trellised vines, and trees growing on the slope to the sea, he could make out part of the white hull of the *Miss Behavin'*. The sprinkler system was spraying on the gentle slope, creating half a dozen distinct miniature rainbows. There was a curved concrete walkway leading toward the dock.

Still paying no attention to Carver or her husband, Lilly Rainer stood poised on the end of the diving board. Carver doubted if she'd had the rumored cosmetic surgery. Even with her hair wet and plastered to her head, she was attractive. It was in her bones. Her features knitted in concentration, she bounced on the board to gain spring, rose high in the air, and jackknifed into a smooth dive with her legs together and her toes pointed. There was very little splashing as she cut the water. She broke the surface and swam with unhurried, powerful strokes toward the side of the pool.

"Lilly swims a lot," Rainer said. "Some years ago she was a top-rated amateur diver. I used to enjoy watching her dive, over and over, each time correcting the slightest imperfection in her previous efforts. Possibly she married me because she knew I so admired, even demanded, perfection."

Carver said, "I suppose you know Henry Tiller died this morning."

Rainer took a sip of margarita then licked the glass rim with a fat pink tongue. Carver wanted badly to reach across the table and slap the glass from his hand, maybe take a few teeth with it. Pearls from swine. "Yes, I do know. You're not the only one who finds out things, Mr. Carver. Who knows things."

"Do you know why I came here?"

"Is it to take me up on my offer of fifty thousand dollars in exchange for your noninvolvement in my affairs?"

"No."

"That's too bad."

"A friend of mine was hurt last night," Carver said.

"Really? The black woman? Miss Jackson?"

"You know about that, too, don't you?"

"No, I only surmise. You can't have any other friends on Key Montaigne." Rainer watched his wife climb the ladder out of the pool again, shake water from her tan body and stride toward the diving board. This time she picked up a towel and sat on the fixed end of the board, facing away from them and staring up at the sky while she dried herself. There was something about the delicate way she worked the towel, like a cat grooming itself. "Mr. Carver," Rainer said, "why exactly are you here?"

"To make sure you understand that if Beth Jackson gets hurt again, you get hurt worse."

"Crudely put," Rainer said.

"There's probably something in Shakespeare that covers it, but what I said will have to do."

"Oh, it does. Chivalry is alive and thriving in your person."

"I'm also here to let you know I think you had something to do with Henry Tiller getting run over and dying. To let you know I'm staying on Key Montaigne and still working for Henry even though he's dead."

"Why on earth would you work for a client who can no longer pay you?" Rainer asked. He sounded genuinely curious, as if dumbfounded that Carver would voluntarily forsake reason and join the world of the mad.

"I was hired by him, and I feel obligated to finish the job."

"Even now that he's dead?"

"Especially now."

Rainer absently ran a hand down his flabby, glistening chest. His breasts were hairless and pendulous, almost like a woman's. Beyond him, his wife continued staring out at the sea. "Morality. Obligation. The work ethic. My God, is it really that depressingly simple?"

"It is."

"I won't act as if I understand."

"Just as well. I'd know you were pretending."

The fat man shifted his weight a millimeter, causing his chair to creak, and looked directly at Carver with his rapacious little eyes. A bead of sweat ran down the center of his nose to its tip, paused, then dropped onto his protruding stomach. He smiled. "I admire how well you control your anger, Mr. Carver."

"If I could control it completely, I wouldn't be here."

"I also admire your loyalty, even though it's foolish. In the way I admire bravery in the soldier who dies for his country in a losing cause. It's a pointless and futile effort, even a mechanical one, yet it requires undeniable courage. The tragedy is that his death is wasted."

"There's no way to know whose cause is lost till the war's over," Carver said.

"Then let's at least get this minor skirmish over with," Rainer suggested. "You're on Key Montaigne because Henry Tiller convinced you I was engaged in some sort of nefarious activity. Now here you sit making no specific accusations, only smearing my character. Perhaps you'll manage to start some rumors about me, cause myself and my wife a measure of discontent here in what we see as our personal paradise. I don't care for that prospect, which is why I offered you money to desist. Well, why *don't* you bring specific charges? Ask Chief Wicke to procure a warrant and search the house and grounds?''

"Because you would not be making the suggestion unless you'd removed any evidence of criminal behavior. And because . . .''

"What, Mr. Carver?'' Rainer laughed. "Ah, you suspect the good chief of police is in my employ? Or on the take, as the people who move in your world call it?''

"I didn't say that.''

"But you do see it as a possibility.''

"Almost everything's a possibility.''

"Not that you'll prove any criminal wrongdoing on my part, Mr. Carver. Not if you stay on Key Montaigne a hundred years.''

Lilly Rainer strode to the table and poured herself a margarita from the pitcher sitting near the umbrella's aluminum stalk. She still gave no indication she knew Carver was there, and she barely glanced at her husband. She seemed to accept the fact she was ornamental and his business was none of hers. She returned to sit on the diving board with her drink, the towel now slung like a cape over her broad shoulders.

Carver gripped his cane and stood up, again ducking the long fringe of the umbrella. Out of its shade he was suddenly very hot. He wondered how Lilly Rainer could endure sitting there in the burning sun. He looked down at Rainer. "I won't stay on Key Montaigne for the next hundred years,'' he said. Then he smiled. "But I'll be here the next fifty, if that's how long it takes. And if you harm Beth Jackson, I'll have some of you no matter how long that takes.''

"Such an extreme and melodramatic warning.''

Carver said, "Think in terms of substance over style.''

"Well, you're a remarkably stubborn man, obsessed in

the way Henry Tiller was. Or perhaps you're even beyond stubborn and you're marginally psychotic.''

Carver said, ''Maybe we know each other's minds better than either of us thought.''

He turned and limped across the sun-baked concrete toward the flagstone walk.

Behind him the *sprong!* of the diving board reverberated and he heard Lilly Rainer enter the water again.

He called, ''Nice dive!'' but didn't look back. He didn't have to. All her dives would be perfect tens. She could afford no less.

26

AFTER HIS conversation with Rainer, Carver was surprised to see activity across the water that night within minutes after he'd taken up position in the blind. Through the infrared binoculars he watched as Davy dollied two large crates on board the *Miss Behavin'*. Hector scurried back and forth between boat and house with smaller objects, what looked like plastic grocery sacks. He was using only one hand, and though the temperature was in the eighties, he was wearing a long-sleeved shirt. Carver was sure there was a wrist cast beneath the sleeve on the arm he wasn't using. Hector, meet Beth, not your standard victim.

Lights glowed on the boat, but it remained at the dock after activity around it had ceased. For a long time there were only dim moonlight and screaming crickets, and a ship's faint running lights passing slowly far out at sea. Sweating, itching, Carver shifted position to ease cramped muscles.

Just before one o'clock Walter Rainer, wearing what appeared through the binoculars to be huge white bib overalls and a white T-shirt, waddled down to the dock and boarded the boat, blending with the craft's whiteness like a radar blip merging with the mother ship. A few minutes later Davy, now empty-handed, swaggered on board. One-armed Hector loosed lines from the cleats, but he didn't hop on board as the *Miss Behavin's* twin diesels revved up and sent a low rumbling over the water. The boat edged away from the dock.

All its lights, including running lights, suddenly winked out, and Carver could barely discern its faint form. Then there was almost total darkness, only the white wake catching glimmers of moonlight as the boat made its way out to sea at a pace that suggested nothing so much as stealth. There was no doubt the *Miss Behavin'* was attempting to leave Key Montaigne without attracting attention.

Carver swept the binoculars from the shimmering wake back to the dock. All quiet and motionless over there. Hector had already returned to the house, apparently its only occupant now other than Lilly Rainer.

An insect stung or bit the back of Carver's left hand, and he rubbed the hand across his thigh, felt another sharp sting, heard something buzz away. Letting the binoculars dangle by their leather strap slung around his neck, he gazed out at the vast blackness of sea and night sky. He wondered why Rainer would leave in the boat when he knew he or Beth might be watching. The fat man had been under surveillance for several nights now and might have known it almost from the beginning, but perhaps the pressure of whatever illicit business he was running forced him to act despite the risk.

Of course, Carver thought, there was the possibility he was meant to observe what went on. That he was being misled and set up for a fall.

Carver was curious about the large wooden crates Davy had wheeled on board. They were about the size of the crates automatic washers and dryers came in, only they seemed not nearly so heavy. Davy had managed them almost effortlessly with the two-wheel dolly, as if they contained very little weight. Maybe they were empty, and Carver was supposed to think they were full. But bales of marijuana, kilos of cocaine, would fit in such crates in Mexico, along with enough ballast to tug them beneath the surface if the *Miss Behavin'* happened to be approached by the Coast Guard and had to jettison cargo.

They might be specially built, with signal and flotation devices so they could be retrieved after danger had passed. That would explain why they were being onloaded at this end of the journey. Carver remembered drug runners off the Mexican coast who'd used technology that way. Barrels of narcotics were jettisoned, then later brought to the surface when radio signals triggered inflatable rings. But the Coast Guard and Drug Enforcement Administration were on to such tricks these days; whatever technology Walter Rainer's crates might contain, there'd be no way to dump them overboard and surely recover them later.

Something touched Carver's shoulder and he sucked in his breath and jumped.

"Me, lover." Beth had approached him silent as a shadow. "After what happened to me here, I figured it'd be smart for both of us to be on hand." She looked out at the cove. "Anything going on across the way?"

He explained to her what he'd seen, what he thought.

She said, "We need to find out more, make sure we're not being suckered."

"Ideas?" Carver asked.

"Uh-huh. It's a great night for a swim. Cool us off."

He considered. He didn't like sequels. Or reruns. "What about Rainer's alarm system?"

"I think I know how to deal with it. You said Hector and Lilly are the only ones left over there. So you keep an eye out for trouble and I'll get in the house and look around."

"Hector's still dangerous, even with a broken wrist."

"Lilly might be more dangerous, but I don't plan on being seen. And it's not likely they got the small boat repaired yet, even if they see us and we have to swim for it."

Carver said, "Where'd you learn about alarm systems?"

"Roberto was paranoid on top of having plenty to worry about. He had everything wired. Times I thought he was gonna have me wired."

"I don't remember tripping a wire over there."

"Figure of speech. You probably got in range of a photoelectric alarm, kind that detects motion when its field is broken. When we get to the other side, you stay just short of where you raised a ruckus the other night, wait for me to neutralize the alarm, then move in close and watch while I see what I can find out inside the house. Good plan?''

"I'm not sure."

But she was already removing her shoes. "Get undressed, lover."

SHE WAS almost as strong a swimmer as he was. Carver liked to think that, anyway. He wouldn't want to test her.

He lay on firm ground now, waiting, wet and afraid and gloriously cool in the ocean breeze. Tonight he'd made the swim with his cane tucked in his belt; it would hinder him if there was trouble, but he knew now the paucity of branches or anything else he might be able to use here as a substitute. He also knew the vulnerability he'd feel without his cane.

Beth had moved off to the side, her dark skin and black shorts and T-shirt invisible in the night. She'd dressed for this before approaching him in the blind, certain she could convince him. She'd been prepared to come here no matter who was on the grounds, no matter what the degree of danger. Well, here they were.

He saw her when she was less than ten feet in front of him, but beyond the point where he'd passed and set off the alarm.

"It was a motion alarm, all right," she said softly. "That means they don't have dogs patrolling, any of that kinda shit. I did my thing with it. You ready to move in close while I get inside the house?" He picked up the excitement in her voice. She was getting her jollies.

"Don't take chances," he warned her.

"That my Fred talking?" And she lost herself in the night.

Carver stood in a crouch with the cane and limped quietly toward the house.

He found cover behind the pool's filtering system. He could see into the three ground-floor lighted windows from where he sat with his bad leg out in front of him. The other lighted window was upstairs, on the third floor.

After about five minutes Beth appeared in one of the ground-floor windows, looked in his direction and gave a slight wave. She must have watched him before breaking in and gotten a fix on where he'd taken cover. She knew her stuff, all right. He tried not to contemplate her background, the kinds of crime she'd lived through as perpetrator or victim. Some areas of the past you left alone.

He continued watching the window where she'd appeared. Now and then he could see her moving around inside, smooth, nimble, seemingly unafraid, her lean dark body more capable than his for this kind of task.

He caught a glimpse of movement in the window two rooms from where Beth was, grabbed his cane and scooted over behind a low wall topped with planters so he could get a better view. Almost knocked over a potted geranium.

There was Hector, slumped in a brown leather chair and reading a magazine. Good. Carver liked knowing where Hector was. He was only two rooms away from Beth, but Carver would know if he got up from his chair. He saw Hector pick up a glass and take a sip of something, his eyes not leaving his magazine.

Carver settled down and continued to watch, occasionally glancing to his right to try to catch a glimpse of Beth. He couldn't see her, but he noticed a moving shadow and knew she was still in the same room. She must have found something of interest there.

Hector shifted in his chair but didn't get up.

Carver's nerves were singing. His mouth was dry. He wished he could be inside instead of Beth, even though he knew that how they were working this made more sense.

He was in close enough to see what Hector was so avidly reading. It looked like pornography, nude figures on the large glossy cover. Tall red letters: NAUGHTY NYMPHETS. Hmm, that should keep Hector involved enough not to know Beth was in the house, as long as she didn't venture into the room where he sat. Carver picked up a pebble. If she went into the middle room, next to the one occupied by Hector, he'd toss it at the window, warn her to get out of there. Carver had a particularly clear view of that room, a kind of den with pale wicker furniture and pastel artwork on the walls.

Uh-oh. Above him! He thought he saw someone in the third-floor window.

There! Again!

It was Lilly. She was standing at the window and looking out at the sea. She was very erect and smiling with a vaguely cruel confidence, like a goddess surveying her domain. He stayed completely still. She hadn't seen him yet, and wouldn't unless she peered down through the darkness.

Then she cocked her head suddenly, as if hearing something that had aroused her curiosity. Drew back from the window and out of sight.

A light appeared in a window directly above the middle room. Lilly was on the move.

Now Beth was in the middle room, looking out the window at where Carver used to be, giving her little "I'm okay" wave.

Shapely legs and a pink skirt appeared in the second-floor window above Beth. It looked in on a staircase, and Lilly was descending!

Motion on the left caught Carver's attention. Hector had put down the magazine and was sitting forward in his chair.

He got up, inserted a finger to scratch beneath the cast on his left wrist, and started toward the middle room.

Carver could only watch. He felt like screaming for Beth to run, but he knew that would only make things worse.

Lilly's head passed from view, she was almost on the ground floor, only seconds from the room where Carver had last seen Beth.

Finally he remembered the pebble in his sweating palm and tossed it at the window. Too hard. It made a startlingly loud sound and almost broke the glass.

Hector picked up his pace.

Lilly was nowhere to be seen.

Neither was Beth.

Carver's heart was the loudest sound in the night.

He could only wait.

Wait.

There, Hector and Lilly were in the middle room! They were looking only at each other, talking. Lilly, in a delicate pink wrap unsuitable for her athletic frame, was waving an arm as she spoke. Hector held on to his cast and gazed around. Shrugged.

Carver got the idea. They'd both heard the pebble striking the window, not nearly as loud as it must have sounded to Carver, and both thought the sound might have been made by the other. That was improbable, but it was the kind of thing he could hope.

He wanted to bolt, but he waited for Beth.

Then he saw her over by the pool filter, searching for him. He stayed low and hobbled toward her, keeping his silence.

She saw him and ran wordlessly to him; the wind had died and he could hear her bare feet pounding the hard lawn. My God, she was grinning!

She whispered, ''Time to make like fishies again,'' and slowed her pace to his as they moved through the darkness to the sea.

When they were a hundred yards from land, the floodlights came on around the Rainer house, and Carver thought he saw Hector walking the grounds.

By the time they'd reached the opposite shore, the lights had been extinguished.

In the cottage Beth showed Carver a soaked and ink-smeared paper she'd brought with her on the swim back. It was illegible now, but she told him the room she'd spent so much time in was an office, and the paper was an unsigned letter insisting that ''the cargo had to be shipped, whatever the danger.''

Might the letter have been a plant, part of an elaborate scheme to set him up?

He doubted it. There was no way for Rainer to be sure the house would be broken into, and the alarm Beth had neutralized would have activated the sound and light show that had driven Carver away on his first visit to the Rainer estate.

He and Beth decided they should proceed on the premise that Rainer had been compelled to load the *Miss Behavin'* and put to sea.

Carver limped into the bathroom and got a towel, but Beth asked him not to dry himself. She wanted to make love wet. He was exhausted but he understood her need. Shared it. They'd been flying on fear and excitement, and it wasn't so easy to land.

Adrenaline took over.

AT BREAKFAST Beth said, "Some night, huh?"

"On which shore?" Carver asked.

She stirred her coffee. "Why wouldn't Rainer just put to sea during the day? You figure he doesn't want anybody being able to swear when or how long the boat's been gone?"

The morning hadn't heated up yet, and Henry's kitchen window was open. There was a breeze, the ancient-new scent of the sea pressing in. Carver took a sip of coffee. Yech! It was in a ceramic mug with a yellow smiley face on it, but it tasted like the coffee from the thermos bottle and didn't appeal to him. He hadn't slept well after last night. He was suddenly sick of Walter Rainer and all the Walter Rainers and the people who sucked up to them and even the people who merely tolerated them. Sometimes he wondered what it would be like to swim far, far out to sea, join Henry Tiller. He admonished himself; he hadn't been haunted by thoughts like that for a long time. Not since he'd been with Edwina. Hadn't allowed it.

"Fred?"

"I figure it's more than the boat coming and going," he said. "He also doesn't want anyone seeing him load or unload those crates, doesn't ever wanna have to explain them. He's got to know that at any given moment he might be under surveillance. But like the letter said, time was beginning to run out on some kinda deal, so he had to take a chance. If we did happen to be watching, we'd only know crates were taken aboard in the dead of night to ferry *something* somewhere."

"Not hard to figure what that something is, though,"

Beth said. She calmly buttered her toast. The cut on her forehead still looked nasty, almost luminous, but her bruised cheek was much better. She healed fast. "Maybe you better talk to Chief Wicke."

"No," Carver said, "not Wicke."

Beth gave him a smile as she laid her knife across the edge of her plate. "Now you're beginning to understand the drug trade, Fred."

He said nothing. Took a bite of toast and chewed thoughtfully.

"What're you thinking?" she asked.

"Wondering where you got this coffee mug with the smiley face on it."

"Back of the cabinet over the sink."

"I never did like this beaming little bastard. I was hoping I'd about seen the last of him." He rotated the mug on the table and saw that its glaze was finely checked. A survivor from the seventies, Carver thought.

Beth said, "The Coast Guard'll be able to intercept that boat on its way back from Mexico, if that's where it's going. It's like Rainer himself, built for luxury, not speed."

"There's plenty of time," Carver agreed. "An intercept's what I was actually sitting here considering. The idea grows on me."

"Wicke won't like it, you going over his head," Beth said, "but some things you gotta do."

That was for sure.

"Think the DEA or Coast Guard'll listen to you?" Beth asked.

"No, but they'll listen to Desoto, or whoever Desoto gets to contact them and request a search at sea."

"Desoto'll be sticking his neck out. Will he do that for you?"

"He'll do it." Which Carver knew was true; the thing was, he hated to ask Desoto to do it. But he remembered seeing Davy wheeling those big lightweight crates on board the *Miss Behavin'*. Being careful with them. Under cover of darkness. Secretly as possible.

"You could tell them about the letter."

"Right," Carver said, "and trespassing and burglary."

"It was only a thought. What if they stop the boat and don't find anything incriminating on board?"

"Then the letter meant nothing and Rainer will have made chumps of us, and his innocent act'll be that much more convincing. He'll be all the harder to nail. But I think something'll be in those crates. And if the crates themselves aren't on board during an interception and search at sea, Rainer's explanation'll be interesting."

"To you, but maybe not to the DEA or Coast Guard. Rainer wouldn't have to explain where he left the crates or why. You're the only one saw them being loaded."

Carver sipped his bitter coffee. "Well, there's some satisfaction in making Rainer jettison valuable cargo, and maybe having to chance going out later and trying to retrieve it."

"That what you're looking for in this, Fred? Satisfaction?"

"Of one kind or another," Carver said.

"I figured," Beth said. "I sure as hell knew it wasn't money." She sank her even white teeth into her buttered toast.

Carver shoved his smiley mug away and stood up. He limped to the phone and called Desoto.

He was playing on the edge again.

And liking it.

27

THE *Miss Behavin'* didn't return that night, but just before midnight the next night it slipped like a dark illusion along the coast and docked at the foot of the Rainer estate. Hector had been expecting it. Through the night glasses, Carver watched as he fastened lines and stood waiting as Walter Rainer made his way up on deck. With his good arm Hector helped Rainer across the short gangplank and onto land. Rainer remained supported by Hector for a few minutes while he became accustomed to being motionless. They waited for Davy, who shut down the boat's systems and then hopped nimbly onto the dock.

Rainer and the two men stood for about five minutes talking, then, with Rainer leading the way, they walked from sight in the direction of the house. The *Miss Behavin'* lay dark at her moorings.

Carver decided nothing more was likely to happen within his view that night, so he left the blind and returned to the cottage. It was a pleasure to get away from the flitting, biting insects that seemed to find him irresistible despite the bug repellent he'd sprayed on himself before taking up position among the branches. Florida insects were survivors; maybe in a few short days they had become immune to and then learned to love the stuff, become insect drug addicts.

After a quick shower to wash the camphor scent of the repellent from his skin, he went to bed and fell asleep listening to Beth's deep and even breathing.

AT EIGHT the next morning he was drawn from sleep by gunfire. He contorted his arm to grip the headboard so he could sit up in bed, coming all the way awake.

No, not gunfire, only a knocking on the door.

Beth, also awake, raised her head and looked sloe-eyed and sleepily over at him. "Gonna get that, Fred?"

Carver figured it was a rhetorical question, since her head dropped back onto her pillow and her eyes closed.

Without answering her, he found his cane and struggled out of bed and into his pants, limped shirtless and barefoot to the front door. Through the small window of the door, the shape of a man banging on the porch screen door was visible. Carver thumped across the porch, and the man stood with his hands at his sides, waiting until the door was unlatched and opened. Still without moving, he said, "Fred Carver?"

Carver admitted he was, then stepped outside and stood barefoot in the sun's warmth. The breeze off the sea was still cool and felt good on his perspiring chest.

"I'm agent Rodney Martinson, with the Drug Enforcement Administration." He flashed ID and extended his free hand, squinting at Carver with something like a smile.

Carver shook hands, thinking he might as well invite Martinson into the shade. "Wanna come up on the porch?"

"Pleasant enough out here, if it's okay with you," Martinson said. He was a medium-height, paunchy man with thinning hair in a short military cut, in his thirties, unremarkable except for a turned-up nose and a pencil-thin dark mustache that belonged on a prewar movie villain. He was wearing a standard gray suit and plain-toed black shoes, as if he'd just been released from an institution. A bureaucrat turned crime fighter. Carver had met him over and over.

He told Martinson sure, outside was fine, and leaned on his cane and waited. He knew why Martinson was here and wondered what he was going to say. Behind Martinson gulls were circling something out at sea, though Carver couldn't make out the object of their attention. Their shrill, demanding cries reached him faintly on the breeze.

"The Coast Guard intercepted the *Miss Behavin'* twenty miles off the coast last night," Martinson said. "Its crew cooperated fully and a thorough search was conducted." Martinson shrugged and shook his head. "No drugs were found. No kind of contraband. The boat was completely legal."

Carver stared out at the circling gulls, the morning sun sparking silver off the sea. "Did the crew have a chance to jettison anything when they knew the Coast Guard was closing in for a possible search?"

"Coast Guard says no, but they do admit they can't be positive about that."

"Why not? Don't they have sonar, all that kinda crap?"

"Yeah, but it's an uncertain world. Hard to be positive about anything."

Maybe Martinson wasn't the typical DEA agent at that. "Were there any large wooden crates on board?" Carver asked.

Martinson's mustache twitched, giving him a wry, man-of-the-world expression. "Crates? No. There was no cargo of any kind. Walter Rainer said the boat had docked at Jurello, a little Mexican coastal town. Said he'd gone there to look over property he might buy. He had a hundred thousand cash in a briefcase. His story is that he speculates in Mexican real estate, usually raw land, buying low by making spot cash offers to desperate owners, then holding the property awhile and reselling at a profit."

Carver was still looking out to sea. "That's bullshit," he said.

"But not bullshit we can disprove," Martinson pointed out. "And it might even be true."

"He'd have to deal through a Mexican real estate agent," Carver said. "The Mexicans are restrictive about Americans doing that kind of business in their country."

"He gave us a name of a real estate broker in Jurello," Martinson said. "We're checking on it."

"If he gave you a name, it'll check out. It's a prearranged cover story."

"Or it's simply true."

"I don't buy it. If you talked to Walter Rainer, you wouldn't buy it, either."

"I'm planning on talking to him," Martinson said.

"Because he's rich and his feathers are ruffled?"

"That'll be how it seems to him, but I want to get an impression of the man, of the setup."

"Setup's what it is," Carver said in disgust.

Martinson frowned at him impatiently. Carver was being difficult. There had been no drugs on board the *Miss Behavin'*. He'd proved out wrong and it didn't set well with him, and now he was being a pain in the ass. "Look, Mr. Carver, you steered us on to this guy, we stirred up the Coast Guard, got the search conducted, came up empty, and you don't like it. I don't blame you, but the fact is that Rainer might be just another eccentric millionaire enjoying himself any way he pleases and it has nothing to do with drug running. You'd be surprised what some people not in the drug trade are doing."

"No," Carver said, "I wouldn't."

Martinson sighed. "Well, I came by to tell you the results of last night's party. Now I'm suggesting something—not instructing you, just suggesting. It'd be best if you quit dogging this Rainer character and making trouble for him. He's got clout and money up the ass, and he can make big trouble back. You keep prodding his hive and you're going to get stung."

Carver felt himself getting angry. Not good so early in the morning; it could set a bad tone for the entire day. He stabbed at the ground with his cane as if jabbing something to death. "I was afraid of this."

"And it's happened," Martinson said. "Empty is empty, Mr. Carver. Legal is legal."

"A hundred thousand in a briercase. Doesn't that strike you as a bit odd?"

"Yeah. And odd is odd. And still legal. You better let this one rest, or you might wind up on the nasty end of a court decision."

"Suppose you search Rainer's house," Carver said.

Martinson gave him an exasperated little smile, working his mustache again. "That's not exactly letting it rest, Mr. Carver. We've no solid grounds to obtain a warrant. And frankly, no good reason to think we might find anything incriminating. The boat was clean, the house'll be just as clean."

Carver thought Martinson was probably right. "I figure Rainer was transporting drugs in wooden crates," he said, "and he jettisoned them at sea when he knew the boat might be searched."

Martinson made a slight motion with his entire body, as if to say sure, that was possible. "So if that's true you have the satisfaction of having cost Rainer a lot of money."

Satisfaction again. "No, I suspect there are location transmitters and flotation devices built into the crates and waiting to be triggered, so Rainer can return when it's safe and pick the cargo back up at sea."

"That kind of thing's been done," Martinson admitted, "but to tell you the truth, it doesn't seem likely in this case. I mean there was no sign of drugs *ever* being on that boat. Coast Guard says there's usually something, even if the boat's legal at the time of the search. It's hard to eliminate all traces of that kind of cargo."

"Hard but not impossible."

"True, like going to Mars."

"Rainer's smart, and he's got the wherewithal to have the boat gone over after every trip, just in case something like last night happens. He doesn't wanna invite suspicion."

"He hasn't," Martinson said firmly. "Except for *your* suspicion, which, as I understand it, is secondhand by way of a late retired cop."

"Secondhand but good as new."

"You're stubborn, Mr. Carver."

"I keep hearing that."

Martinson studied him, sweating now in his gray suit. The sun was suddenly getting very hot, promising a temperature like Hell's today. "Tell you what," Martinson said, moving back a step, obviously trying to get the conversation over so he could get out of the heat, "I'll keep an open mind. You stumble on something more solid, you let me know."

"And you'll what?"

He handed Carver a card and smiled. "Act on it, of course." He nodded, still smiling, and turned and walked toward a gray Dodge sedan parked in the wavering shade of a palm cluster, his gray suitcoat unbuttoned and flapping like wings in a gust of wind off the ocean.

Martinson didn't look at Carver as he started the car and drove away slowly, as if he didn't want the tires to crunch too loudly in the driveway. He probably knew Beth was sleeping inside the cottage. Probably knew a lot more than he was saying. Carver hated government types.

He stood with both hands on the crook of his cane, not moving until he heard the car accelerate on Shoreline, heading in the direction of Fishback. The futile search of the *Miss Behavin'* hadn't helped matters. He decided that now he'd have to come up with incontrovertible proof before Rodney Martinson would act, maybe photographs of Walter Rainer powdering himself with cocaine. He glanced again out to sea, where the gulls had been soaring, but now there was only empty blue sky, then he went back into the cottage.

Beth was up, in the kitchen making coffee.

"You hear any of that?" Carver asked.

"Yeah, all of it. I was standing on the porch eavesdropping." She poured water into the coffee brewer and stood staring at it as it began to trickle dark and transformed into the bulbous glass pot. "So where do you think this leaves us?" she asked, still not looking at Carver, hypnotized by the coffee.

"More or less where we were before I called Desoto," Carver said.

"Not quite."

"Meaning?"

She turned away from the brewer to look directly at him. The coffee was heating up, making the kitchen smell good, but Carver had no appetite this morning. She said, "Meaning people like Rainer, once they got you on the run even a little bit, they go on the offensive and they do it right now. You think they were ruthless dealing with poor Henry Tiller, just you watch them kick into high gear. I understand their kind; I was married to one and knew dozens of others, and I know what millions of dollars of drug money can do to people, how they think it puts them beyond the law, how it burns in the blood and rots and warps them. They got the killer instinct, Fred. Not like it's talked about in sports, I mean the *real* killer instinct.''

Carver stood trying to plumb the depths of his thoughts, pushing down through shadows and ugliness and dead faces and dead emotions. Down through the past. Did *he* have the killer instinct?

''You gotta be much more careful now, Fred. You understand?''

There was a current of fear, of pleading, in her voice that surprised him. He knew that not much scared her.

They both heard the soft creaking sound at the same time and turned toward it.

Someone on the porch.

28

CARVER STAYED well to the side of the door and peered out through its tiny window. He caught a glimpse of red hair, a green barrette shaped like a leaping dolphin.

Effie.

He opened the door and she grinned at him. Beyond her, through the screen, he could see her bike leaning against a tree in the shade. Its handlebar basket was stuffed with cleaning equipment. Effie was cradling a spray can of Lemon Pledge and a rag in her right hand. "Thought it was past time I came over and cleaned," she explained.

Carver shifted his weight over his cane and moved aside to let her in. She was wearing a green T-shirt, black shorts, her big jogging shoes without socks. Her long, coltish legs were marked with mosquito bites.

"Hi, Miss Jackson." Beth had wandered in from the kitchen.

"Told you to call me Beth."

Effie's grin got wider. "Beth, then." She stopped and looked at Beth, wearing her robe and apparently nothing else, then at Carver, still shirtless and barefoot. "I come at a bad time?" She leered ludicrously, trying to look sophisticated and knowing.

"Not if you want some breakfast," Beth said.

"Thanks, but I already ate." Effie put the Pledge and

rag on a table. "Be right back." She hurled herself out of the room like a ten-year-old rushing to play, then returned in a few minutes with her arms laden with cleaning solvents, brushes, a squeegee, and a box of steel-wool pads. She dropped the squeegee, hurriedly stooped and picked it up, dropping a can of mildew remover that rolled when it hit the floor. "Damn!" she said, then looked embarrassed and carefully transferred items one by one to the table to surround the Lemon Pledge. She stared at Carver, did a little bounce in her joggers with the blue checkmarks on them. "I feel terrible about Mr. Tiller," she said.

"We do, too," Beth told her, before Carver could reply.

"I mean, like, I wanna go to his funeral or something. You know, show some respect for the dead."

"He's going to be buried up north," Carver said. "Tomorrow morning. He'd understand why you can't be there, Effie."

She seemed close to tears. "He was my friend, really. Not just some old man I cleaned for."

"I know. That's how he saw it, too." Carver thought he'd better change the subject, but Beth beat him to it.

"I'm gonna cook some eggs and bacon," she said. "You sure you already ate?"

Effie tried another grin but didn't succeed. Henry was still on her mind. Death and youth. Her young, mobile mouth twitched and turned down at the corners. "Yeah, I'm not hungry at all." She sniffed, wiped her nose with a straight-up motion of her palm. "I'll start in the bathroom, if I won't, like, be in the way."

"That's fine," Carver told her.

He started to return to the kitchen with Beth, when Effie stopped gathering her cleaning supplies from the table and said, "Mr. Carver, I don't want you to think I went against your wishes or anything."

He twisted his upper body over his cane and looked at her. "Why would I think that?"

"I mean, I didn't go asking for information, but a friend of mine, Bobby Curlin, works at a Texaco station on Highway One up on Marathon Key, and we was just talking, and when I mentioned that Davy gorilla, that was when

Bobby said him and his van stopped for gas real frequent at the station. Davy always does a lotta driving north and south and that's where he always gasses up his creepy black van. It's a self-service station, and Bobby said whenever Davy finishes pumping gas he pulls the van way out and parks it at the edge of the lot before he comes into the station and pays. Anyway, you said I wasn't to take any chances, but Bobby kinda volunteered to sneak over and try and peek in the van next time Davy gasses up and is inside at the register.''

Carver felt a twinge of horror. A teenage gas station attendant might get himself killed because of him. ''Tell . . . Bobby, is it?''

She nodded.

''Tell Bobby not to sneak anywhere or peek anyplace,'' he said.

''Well, I'm afraid he already did it.''

Oh, Christ! ''No more,'' he told Effie, too angrily. She winced, but her eyes stayed fixed on his face. ''No more of that, please,'' Carver said more gently. ''I don't want you or any of your friends hurt.'' He thought of Davy and his sharpened steel cargo hook. His burden of sadism. ''And believe me, Effie, it's possible.''

''Bobby said he wasn't afraid.''

''All the worse,'' Carver told her. Teenagers! He'd never had much luck dealing with teenagers, and wondered again how it would be when his own daughter reached her teen years.

Effie was still looking at him, her young face serious beneath the freckles.

''Fred just doesn't wanna be responsible for putting you in harm's way, honey,'' Beth said softly.

''He wasn't.'' Not looking away from Carver, Effie now had the same expression he'd seen on much older and more experienced women. Or maybe experience had nothing to do with it. ''Ain't you gonna ask me?'' she said, faintly smiling, dangling bait. Sure, he hadn't wanted her or any of her friends snooping around, but now that she'd acted, now that she knew something, where did he stand? Was he going to be such a hard-ass he wouldn't ask for or use any of her information?

"All right," Carver said, tapping his cane on the floor, "what was inside the van?"

"Well, with the windows tinted so dark, Bobby couldn't see much. Looked like a rolled-up carpet or something laying in the back, and a big wood crate."

"Crate?"

"Yeah, but there were like spaces between the boards, and Bobby could see it was empty."

Spaces. So laden with cargo, the crate would sink almost instantly if shoved overboard at sea. "Anything else?" Carver asked.

"Nope. That Davy creep came out from inside the station, so Bobby had to beat feet outa there or he'd have been seen."

"Is he sure he *wasn't* seen?"

"Says he is, and I think we can trust him."

"*You* can trust him," Carver said. "I never even met him."

"Well, Bobby's a straight-ahead reliable dude."

"How old is he?"

"Fourteen and a half. Same as me." She stood up taller. "Plenty old enough, no matter what you think."

Carver looked at Beth. Said, "Jesus!" Beth smiled.

Carver said, "Did Bobby mention which way the van turned on Highway One when it pulled outa the station?"

"Sure he did. The van went north. Came in from the south, then gassed up and went on north."

"You're right," Carver said, "Bobby's a reliable dude." The fact that the crate was empty meant Davy wasn't hauling contraband north, at least on that trip. Carver had envisioned drug shipments from Mexico to Florida, then north to the major markets in the greater United States. Of course, there might be other reasons for Davy's trip north, this time not involving a drug shipment. Carver knew what he'd have to do to satisfy his curiosity.

"Guess I better get busy," Effie said, making a circular motion with a commode brush.

"Tell your friend Bobby I said thanks," Carver told her,

"but also tell him not to do anything from now on other than observe, and from a distance." To impress her with his seriousness, he added, "It looks as if Henry Tiller was murdered. Keep that at the top of your mind."

But she didn't seem impressed. His somber advice glanced off the armor of her youth; he could almost imagine it dropping useless to the floor. Well, what had he expected?

She said, "I knew the day I heard he was run down it was somebody tried to kill him."

She scooped more cleaning supplies from the table and sashayed into the bathroom. Carver heard the toilet flush and whine, water pipes knocking.

"Young, huh?" Beth said, knowing what he was thinking.

"Only fourteen."

"I didn't mean in years," Beth said, the woman who'd matured by twelve in a Chicago ghetto. "It's her naiveté's gonna get her into trouble. Not like you, Fred. It's your bullheadedness gonna do you in someday."

"Why don't you try thinking of me as simply resolute?" Carver asked, irritated.

"Resolute ain't psychotic, baby."

He was even more irritated by the way she'd fallen into the slip-and-slide lilt and slang of her youth; she did that sometimes for effect. He said, "I love it when you call me insane."

"Yeah? Well, that can be a turn-on for some."

The scent of Pine Sol was drifting in from the bathroom. "If you think I'm an obsessive nutcase, how come you stay with me?"

"Huh? It's why I love you. Even though it's what makes you do things that're downright dumb and dangerous. It's like living with a sky diver."

He shook his head, then limped toward the phone.

"What you doing now, Fred?"

"I'm gonna make a call to Miami."

"Have to do with our friend Davy?"

"Sure does."

She smiled wickedly. "Geronimo!"

| 29 |

CARVER INSTRUCTED Beth not to stake out the Rainer estate that night. He'd rented a Ford Taurus from Hertz, dark blue and inconspicuous and powerful, and that evening sat parked where he could see anyone entering or leaving the Rainer driveway.

His hopes had been high, but after the gray Lincoln pulled into the drive, Hector at the wheel and Walter Rainer almost reclining in the backseat, no other vehicle came or went.

Carver returned to the cottage, but parked the Ford on the far side of the structure where it wouldn't be noticed.

After waking around nine-thirty, he ate a hurried breakfast of toast and jelly, not minding that he'd burned the toast. Leaving Beth still asleep, he took his coffee and the day binoculars out to a shady spot, settled into an aluminum lounger and watched the Rainer estate. The sun had climbed high and brightened the sea and was lancing warm beams through the palm fronds. Shade or not, Carver didn't want to stay where he was for very long.

After half an hour he saw Davy amble down to the *Miss Behavin'*, hop on board, and fifteen minutes later return to the house. He was wearing jeans and a black T-shirt. Even from this distance the tattoos on his muscular arms were plainly visible. Carver never could figure why anyone would have themselves tattooed; the permanency of it would bother him. Maybe permanency bothered him, period.

He sipped coffee and from time to time raised the binoculars to his eyes, though he'd fixed on the spot where the van would have to pass if it left the garage, and he could surely spot it with the naked eye.

A few minutes past noon, when the heat had almost driven him inside, the van did back from the garage. Carver watched it slowly maneuver in the driveway like a huge black roach among lush foliage, then start forward. When it was out of sight, he tossed away the rest of his coffee in a sun-illumined amber arc and watched it splatter on the sandy soil. Then he limped to the Ford and drove down to Shoreline, parked and waited. If Davy was driving north, he'd have to pass Carver, and soon.

Carver tapped his fingers on the steering wheel. Switched the air conditioner to a higher setting. Doublechecked the fuel gauge to make sure the Ford had plenty of gas in its tank. Waiting again. He spent so much time waiting.

Davy's black van didn't pass. He was probably driving south into Fishback, maybe on an errand for Rainer. Or maybe to knock back a few beers at the Key Lime Pie bar, get lucky and find somebody who wanted a fight. But even Davy couldn't do battle every day and odd hour. Guys like that were like generals and TV weathermen; it was hard to imagine what they did with their leisure time.

When he was sure Davy would have passed him heading north, Carver drove back to the cottage. He hated this kind of thing, the intermittent watching that might lead to nothing. He'd done too much of it in his life, spent too much time trying to get inside other people's minds, only to be thrown by the complexity of the human condition. It could be he was wrong about Davy, and the black van might never again travel farther north than Marathon Key.

Beth wandered out to where he was sitting in the lounge chair, waiting for Davy's return to the Rainer estate. She laid a hand gently on his shoudler, and he realized his back muscles were tight. He made a conscious effort to relax them, leaning forward in the chair and working his shoulders back and forth.

"Getting hot enough to bake beans out here," Beth said.

"Been hot."

"You're sweating. I can feel the dampness through your shirt. You wanna give me the binoculars and go inside for a while in the air-conditioning, I'll sit in for you."

"I'm okay. If I went in there and cooled off, I'd really feel it when I came back out."

She clucked her tongue. "You're one hardheaded individual, lover. Might be you'll sit here forever and nothing'll happen over at the Rainer place."

"Then it'll take forever," Carver said.

"You're starting to tighten up again." She kneaded his back with her long fingers, knowing how. Knowing him. Had she done this for Roberto Gomez? Carver hunched his shoulders, then let them sag. "Go on in and get some sleep, Fred. My eyesight's good as yours. Won't hurt a thing if I keep watch out here for a while."

He knew she was right and he was playing hardcore.

"You don't trust me?" she asked.

"I trust you." He stood up, stretched, grinned at her, then limped through harsh sunlight into the cottage.

He took a shower and lay down for a while. Even slept. Davy would probably spend quite some time in Fishback, and there'd be nothing to see on the Rainer grounds. Carver figured it was time-out in whatever dangerous game they were playing. When it got dark, he'd use the Hertz and move in closer.

AT TEN-THIRTY that night, while Carver was parked in the shelter of a cluster of palm trees off Shoreline, the chain-link gates across Rainer's driveway eased open and the black van nosed out onto the road.

It was only after the gates had closed and the van was a hundred yards down the highway that Davy—if Davy was the driver—switched on its lights. Carver smiled, started the Ford, and eased onto Shoreline at a safe distance behind the van, traveling north.

When they crossed the bridge to Duck Key, his heart began hammering. This was what he'd been waiting for, Davy embarking on one of his many runs north for whatever mysterious reason. Carver figured the destination was Miami. He hoped so, anyway. He had set things up for Miami. The only problem was, he needed Davy to light somewhere in Miami for a while, give him a little time. As late as it was, maybe Davy would stop at a motel in or close to the city and conduct his business tomorrow. He must sleep like other people, or maybe with his eyes open, like a fish. If he didn't stop at a motel, maybe Davy would pull in somewhere in Miami for a snack or a cup of coffee to keep him alert, and he could get to a phone.

The van stopped at the Texaco station on Marathon Key, and Carver parked well up the road and watched Davy pump gas. Then, as Effie's friend Bobby had described, he drove to the far end of the lot, walked inside the brightly lighted station/convenience store and settled with the cashier for the gas.

Davy popped a piece of candy or gum into his mouth as he walked back to the van, dropping the wrapper on the ground. When he drove from the station and pulled the van back onto Route 1, Carver followed.

The highway was almost deserted, and the van made good time. Carver rode well behind it in the Ford, able to keep its taillights in view easily on the straight ribbon of road. Now and then he'd drive with his headlights off, so if Davy was checking the rearview mirror he'd assume the car behind him had turned off the highway. A new set of headlights five minutes later wouldn't alarm him.

Just after one o'clock the van's taillights flared bright red as it slowed and made a left into the lot of what a large red and green neon sign proclaimed to be Guzman's Drop Inn Motel.

Carver parked the Ford on the gravel shoulder and left the motor idling. He watched while Davy checked in at the motel office, then drove the van to an end room and parked it. After carefully locking the van, Davy went into the room carrying a small duffel bag.

This was all fine with Carver. He drove back to a phone booth he'd noticed and called Van Meter.

LLOYD VAN METER was one of the more prosperous private investigators in Florida, with offices in Orlando, Tampa, and Miami. He was almost as fat as Walter Rainer, and he dressed expensively but in the depths of fashion. He'd been expecting Carver's call, and when Carver arrived at the shopping mall lot where Van Meter said he'd be waiting, Van Meter was standing outside his white Cadillac, wearing a yellow suit that looked luminous in the moonlight. Carver hadn't seen him for a while. He still had his full white beard, which lent him an oddly biblical look even in his bizarre clothes, an overweight Moses with an Elton John wardrobe.

Theirs were the only cars on the lot. Carver got out from behind the steering wheel, slammed the Ford's door behind him, and limped over to Van Meter. He saw that up close the suit had a checked pattern.

Van Meter grinned as if about to change water to wine. Or maybe he could cure Carver simply with the laying on of pudgy hands. He said, ''You step in some shit, Fred?''

''Just working a case, that's all.''

''Uh-huh. Not like an independent soul such as you to ask for help.''

''I knew you were in Miami,'' Carver said, ''and you're the most progressive investigator I could think of. A leader in our field.''

''Meaning I'd have whatever kinda electronic gizmo you needed.''

Carver smiled, stood facing him and waiting.

Van Meter turned around and with great effort reached in through the Cadillac's lowered window and straightened up with a shoe box in his beefy hand. The box was lettered GENUINE CHEROKEE MOCCASINS. Carver glanced at Van Meter's feet and saw huge two-tone leather moccasins with oversized silver-tipped tassels. Surely no Cherokee had ever stalked game in such footwear. ''What you asked for's in here,'' Van Meter said, and lifted the box's lid as if it were hinged.

Carver saw among wadded white tissue paper the square black receiver with coiled black cord wrapped around it.

"This ain't like the one I loaned you once before," Van Meter said. "You do what I told you and rent a car with a cigarette lighter?"

"Car's got every toy made," Carver said.

"Except one of these."

"True."

Having made his point, Van Meter said, "You just plug this gizmo into the lighter socket. It's your receiver and'll sound a kinda high-pitched beeping, gets louder and closer together as you get nearer to this gadget." He held up a metal disk the size of a quarter only slightly thicker. "That's your transmitter. Magnetic, or it's got stickum on the back if you peel away the paper. I put a spare in the box for you, just in case, though the damned things never go wrong. Pretty simple, really, this little watch-battery-powered disk is your signal sender, like a miniature radio, and the box is your receiver. Basic as a kid's toy. Activate the disk like so, stick it on whatever it is you wanna follow, plug the receiver into your cigarette lighter, and you're off and away on your big adventure."

Carver said, "You make it sound like fun."

Not smiling, Van Meter said, "Don't shit me, Fred. You know it can be fun, once you get the transmitter in place. But planting it on the subject's car can be the nasty part. You need any help with that? A diversion? That kinda thing?"

"I don't think so. My guy's sacked out in a motel over on Route One."

"You hope."

"Well, that's life, hoping, running the risk. I think I'd be better off just walking up and sticking the transmitter to the bumper of his parked van than having you set fire to the motel for a diversion."

"Maybe you got a point. I get accused sometimes of doing things too flamboyantly."

"It's true, Lloyd, but then that's you."

Van Meter frowned as if he might cast fingertip lightning Carver's way. He really would look at home on a stained-glass window. "Meaning?"

"Well, there's not much about you that screams accountant."

"That a compliment?"

"Sure, unless you're an accountant."

Van Meter stroked his long white beard. "I ain't some accountant, and I can cover your back if you need it. I'm serious about the offer, Fred. Don't be too proud to accept, wind up hurt bad or dead. Hell, *I* might call on *you* sometime. Buddies, fellow pros, that kinda stuff, hey?"

"You are helping me, Lloyd. Lending me the latest in secret agent paraphernalia." Carver held up the shoe box. "For which I'm grateful."

"That's old, old technology, Fred, like the microphone in the martini olive. You worry me, the way you don't keep up with things. World's gonna pass you by on microchip skates."

"I like being old-fashioned."

"Yeah, like the town marshal without deputies." Van Meter shook his massive, shaggy head and opened the Caddy's driver-side door. Bathed in the glow of the courtesy light, his gigantic pseudo-Indian moccasins took on a yellow hue that matched his suit. Had he found color consciousness? "I'm driving home and going to bed, Fred," he said somberly, "maybe read about you in tomorrow's papers."

"I'll get this receiver back to you soon as I can," Carver told him. "Thanks, Lloyd."

Van Meter waved a pudgy hand. "Sure, stuff it in a padded envelope and put it in the mail, if you can't come by the office in the next few days. And if it gets shot or somebody breaks it over your skull, don't worry about it; it's already depreciated out for tax purposes." The big Cadillac's engine turned over and it glided away, white and ghostly in the deserted parking lot.

Carver used his cane to wave good-bye to Van Meter, then lowered himself into the Ford and drove back to the motel.

* * *

BOLDNESS WOULD be the right tactic here, he decided, after parking the Ford on the street near Guzman's Drop Inn. He could see Davy's van still squatting on its over-sized tires at the far end of the row of rooms. Light from a sign in the next block shone on its smooth black surface. The glow from the motel's neon sign illuminated the near side of the van so there were no concealing shadows.

The lights were out in Davy's room. Carver sat in the Ford sweating and waiting until another hour had passed. When he figured Davy would surely be asleep, dreaming whatever dreams a man like that dreamed, he climbed out of the car and limped along the edge of the motel lot, where he wouldn't be visible from the office. The slight breeze that played over him was warm, and he began per-spiring more heavily. He was hotter than he'd been today in the lounge chair; his shirt was molded like shrink-wrap to his body.

Still in deep shadow at the edge of the lot, he stood for a few seconds listening to the hum of distant traffic, the chirping and droning of night insects. Then he drew one of the quarter-sized transmitter disks from his pocket, twisted its rim as instructed to activate it, and limped quickly, but not too quickly, directly to Davy's van.

He felt totally exposed and vulnerable on the wide lot, unable to maneuver with the cane. If the motel desk man or a guest saw him and suspected something was going on, there was no way to flee. If Davy saw him, it would be stand and fight time. Tonight, right now, Carver didn't feel like fighting.

He reached the van and casually as possible attached the beeper to the inside of the back bumper, first peeling the paper from the back so the disk would be affixed with adhesive as well as magnetism. He tapped it with his fore-finger. It seemed firmly mounted.

As he straightened up, one of the motel doors opened and a man in shorts and a sleeveless white undershirt stepped out. He saw Carver, looked surprised, then nod-ded.

After nodding back, Carver moved around, kicked the van's left rear tire as if he owned the vehicle and was checking on it, and watched the man walk to a lighted break in the motel's line of rooms. There was a soda machine there, and a couple of vending machines that dispensed junk food.

Carver walked around to the far side of the van and stood listening to the *clunk! clunk!* of the soda machine reluctantly parting with its wares. He tried to peer inside the van's tinted windows, but the light reflecting on the outside of the glass made that impossible.

The man in the shorts and undershirt didn't look at him as he returned to his room with two soda cans. He was wearing rubber thongs; Carver could hear them slapping his heels as he trudged to within twenty feet of the van, opened the partly latched door to his room, and disappeared inside.

Breathing easier, Carver used a more circuitous route to reach the edge of the motel lot, then made his way back to the rental car. He drove around the block and parked where he could still see Davy's van, but where Davy wouldn't notice him as he checked out tomorrow and drove from the motel.

Carver got the square black receiver from the shoe box and plugged it into the cigarette lighter socket. Immediately it broke into deafening cricketlike beeping, as if it were a geiger counter on top of a pile of uranium. He fumbled for the control knob and turned down the volume. Whew! Much better.

Satisfied that the transmitter and receiver were working, he twisted the car's ignition key to Off so the lighter socket was dead.

With a final glance at the black van, he settled back in the Ford's deep upholstery and allowed himself to doze lightly, never falling completely asleep, maintaining a twilight level of awareness. He'd done this sort of thing before and had the knack.

Though the car's windows were down, it was warm inside and would stay warm. He knew he wouldn't get much rest, but it was unlikely Davy could leave tomorrow without Carver knowing about it through his hunter's sixth sense that seldom failed him.

The game was on and Van Meter was right: an essential part of him was enjoying it.

Enjoying the hell out of it.

He rested his bald pate on the padded headrest and crossed his arms, leaving his eyes narrowed to slits, feeling miserable and elated at the same time. Not quite sleeping.

Eager for morning.

| 30 |

JUST AFTER nine o'clock Carver knuckled sand from his eyes and watched Davy's black van jounce over the raised concrete apron as it drove from the motel lot. It hadn't stopped at the office; apparently Davy had paid cash, or the desk clerk had run his credit card through the night before. If Carver hadn't been half awake and watching, he would have missed him. Davy was a guy usually better missed, but not this time.

Carver worked the ignition key and the Ford's engine kicked to life and smoothed out. He pulled away from the curb and hung steady about a block behind the van. The beeper receiver rested next to him on the seat, already plugged into the lighter socket, but he didn't switch it on. There was no sense using it as long as he could see the boxy black form of the van. The sun hadn't gotten mean yet, and he drove with the window down, enjoying the cool breeze. Despite a stiff neck and the foul taste in his mouth, this wasn't half bad; he felt as if he had things more or less under control and was shaping events.

The van stopped at a McDonald's, and Carver waited, hungry, while Davy ambled inside and had breakfast. He was pleased to see that Davy acted nothing like a man suspicious of being followed. Carver could see him through the window, leaning back in his plastic chair and raising and lowering his plastic fork.

When Carver's stomach growled, he was tempted to chance getting something from the drive-through window, but he decided against it. Davy might happen to glance in his direction during the exchange of cash for McMuffin. So he sat with the Ford backed into one of the lot's yellow-bordered parking slots and waited, trying not to notice the fuzz on his teeth, or that he needed to use the rest room. These were occupational discomforts. He should have brought his plastic Porta Potti.

Finally Davy swaggered from McDonald's as if leaving a just-docked freighter. Without glancing around, he climbed up into the van and drove from the lot. Carver started the Ford's engine, glad to switch on the air conditioner now that the sun was higher and more serious. But he didn't pull out of his parking slot.

Tires squealing, the van had made a U-turn and was bouncing back in through the McDonald's exit, speeding the wrong way past irate drivers lined up at the drive-through window. Horns honked. A woman yelled something indecipherable. Carver ducked out of sight and listened to the van roar past. He realized he was smiling. Davy, Davy, you seafaring scoundrel!

He knew Davy was making sure he wasn't being followed. When Carver figured the van had exited from the entrance driveway, he switched on the receiver, sat up behind the steering wheel and followed the beeps instead of the van itself.

It was the first time he'd ever tried to keep track of another car this way, and after some initial doubts, he found it much simpler than he'd anticipated. The variance in tone and volume of the beeps emitted by the receiver was easy to detect, and any change in the unseen van's direction was noticeable. And when the intermittent beeping became fainter, Carver sped up and regained volume, knowing he was keeping the distance between Ford and van more or less constant. His curiosity about where Davy might lead him became sharp and goading.

Then the beeping got suddenly very loud and began a

fluttering beat that was almost an unbroken electronic scream.

Startled at first, Carver realized the van had stopped.

He steered the Ford to the outside lane, slowing to around fifteen miles per hour. Davy must be parked somewhere ahead. Keeping his speed slow, Carver peered through the windshield, scanning the sunny street, not wanting to stop too close to the black van.

But before he saw the van, the beeping abruptly changed tone and began to fade again. Davy was on the move after only a brief pause. Okay, so maybe he'd only stopped for half a minute at a traffic light. Carver urged himself to be more alert, to think of that sort of thing and not jump to conclusions.

His cane shifted sideways where it leaned against the seat, its crook bumping the receiver as he veered the Ford back to the outside lane and picked up speed to keep the volume constant.

After about five minutes the beeping grew louder again, changed tone.

The van was motionless again.

But not for long. The high-pitched beeps grew farther apart and fainter. The van was now on the move, probably after another brief wait for a traffic signal to change.

Only Carver didn't pass a traffic light for the next five blocks, and he was sure the van wasn't farther ahead of him than that. This was—

Uh-oh. The beeping indicated the van was stopped once more. Carver pulled the Ford to the curb and waited, this time for almost two minutes. Longer than any traffic light.

Beeep beeep . . . beep . . . beep . . . beep . . .

Davy on the go again, according to the tiny transmitter on the van's bumper.

Stop, start, stop, start. What the hell was the game here?

Carver studied the wide, four-lane avenue ahead of him. Heavy Miami traffic, even this late in the morning. Lots of pedestrians on the sidewalk, window shopping, standing at—

Goddamnit!

He swerved around a pickup truck and goosed the Ford's

speed up to fifty, flying past slower traffic in the curb lane.
The beeping got louder and louder.

Became almost unbearably loud and constant.

And Carver saw the bus.

He parked.

Watched the bus pull away after picking up passengers.
The beeping receded.

Two blocks farther down, when the lumbering vehicle
angled to the curb to pick up and drop off more passengers, the beeping flared again. It faded as the bus rumbled
away, leaving a dark haze of diesel exhaust.

Carver's heart took a dive. He swerved the Ford to the
curb lane and parked, switching off the receiver. Then he
slapped the dashboard hard enough to sting his hand and
make something drop with a tiny tinkling sound somewhere in the car.

Davy had figured it out, maybe even seen him plant the
bumper beeper on the van last night at the motel. He'd
tricked Carver, been toying with him. Placed the beeper
on the back of a bus while he went about his business,
leaving Carver to start and stop along the vehicle's route.
Davy's little joke.

Not funny to Carver.

After sitting for a while seething and trying to think in
the glaring sunlight, he decided there was only one way
he might salvage something from this trip north. Still
smelling diesel fumes, he almost broke the Ford's key
twisting it in the ignition to restart the engine. Then he
drove to the Blue Flamingo Hotel. There was the slim
possibility the Evermans had checked back in. And if they
hadn't, he could talk to some of the other residents and
try to get a line on where they might have gone.

And there was another possibility. He was sure Davy
was wily enough to figure out his trail might be picked up
again at the Blue Flamingo, yet Davy's arrogance and sadistic streak might compel him to go to the hotel for no
reason other than to taunt Carver. How likely that was,
Carver wasn't sure, but he decided to give psychology a
chance.

He'd leave the Ford parked out of sight, then check into

one of the nearby hotels that was a notch above the Blue Flamingo and buy some shorts and sunglasses, a hat to protect his bald head from the sun. Maybe he'd smear a glob of that white suntan lotion on his nose, become unrecognizable. There was no shortage of men who walked with canes in this area. He could wander unobtrusively down Collins Avenue, or possibly along the beach like a shell collector, and wait to see if Davy showed up at the Blue Flamingo. Carver the man of a thousand disguises.

If Davy showed, Carver would attach the second transmitter to the van, this time someplace where it wouldn't be noticed.

If Davy didn't show, at least Carver would return to Key Montaigne with an enviable tan, and feeling qualified to drive a bus in Miami.

31

CARVER DROVE back to Key Montaigne the next morning still wearing his tourist garb and sunglasses, the bridge of his nose painfully sunburned despite the glob of white lotion he'd smeared and left on it. He'd missed a spot. The sun had found it.

No one at the Blue Flamingo even knew who the Evermans were when he'd asked about them. It was a place where questions weren't welcome, and that included the ones posed by Carver. And Davy hadn't reappeared in the vicinity of the old art deco hotel. At least not in any way Carver could detect. So much for abnormal psychology.

He hadn't rushed leaving Miami, figuring why not temper his disappointment with a large and leisurely breakfast, then a cigar.

He'd indulged himself at the Osprey restaurant, overlooking the ocean, and decided he'd return there sometime when he got back to Miami. After breakfast he walked along the beach smoking, even though he'd had more than enough of the sun while staking out the Blue Flamingo. It felt good to be among the hundreds of tourists; his was a lonely line of work, and even this impersonal human closeness helped relieve the pressure of solitude.

By the time he'd driven to Key Montaigne and returned the Ford to Hertz, it was well past noon. Since his sunburned nose still hurt, he drove the Olds with the top up. Beth was sitting on the screened-in porch when he parked in front of the cottage and climbed out of the car in his red and black striped shorts, T-shirt with the flying fish on it, long-billed white cap, and reflector-lens sunglasses. She walked out and stood on the porch steps with the door open, staring at him.

"Been in some kinda accident, Fred?"

"What's that mean?"

"Nothing. What's that white gunk on your nose?"

"Sunscreen. Makes it feel better."

"Oh. I'd ask you how it went up in Miami, but I can tell by your face it didn't go well." When he got close enough, hobbling up the steps with his cane, she kissed him on the chin, well below nose level. "Want a beer?"

He nodded and lowered himself into one of the chairs on the porch, then sat tracing idle patterns on the floor with the tip of his cane. It was dim there compared to the brilliant sunlight beyond the dark screen, almost cool.

She returned with two opened cans of Budweiser, gave him one and settled into the metal glider with the other. She had her hair pulled back and tied with a yellow ribbon today. The ribbon matched her shorts. She looked cool as ice cream and twice as—

"Been some news here while you were gone," she said, interrupting his thoughts, even his plans. "Came over the local radio station this morning. The head of the Oceanography Research Center was found dead. Hanged himself, news said."

Carver planted the tip of his cane on the floor and pushed himself up straighter in the chair. "Dr. Sam?"

"Yeah. Only the news called him Dr. Bing."

"Who found him?"

"His assistant—that Katia woman. S'posed to have come in for work around eight this morning to open the aquarium for tourists, and there the good doctor was hanging."

Carver breathed out and sat still for a moment, digesting what Beth had told him. "They calling it suicide?"

"Sure. According to Chief Wicke, there was no doubt."

"Bing leave a note?"

She shrugged, sipped Budweiser, wiped a bit of foam from her upper lip. "News didn't say."

Carver set his beer can aside and stood up, leaning on the cane.

"Guess I don't have to ask where you're going?" Beth said.

"Guess not."

"Want me to come along?"

Carver stood thinking about that. Beth had a way with distraught members of her own sex. She'd suffered and she understood *their* suffering, and she might notice something he'd miss in a conversation with Millicent Bing or Katia. "It'd be a good idea," he said. "You ready to go?"

She didn't move. "Only on one condition."

He cocked his head and looked questioningly at her. What had she cranked up to throw at him now?

"You gotta change clothes, Fred, get rid of that white stuff on your nose."

Easy enough.

HE'D EXPECTED to see police cars parked at the research center, but the lot was empty. The law had come and gone, shaping death to the brisk, efficient routine of bureaucracy and making it seem comprehensible to the only species that thought about it before it happened. A cardboard sign next to the parking lot entrance, printed crudely in thick black marking pen, informed visitors apologetically that the center was temporarily closed.

With Beth beside him, Carver limped to the tinted glass entrance, hoping someone was still inside. There must be chores here that had to be done, cleaning tanks, feeding sea life, whatever was necessary to maintain a patch of ocean on dry land. He noticed the *Fair Wind* still at its dock and riding gently on incoming ripples, as if dancing lightly to the music of the wind through its myriad antennae. The breeze off the ocean made the place seem sad and desolate, touched by undeniable mortality. Death itself could haunt.

Carver pounded on the door with the crook of his cane.

"Place *feels* unoccupied," Beth said.

But it wasn't. The door opened about six inches and Katia Marsh peered out. There were deep crescents of grief beneath her eyes; she'd been crying and it hadn't helped much.

"We're closed," she said, "Dr. Sam—"

"I know," Carver told her. "We heard about it on the news. This is my associate, Beth Jackson. Can we come inside, Katia?"

She hesitated a moment, then stepped back and opened the door wider so they could enter. Before closing the door, she glanced around outside, as if suspecting they might be the advance guard for an army of interlopers. Maybe she feared the news media. Or the police converging on her again.

It was blessedly cool in the research center. The only sound was an air-conditioning unit, or possibly a filtering system, humming away somewhere.

"I was cleaning some of the displays," Katia said, "trying to keep busy." With a weak smile she turned and walked to the door leading to the live exhibits. Carver and Beth followed her through the door and down the steel steps. Beth looked at the circling shark behind the glass wall. It looked back at her. She shivered.

Katia picked up some kind of instrument, a screened scoop on the end of a wooden handle, and began listlessly skimming the surface of the shallow water in which a small sea turtle was displayed.

"Is this where you found Dr. Sam?" Carver asked.

The sifter jerked, causing ripples in the shallow water. Beth looked hard at Carver, somewhat the way the shark had looked at her.

"I'm told you were close to the doctor," she said to Katia. "We're sorry about what happened. Really."

Katia dropped the sifter and rubbed her eyes with knuckles still wet from the tank. Carver felt guilty for being cynical enough to wonder if there'd been anything beyond business going on between the late doctor and his attractive young assistant. He said, "I'm sorry about Dr. Sam, and sorry to have to ask you these questions."

"Why *do* you have to?" Katia asked, staring at him with red-rimmed eyes.

"Because Dr. Sam's death might be linked to Henry Tiller's."

"Henry Tiller was struck by a hit-and-run driver, and Dr. Sam committed suicide."

"Henry was murdered," Carver said.

"Maybe. But I still don't see the relevance." The skeptical scientist in her.

"I don't know that there actually is any," Carver admitted. "But I'm asking you to understand I need to make sure."

Katia shrugged, apparently not understanding, but also not wanting to argue. "I found him in there," she said, motioning with her head toward a closed door. "It's a storeroom. I unlocked and opened that door to get something, and there—I mean, the first thing that happened was I smelled the stench." She bowed her head. Carver distinctly saw a glittering tear fall from her cheek to the floor, where it seemed to shatter like crystal. Beth moved close to her and wrapped a long brown arm around her. Carver had seen hangings. He knew the doctor's sphincter had relaxed during death and his bowels had released. "Then I saw his legs, one stockinged foot, a black silk sock. He'd kicked off one of his shoes when he shoved away the boxes he'd been standing on. He was suspended by a rope around his neck, hanging from one of the steel beams up near the ceiling. I saw his face and backed away. Got out of there." She buried her face in her hands and sobbed for a minute while Carver and Beth said nothing. Carver felt like hugging the girl himself, assuring her that grief would pass, or at least become tolerable with time. But he knew he couldn't. Shouldn't. Felt helpless. He truly hated moments like this. Beth held her tighter, patting her gently and rhythmically on the back.

Finally Katia composed herself, lowering her hands and standing up straight, managing a kind of tear-streaked dignity Carver admired.

"You mentioned the door was locked," he said.

"It usually is locked, but it must not have been this

morning. When I turned my key in the lock, it must have already been *un*locked and I didn't notice. Or maybe it *was* locked; Dr. Sam might have locked the door from the inside.'' She clenched her teeth, making her jaw muscles dance. ''God, does it really make any difference? This is like some sick game!''

''Can I have a look at the room?''

Katia nodded, walked to the door and unlocked it with a brass key on a ring of at least a half a dozen keys. Instead of opening the door, she shied away from it, returning to her work at the tide pool displays. Beth stood near her, watching her, not looking at Carver.

Carver opened the door. The room wasn't much larger than a closet, and the smell of human feces still permeated the warm, motionless air. The hum of whatever was running was louder in here. He found the light switch and flipped it upward. A fluorescent ceiling fixture fought through its birth pangs and winked on.

The police were finished with the death scene, and the rope Dr. Sam had used was removed from the steel girder supporting the concrete ceiling. The small room was lined with metal shelving that held cardboard boxes. Two boxes that contained computer paper sat on the concrete floor, probably the boxes Dr. Sam had stood on, then kicked away after slipping the noose over his head.

Carver examined the door and saw that the only way to lock it from the inside was with a key. Interesting. Maybe meaningful. He switched off the light, stepped outside and closed the door, glad to be out of the close, oppressive room. Here the air was cooler and didn't smell of death.

Carver limped over to where Katia was now sprinkling flakes of food into one of the trays. BALANCED NUTRIENT, read the label on the otherwise plain white box. ''How's Millicent Bing taking her husband's death?'' he asked, watching the irregular flakes float like debris on the surface, glad he wasn't a fish.

Katia didn't look up. ''I think she's still in shock. I offered to go over and stay with her, but she said she'd rather be alone. Said that was how she handled grief.''

''Did Dr. Sam leave a suicide note?'' Carver asked.

Katia shook her head no.

Carver thanked her for talking with him, then said, "You gonna be okay here?"

She put down the balanced nutrient and forced a smile. "Yeah, I think so. I'll stay busy. That's how I handle *my* grief."

"What'll happen to the research center now?" Beth asked.

"I don't know," Katia said. "I haven't thought about it yet."

"If you change your mind about how you want to handle your grief," Beth said, "phone me and I'll come over."

This time Katia's smile was genuine even if fleeting. "Thanks. I appreciate that."

"We'll find our way out," Carver told her. Beth followed him as he limped up the steel stairs to the ground-level exhibit.

Outside in the brilliant sun, Beth said, "The girl thought a lot about her employer."

"More than she should have?" Carver asked.

"Think there was more than something fishy going on there?" Beth said.

"It was a serious question."

"Okay, Fred. Bad joke. I didn't pick up that Katia and the doctor were romantically involved, but it's not impossible. Might not mean anything even if they did have something going."

"Far too many *mights* in this world," Carver said. He lowered himself into the Olds as Beth walked around and got in on the passenger side.

As soon as he started the engine, he switched the air conditioner on High.

Beth crossed her long bare legs, then stretched the front of her shirt to pat perspiration from her forehead. "Think Dr. Sam really committed suicide?" she asked.

"Might have," Carver said.

32

MILLICENT BING hadn't answered the phone when Carver called to offer condolences and ask if he could come over and talk with her. He suspected she was home, though, so he left Beth at the cottage and drove to the Bing house. Mr. Persistence.

The breeze still pushed steadily in from the sea, the leaning palm tree's fronds still rattled on the green tile roof, and if she was inside the house, Millicent wasn't making herself available.

Carver stood for a while in the heat, keeping an eye on the bees in the bougainvillea, occasionally knocking on the door, finally leaning on the bell's brass push button and listening to the rolling repetition of chimes from inside the house. Then he gave up and headed back to the Olds.

As he jockeyed the big car down the driveway, he braked near the mailbox, wondering. Carver cranked down the car window and lifted the mailbox's aluminum door. He pulled out two sun-warmed envelopes.

One was an advertisement for life insurance—too late. The other was personal, addressed to Millicent Bing in pencil. It had a Forest, Ohio, postmark, and the return address was a rural route number.

Carver looked at the neatly scripted address, remembering a hated fifth-grade teacher who was a disciple of the Palmer penmanship method. Then he pried open the envelope's flap carefully, tearing it only once and very slightly.

Inside was a sheet of lined notepaper on which a letter was composed in the same light pencil and precise handwriting that was on the envelope. The letter was dated three days ago. It asked how "Milly" was, and by the way how was brother Sam. Then it told about the successful removal of a brain tumor from someone named Dwayne, complained about federal farm policy, mentioned new furniture in the den, and expressed the wish that Milly and Sam would come up for a visit. Milly should lean on Sam about driving north, it said. It was signed "Love, Sandy."

After copying the return address, then licking what mint-flavored glue remained and resealing the flap, Carver replaced both envelopes in the mailbox. He glanced back at the house. There was no sign of anybody peering from the one visible window. He'd taken a chance, tampering with Millicent's mail, but surely if she'd seen him she would have stormed out of the house and objected. Or phoned the police. But he'd had to risk it; there was always the possibility Dr. Sam had written a note and mailed it to his wife. Suicides did that sometimes, trusting the postal service more than whoever might discover the body. The uniform, maybe.

If Millicent *had* seen him and phoned the law, Carver would soon find out. He accelerated along Shoreline, keeping pace with and then outdistancing a large white gull winging parallel to the coast. He was curious as to what Chief Wicke would have to say about Dr. Sam's suicide.

"AUTOPSY?" WICKE said, leaning back in his desk chair and clasping his hands behind his head. "Why the fuck should there be an autopsy? Man died of asphyxiation brought about by the rope around his neck. Hell, the only thing more purple than his face was his tongue."

"I'm not suggesting it wasn't suicide," Carver said,

"or that Bing didn't die of strangulation. But what about bruises or marks on the body indicating he *didn't* just climb up on those boxes, slip the noose over his head, and kick away his life?"

Wicke looked at Carver with exaggerated tolerance and shook his head. "You saying Dr. Bing was made to hang himself?"

"Under the circumstances, I wouldn't take anything for granted."

"I seen hanging suicides before," Wicke said, now with an edge of impatience. "Believe me, Bing did it to himself without any help."

"But you didn't have the M.E. check the body for any sign of coercion? Any results of a struggle?"

Wicke dropped forward in his chair, propping his elbows on his green felt desk pad. When he did that, the breeze from the air conditioner sent a strong whiff of deodorant and perspiration across the desk. "I looked over the body myself, Carver, at the death scene and later." He brought his hands together and laced his thick fingers. "No marks."

"No note, either?"

"Dr. Sam didn't leave a note, not unless he mailed it."

Carver saw no change of expression at the mention of mail. Apparently he hadn't been seen at the Bing mailbox. He said, "Were there any keys on the body?"

"You're thinking about the girl saying she unlocked the door," Wicke said. "Well, there were keys in Bing's pants pocket, and one of them fit the lock to the storage room. The girl said she couldn't be sure if the door was actually locked when she inserted her key and turned it, but so what? Bing coulda let himself into the room and locked it from the inside so he wouldn't be disturbed. Maybe he knew his assistant would open the door in the morning, wanted her to discover him instead of having his wife go to the research center looking for him and finding him like that. Does that make sense, Carver?"

"Kind of."

"So forget keys, forget Walter Rainer, forget Henry Tiller. Dr. Sam's death's got nothing to do with either of them."

"Any thoughts on why he did commit suicide?"

Wicke shrugged, as if to say it wasn't his business to harbor curiosity. "Who knows why people kill themselves? Sometimes there's some big problem in their lives plunges them into depression, other times it just seems to come on them like a black mood and they give up on life and slit their wrists or jump in front of a train or string themselves up like Dr. Sam. You were a cop; you oughta know suicides can be unpredictable as lightning."

"Sometimes people close to the victim have an idea why it happened," Carver said. "You talk with Millicent Bing?"

"An hour after Dr. Sam's body was discovered," Wicke said. He frowned. "I was the one broke the news to her."

"How'd she take it?"

"Like I just told her her husband was dead."

"I mean, she have any idea why he might have killed himself?"

"About as many ideas as you and me."

"You got any inkling at all about it? I'm not talking facts, I'm asking about your cop's instincts."

"Ho-ho! Like Henry Tiller's instincts?"

"Just like."

"Okay. Maybe Dr. Sam's business was going bad, maybe he had something hot going with the young assistant and it turned cold, maybe his sex life at home was all messed up, maybe it was male menopause. Point is, who gives a fuck now? I mean, the man's dead. Better to have worried about all this when he was alive and prevented him from hanging himself. But it's too late for that now, so it's on to other business for me. And that oughta be the way you look at it. You been in your line of work long enough to know the world don't screech to a halt for any one person's death."

"It does for the person who's dead."

"Well, there's no sense getting all overwrought about it after the fact."

Carver gripped his cane and stood up. "You're probably right."

Wicke smiled dubiously at him. "Now, why are you telling me that, Carver?"

"Because I believe it." He thanked Chief Wicke for his time and limped toward the door.

"Carver," Wicke said behind him, "don't get any ideas about looking over the body. Dr. Sam's remains are already on the way to his family in Ohio."

Carver opened the door, paused and looked back. "How come everybody dies here gets shipped north? Isn't anybody ever buried on Key Montaigne?"

"We got sandy soil here," Wicke said. "They come back up when the tide's in." He wasn't smiling. Man could probably play good poker.

Carver said, "I sorta lean toward that male menopause theory."

Wicke said something to him after he'd closed the door and was limping away, but he wasn't sure what.

33

CARVER HAD stopped for a few beers at the Key Lime Pie's bar after leaving Chief Wicke, thinking he might overhear something significant about Dr. Sam's death. But none of the natives was discussing it. Maybe they'd already talked themselves out on the subject, or maybe everyone knew who Carver was and thought it safest to stay silent, therefore uninvolved and still alive, unlike Dr. Sam.

When he returned to the cottage, he phoned Katia Marsh and asked her if she'd again arrange for him to talk with Millicent Bing.

"You're too late," Katia told him. "She's gone."

"Gone where?"

"From Key Montaigne, and she's not coming back. She wouldn't tell me where she was going. I assume it's wherever Dr. Sam's funeral's going to be. I wanted to go to the funeral, but she told me it'd be better if I didn't, that Dr. Sam'd want me to stay here and take care of the research center. And of course somebody *has* to do that; the exhibits require constant care."

Carver wiped his hand over his perspiring forehead, touching the burned part of his nose with his wrist and causing instantaneous pain. "Don't you have any idea where Dr. Sam's going to be buried?"

"Someplace in the Midwest, I think."

"Ohio?"

"It'd make sense. That's where he was from. Both he and his wife, in fact. She's from Columbus and he was from some little farming town. Can't think of its name. So far from the ocean; maybe that's why the sea fascinated him."

"I heard he had a sister."

"I don't know. It's possible. He never talked much about his family or early life. It seemed his life started when he went to college at Ohio State, then did postgrad work at the University of Michigan and Florida State." Her voice took on a sad tone. "He was a pure scientist, Mr. Carver, a dedicated researcher. Why somebody like that—" Her voice broke, and he thought she was about to break into sobs, but after a moment she said, "Damnit! I'm sorry."

He told her not to be, he understood. He wondered if he did. The relationship of Dr. Sam and Katia still wasn't clear to him.

"I went to Millicent's house to try and comfort her," Katia said. "She told me good-bye. A truck was there and two men were loading it with boxes of possessions. Millicent said she'd arrange to have the furniture put in storage before listing the house with a real estate agent. She told me she never wanted to see Key Montaigne again." Another pause, but not to compose herself. "She was grief-stricken, of course, but something else, too. I got the impression she was scared, Mr. Carver."

"Of what?"

"I have no idea. But she was definitely unwilling to tell me where she was going."

Carver knew whom Millicent Bing was afraid of, but he wasn't sure of the reason for her fear. "You gonna be okay?" he asked Katia.

"Me? Sure. Florida State's been in touch. Some of our grant money flowed through them. They assured me the research center would stay open. I might even be in charge, carry on Dr. Sam's work with sharks. Nothing would please me more. We were learning so much . . ."

Carver left her to her future and hung up.

He sat by the phone for a while, thinking. If Millicent

did travel to Ohio for Dr. Sam's funeral, her fear might cause her to leave immediately afterward and he might never locate her.

He limped in to where Beth was slouched on the sofa watching the world going to hell on CNN news. "Wanna do something for me?" he asked. On the TV screen a missile screamed into an ancient radio-controlled aircraft and exploded.

She smiled at him and struck a suggestive pose with only the slightest shifting of her lean body, more a change of attitude than position. "I ever turn you down?"

"Comes under the category of work," he said, watching the debris of the plane flutter down from a lingering cloud of black smoke. The CNN correspondent, a pretty blond woman in combat fatigues, was saying. " '. . . Pinpoint accuracy and complete destruction. Smart weapons, Bernie."

"I only do it for love," Beth told him with mock disdain.

"Detective work. I need you to find the phone number of a Sandy in Forest, Ohio. Last name might be Bing."

"Relative of the late Dr. Sam?"

"Sister."

"Shouldn't be too hard," she said, using the remote to switch off the TV. "Forest can't be a very large place. When I find the number, want me to call it?"

"No, I better do that. But later. Right now I'm going over to Millicent Bing's house while there's still plenty of light." He'd learned how quickly darkness could fall in the Keys.

"I gathered from your phone conversation that she'd left Key Montaigne," Beth said.

Carver nodded. "Doesn't matter. I won't need anyone to show me around."

Beth was moving toward the phone as he limped from the cottage into the early evening heat.

HE PARKED the Olds as close as possible to the side of the Bing house, so it wouldn't be noticeable from Shoreline. The low sun angled beneath the palm fronds to warm

the front porch as he brushed away a bee and tried using
his honed expired Visa card to slip the lock. The only
result was a kink in the plastic card. Carver made his way
around to the back of the house, limping through tall grass
that found its way beneath his pants cuffs and tickled his
ankles. Each of his dragging steps raised a cloud of tiny
insects.

One of the back windows was unlocked. He managed
to inch it upward enough to get his fingers curled beneath
its aluminum frame, then he slid it open far enough for
his body to fit through. After dropping his cane inside the
house, he draped his arms over the sill and used his powerful upper body to raise his impaired lower self and wriggled through the window to fall onto soft carpet.

He sat there leaning back on his palms, his stiff leg out
in front of him.

The air-conditioning was turned off and the house was
almost as hot as the sultry evening outside. Silent, too,
except for the leaning palm tree's fronds rattling over the
tile roof as the wind blew. It sounded as if someone might
be walking around up there with skeleton feet.

Carver levered himself to his own feet with his cane and
looked around. He was in a small office: gray metal desk
with black leather swivel chair, two-drawer oak file cabinet, table with a small copy machine on it, gray metal
stand supporting a gray IBM typewriter, the old-fashioned
kind with the manual carriage return. On the wall behind
the desk was a framed photograph of Dr. Sam wearing
swimming trunks and standing in front of Victor the shark,
circling behind him on the other side of the aquarium glass.
The camera had picked up very little reflection from the
glass, and the photo was striking, almost as if the doctor
were casually standing underwater only a few feet from
the huge carnivore.

Already sweating, Carver limped over to the desk and
opened the drawers. All four of them were empty except
for a three-foot strand of soft rope in the left-hand bottom.
Carver wondered if it was cut from the length of rope Dr.
Sam had used to hang himself. There was a combination
phone and answering machine on the desk. Its counter

registered no messages. Carver lifted the receiver. The phone was dead. He went to the oak file cabinet and wasn't surprised to find it as empty as the desk. The contents must have been in the boxes Millicent had shipped north. Carver examined the typewriter and saw that it contained no ribbon. He lifted the rubber flap of the copy machine to make sure nothing had been overlooked there. Sighing, he sat down in Dr. Sam's desk chair, trying literally to put himself in the late researcher's place, contemplating death as Dr. Sam himself must have before seeing it as an acceptable option.

After a while Carver decided he wasn't gaining any insight, then left the office. In the hall he noticed a thermometer, switched it to Cool and rolled the setting back to seventy. Nothing happened. The utilities had been turned off.

Carver had been inside longer than he'd thought. The sun was dropping fast and the house's interior was already dim. He'd better finish here soon as possible.

The rest of the house was much like the office. The essential furniture was there, chairs, end tables, pieces far too large to pack, even a few knickknacks. But the place was like a recently vacated hotel suite; all signs of its previous inhabitants had been removed.

In the master bedroom Carver slid open a mirrored closet door and found that Dr. Sam's clothes had been removed as well as Millicent's. There was some indication of previous occupancy here, however. A wire hanger on the floor. Another wedged where it had fallen into an old pair of rubber boots. In a dusty corner lay some wadded panty hose. Carver ran his hand over the closet shelf, hoping something there had been overlooked, but found nothing but a dog leash. It was leather and looked almost new. He tossed it back up on the shelf and was about to leave the house when he remembered another door off the hall. A third bedroom. In the fading golden light he limped to the door and opened it.

The room was small and contained no furniture other than a straight-backed antique wooden chair of the sort designed by puritans to entertain nonbelievers. The win-

dow faced west, so this room was brighter than the main
bedroom. Carver checked its closet and found it empty.
Even its shelf had been removed. He was about to close
the door when he noticed two thick steel eye hooks
mounted on the back closet wall. A few inches beneath
them the paint had been scraped from the plaster. Near
the floor were similar scraped areas, and two more eye
hooks.

Carver shut the closet door and looked around the room
carefully. There were no marks from picture frames or
decorative hangings on the pale beige walls, but a few feet
from the ceiling were areas of scratched paint, and several
round holes about a quarter inch in diameter, approximately the diameter of the eye hooks in the closet. Carver
noticed plaster dust on the brown carpet beneath the holes.
Something had recently been unscrewed from the walls.
He found similar round holes, and more white dusting of
plaster, down low along the baseboard. In this room there
were numerous stains on the carpet that weren't in evidence anywhere else in the house, a few stains on the
walls. Considering it contained no furniture, the room
showed a lot of wear.

Carver limped back to the master bedroom and looked
around for similar holes and plaster dust, but found none.
Then he examined the brass headboard of the king-sized
bed.

He remembered a Key Montaigne phone directory on
top of the oak file cabinets in the office. He got it and
looked up Katia Marsh. Her number was listed for an address on Kale Avenue in Fishback. He tore the page from
the directory and stuffed it into a pocket, then he got out
of the dim and stifling house, leaving by the front door
and letting its lock click loudly and decisively behind him.
Millicent Bing must have heard that same sound, her past
locking shut as she walked away from it. No going back;
a new life lay ahead, ready or not.

He drove down Shoreline and turned the Olds into the
research center driveway. Dusk was dying, and a gigantic
tropical moon had taken over the sky. There were no lights

showing in the low, angular building, and the *Fair Wind* rode darkly at her moorings.

Carver sat for a moment with both hands on the steering wheel, staring out at the ocean fading from green to black, breathing in the scent of the sea brought to him by the warm breeze wafting in through the car's open windows. Around him nocturnal insects had begun their constant and cacophonous scream that might last till dawn. Down near the shore tall palm trees were swaying their fronds like lean, elegant women tossing their hair to dry it in the wind. He didn't like the suspicion that was taking root in his mind. It only served to make matters more complicated and mystifying. Or maybe simply less related.

He drove from the parking lot and aimed the moonlit hood of the Olds toward Fishback.

34

KALE AVENUE was a narrow street that ran off of Main two blocks down from the Key Lime Pie. Katia's address turned out to be a huge gray Victorian home that had been converted to apartments. The darkly shadowed face of the three-story house was almost invisible behind banana and oleander trees.

Carver limped up onto the wide front porch. Two old women were perched on a long bench that was probably an ancient church pew, but neither of them looked at Carver. On the porch ceiling a paddle fan with a schoolhouse light slung below it slowly rotated, creating a slight breeze and enough illumination for Carver to study the bank of brass mailboxes and find Katia's apartment number. Dozens of moths circled the light beneath the fan, their frantic arching and darting causing faint shadows to flit over the porch. He opened a screen door and climbed a narrow flight of stairs to the second floor, found a door marked 2-C, and turned a brass crank that made a rasping noise inside the apartment. He stood waiting. Someone was cooking Italian somewhere in the house. The garlicky aroma prodded Carver's appetite.

Floorboards creaked, and light in the door's fish-eye peephole rolled like a wild pupil, then was steady. He knew Katia was studying his distorted image in the hall.

Then the door opened and she smiled out at him. She was wearing a faded pink robe and was barefoot. He saw that her toenails were painted bright red. Her features seemed puffy and her hair was mussed, as if she'd been sleeping, but her blue eyes were alert. "Mr. Carver!" she said in a surprised voice, as if he were an unexpected gift.

"Evening, Katia." He returned her smile. "I know it's past business hours, but I drove by the research center and you weren't there, and I need to talk to you again about Dr. Sam's death."

She appeared doubtful for a moment, then she said, "Well, I don't see why not." She opened the door wider and stepped back to let him in.

Her apartment had high ceilings but was small. The living room was crowded with Victorian furniture suited to the house. Some of it was threadbare, but other pieces had been refinished or reupholstered. Oval mahogany frames hung on the walls from gold-braided cord hooked over crown molding. Each of them held antique photographs of the sort that made their subjects appear either hopelessly stern or zanily cross-eyed. Either way, people you'd just as soon not meet. On a coffee table with Queen Anne legs that were no compliment to Queen Anne, half a dozen glossy *Smithsonian* magazines were scattered about, but not for show; they were dog-eared and well read. In a tall window, a round-cornered air conditioner that might date back to Victorian times was spitting out cold air along with flecks of ice that caught the light from an ornately shaded marble and brass floor lamp. The room smelled musty but was cool, almost cold.

Katia motioned with her arm, inviting Carver to sit on a plush maroon sofa with a lot of carved wood on it. He sat down, finding it comfortable, and leaned his cane against the wood and velveteen arm. From where he sat he could see into a tiny kitchen with yellowed stove and refrigerator. The refrigerator had round corners like the air conditioner.

Katia lowered herself into a dainty chair across from him. Her robe rode up on her bare legs, better than Queen

Anne's. She asked Carver if he cared for anything to drink, but he declined. That took care of the amenities.

He said, "I had a look around inside the Bings' house this evening."

She arched a surprised eyebrow. "Millicent was there?"

"No."

"Oh." She nodded, understanding. "Is that legal?"

"I found the door unlocked."

Katia smiled, knowing he was lying and an unlocked door wouldn't make trespassing legal anyway, but she didn't press him on it. She looked like a teenager in the soft lamplight. "I imagine Millicent cleaned out most everything but the furniture."

"She did a good job of that," Carver said.

"But you found something, or you wouldn't be here."

"I didn't exactly find anything, but I saw evidence of something. Why do you suppose Millicent left so abruptly, and in such a way that she wouldn't have to return?"

"Well, she had to go north to her husband's funeral, so why shouldn't she try avoiding another trip down here to settle her affairs? Makes sense to me."

Carver watched the light play over the flecks of ice shooting from the air conditioner, wondering if a rainbow might be possible. He said, "You touched on another reason last time we talked."

Katia didn't have to search her memory. "You mean when I said she seemed scared?"

"Uh-huh." Carver waited.

"That was just a feeling I had. Nothing definite."

Time to broach the subject. "Katia, would you have any idea if Dr. Sam and Millicent engaged in what might be called kinky sex?"

She looked surprised but not shocked. Then she laughed nervously. "Well, they sure wouldn't tell me about it, would they?"

"Not intentionally. What I mean is, do you remember anything slipping out about the subject during conversation?"

"No, I don't think so. Anyway, this is a conservative

part of Florida, so what exactly do you mean by kinky sex? Anything other than the missionary position?''

"Sadomasochism. Chains, whips, leashes, that sort of thing. Happens even in Florida.''

An incredulous expression passed over her young face. "Dr. Sam? Millicent? You've got to be kidding!''

Carver gave her a minute to let the idea settle in. "People tend secret flames, Katia, and sometimes the heat consumes them. They lead private lives that are often unlike the ones they present to the world. Sort of existing on two levels. You get a little older you'll realize that, if you don't know it already.''

"Sure. And whatever two consenting adults do, especially if they're married, is their own business.''

"Couldn't agree more. I'm a little kinky myself.''

She squinted at him, unable to quite figure him.

"We're not talking about a crime here,'' he told her.

"We might be, in Florida,'' she said. "But that doesn't matter a fig to me. It's just that with Dr. Sam and Millicent I think the idea's way, way off the mark. He was obsessed with his work and there wasn't room for much else. And Millicent never struck me as . . . well, the carnally adventuresome type. I don't recall Dr. Sam ever saying anything even remotely sexual. God, this was a middle-aged couple, Mr. Carver.''

Ah, the young, he thought. He said, "Maybe their sex life had gone stale and they were experimenting.''

"Oh, sure, maybe. But how would I know, even if it was any of my business? And how would you know?''

"I *don't* know,'' Carver said. "Not for sure. I found some eye hooks, and some holes drilled in the wall that were spaced as if they were used to constrain somebody. There were marks on the paint that might have come from chains or manacles being scraped over the plaster. Discoloration from perspiration. I found a leather leash in the closet.''

Katia pressed her knees together tight enough to whiten the flesh. She looked thoughtful. Said, "The Bings didn't have a dog.''

"You wouldn't guess it by looking at the carpet where I found most of the drilled holes," Carver told her.

She seemed confused, and passed a hand down her cheek vaguely, as if feeling for an injury, and shook her head. "Listen, even if what you found does mean anything, so what? I mean, Dr. Sam and Millicent's sex life couldn't be relevant to what you're investigating: Henry Tiller's death, whatever you think's going on over at the Rainer place."

"Don't forget Dr. Sam's suicide," Carver said.

She frowned. "I don't see the connection."

"Could be there isn't any. That's one of the things I'm trying to determine."

Katia stared at the dark window as if she could see out of it. Then she stood up and clutched her robe around her. "I keep getting images of Dr. Sam and Millicent," she said, making a face as if she'd found a roach in her stew. "I don't like what I see. If you don't mind, I think I've had about enough of this conversation."

Carver set his cane in the flowered Victorian carpet and gained his feet. "I don't blame you," he said. "I don't like asking you about it, but you were the one who might know."

"Well, I don't know. I mean, neither Dr. Sam nor Millicent ever said or did anything that gave me any insight into their sex life. They simply didn't talk about that kind of thing. Not that I was curious. I didn't consider it any of my affair when Dr. Sam was alive, and I consider it even less my business now that he's dead."

"I wouldn't argue," Carver said. "Whatever they did in the privacy of their home, it's most likely irrelevant." He limped across the faded flower pattern to the door and opened it.

"You don't really believe that, do you?" she said behind him.

He braced with the cane and twisted around to face her, one foot out in the hall. The pungent scent of spicy Italian cooking wasn't so appetizing now. "I don't know what to believe," he said. "I honestly don't know."

"I'd appreciate it if you wouldn't dirty Dr. Sam's memory by speculating with the wrong people about his sex life.''

''You have Chief Wicke in mind?''

''Yes, among others. Talking to him might make any nasty rumor sort of semiofficial and lend it credibility. I mean, the idea's nauseating. It isn't dignified, and Dr. Sam was a dignified scientist. Let's leave him with that.''

''And Millicent's still alive,'' Carver said. ''We wouldn't want to drag her private life out for everyone to see.''

''Of course not.'' Katia looked angry for a moment. ''I wasn't forgetting Millicent.''

''I trusted you to tell me the truth,'' Carver said. ''You can trust me to do what I can. But I can't promise, because I don't know where this'll lead.''

''What you suspect about Dr. Sam and Millicent,'' she said confidently, ''won't lead anywhere at all. It's simply not *them.*''

''I expect you're right.''

She gave him her young, naive smile, the girl who knew more about sea life than life on land.

35

Beth was in the kitchen eating a tuna salad sandwich and drinking beer when Carver got back to the cottage. He pulled a Budweiser from the refrigerator and sat down across the table from her. She was wearing a gray Florida State T-shirt and faded Levi's, dressed to take her turn in the blind and keep up surveillance on the Rainer estate. He didn't want her back in the blind, was getting worn-down from fearing for her. Obstinate, heedless woman.

A hard-shelled bug of some kind flew against the window and bounced off, sounding like a thrown pebble. Carver took a sip of beer and said, "There's no point in watching the Rainer place any longer. We've seen all we're going to see."

She swallowed a bite of sandwich. "I wasn't sure what you had in mind. Thought I better be ready."

The sandwich smelled good. He noticed a brown ceramic bowl containing tuna salad on the sink counter and limped over to it, got two slices of white bread and set about constructing a sandwich of his own. "Call Forest, Ohio?"

Beth nodded. "Turns out to be a little town out in the middle of farm country. Everybody knows everything about everybody. Key Montaigne north."

"Only without Walter Rainer."

"Yeah. Anyway, there's only one Sandy listed, and her last name's Bing. I called a gas station near Forest, said I was looking for the address of somebody named Bing to send some money lent me to get a flat tire repaired some weeks ago. Guy at the station liked to hear himself talk, so I kept quiet and let him run on fast-forward. He told me there were lots of Bings in and around Forest, family's prominent in the town. There used to be a large Bing farm, but now it's been parceled out for homes and a feed store. Sandy and Sam Bing are the daughter and son of Bings who still work the land. That was just the way the gas station guy put it, 'work the land.' Dr. Sam's death's the talk of Forest, as you might expect; his funeral's tomorrow and most of the locals are attending. Sandy was married to a guy named Merchant, but they got divorced last year and she's back to using her maiden name." Beth drained beer from her glass. "I got her phone number and the number of the Bing farm."

Carver grinned, amazed as he often was by her ability to ferret out information. "You did better than okay." He sliced the sandwich in half diagonally and sat back down at the table, hooking the crook of his cane over the back of the chair next to him.

"Thanks. Speaking of cars, some bastard went at mine under the hood and made a mess of the engine. I got a call in for Effie's father to tow it to his station for repairs."

"Davy or Hector," Carver said. "Trying to decrease our mobility. Or maybe just more fun and fright tactics. The Olds'll probably be next, if they get a chance at it." He subdued the heat of his anger so he could eat.

"I didn't figure it was mischievous kids," Beth said. "How'd you do at the house?"

Between bites of sandwich, he told her about what he'd found in the Bing house, and his conversation with Katia Marsh.

"Katia's right," Beth said. "The fact the good doctor and his wife were likely doing S and M probably doesn't have anything to do with anything. Lotsa uptight conservatives and fundamentalists in Florida. They're heavy into this kinda thing, but their consciences won't allow them to get involved in honest crime. A night now and then with ropes and nipple clamps is all they need to let off steam.''

Carver studied her, trying to figure if she was putting him on. He decided she was serious. Not for the first time he wondered about her life with Roberto Gomez. Maybe it was best she hadn't told him everything and never would.

"You think you're getting anywhere with all of this?" Beth asked.

"Either that or I'm being taken somewhere." Carver finished his sandwich, then looked at his watch. Ten o'clock. Not too late to call Ohio. "You got those numbers handy?"

"They're written on the tablet by the phone."

Carrying his beer can, he limped into the living room and sat down by the phone. The air conditioner was off in there, and the ratchety clamor of cicadas in the lush foliage outside was shrill and loud, almost as if it were coming from inside the cottage. He decided to punch out Sandy's number instead of that of the Bing farm. She'd written to Millicent and inquired about her brother; Sandy and Dr. Sam had been at least that close at the time of his death.

She answered on the third ring. Her voice was slow, dragging, as if she might be tired or drugged. Grief pulling her down.

Carver told her his name, said he'd been a friend of Dr. Sam's and that he sure hoped he hadn't gotten her out of bed. He was assured he hadn't.

"I'm sorry about your brother," he said.

"We all are. Everybody who knew him's sorry." She spoke with a slight midwestern lilt, not unpleasant.

He said, "I'm trying to get in touch with Millicent."

"She ain't here."

"Oh? She said she was flying in for the funeral."

"Yeah, but she ain't got here yet. Had a long layover in Atlanta. Plane had a mechanical problem and couldn't take off till it was fixed. Dave drove to the airport to pick her up."

Carver didn't ask who Dave was. "When Millicent gets there," he said, "will you give her a message from me?"

"Don't see why not."

"Ask her to phone me about Dr. Sam. Tell her I'm a friend, that this has to do with his work and how he'll be remembered here in Key Montaigne and it's vitally important. She needs to talk to me for his sake and for hers." He gave her the phone number of the cottage.

"That the entire message?" Sandy asked, obviously curious.

"That's it. She'll understand."

"Wish I did." She sounded wistful, not as if she was just talking about his message for Millicent, but maybe life in general. And death.

He told her again he was sorry about Dr. Sam, then hung up. Millicent Bing would probably phone Katia first, then, if he'd read Katia right, she'd urge Millicent to call him. Then maybe he could find out why Millicent was frightened when she left Key Montaigne. It must have to do with Walter Rainer. Maybe, Carver thought, if he promised her anonymity and the chance to bring Rainer down, she just might confide in him. He was sure she knew something, knew what Dr. Sam had known. And maybe she wasn't as sure as everyone else seemed to be that her husband's death was a suicide.

"Think she'll call?" Beth asked from the living room doorway. She was leaning with a shoulder on the doorjamb, her fingertips inserted into the pockets of her tight Levi's.

"She might. She'll be curious, and the phone call's no risk to her. When the funeral's over tomorrow and she leaves Forest, she probably plans on dropping from sight."

"What now?" Beth asked.

"Bed." He wiped a hand down his face, starting high on his bald forehead. *Ouch!* Hurt his nose again, still tender from too much sun. "Jesus, I'm tired!"

"Too tired?"

He thought about it, looking at her there in the doorway. "Well, maybe not."

She hip-switched over to him and gracefully settled

down on his lap. his cane clattered to the floor as she draped a long arm around his neck and bit his earlobe, flicked her tongue in his ear.

"Definitely not," he said.

Smiling, she swiveled from his lap, bent low and retrieved his cane. He enjoyed watching that.

The screaming of the cicadas was deafening as he limped beside her to Henry Tiller's bed.

36

THE MORNING sun punched through the parted curtains and bisected the bedroom with a golden brilliance thick as syrup. Carver blinked sleep from his eyes and looked over at Beth. She was lying on her stomach, her face scrunched into her pillow so the morning glare wouldn't disturb her. He remembered last night, and his hand reached out for her, almost touched the smooth curve of her bare back, softened by sunlight.

Then he caught a glimpse of his watch and withdrew his hand. It was ten minutes to eight. Dr. Sam would be put in the ground soon in Ohio. Millicent was probably up and dressed.

She hadn't returned his call last night. If she'd decided to call this morning, it would happen after the funeral. That gave him a few hours to do something other than sit by the phone. A few hours he should try using to his advantage.

He carefully worked himself out of bed so he wouldn't wake Beth, located his cane, then limped through the dust-moted pattern of sunlight into the bathroom, feeling warmth on his bare calves and feet.

By eight-thirty he'd showered and dressed and was in the kitchen sipping steaming black coffee from one of Henry's smiley mugs. At twenty minutes to nine he carried his coffee into the living room and called Effie Norton's home number. The phone at the other end of the connection rang five times, and Carver was about to hang up when a man answered with a mumbled unfriendly hello. He had a deep voice that suggested a bear disturbed during hibernation.

"Sorry if I woke you," Carver said. "I'd like to talk to Effie."

"S'who is this?"

Carver told him.

"I'm Vic Norton, her father," the man said. "And you didn't wake me up. In fact, I was meaning to get by this morning and talk with you. Effie's mom and I don't think it's a good idea, her getting involved in whatever it is you're doing here on the island."

"I've been trying to tell Effie that myself," Carver said.

"Then why you calling? Gonna try telling her again? Or do you need the place cleaned?"

"Neither. I just wanna ask her one question. There's no danger in her answering, believe me."

"Uh-huh."

"She still in bed?"

"Naw, she's awake. Out in the yard helping her mother trim hedges. We was all doing yardwork, trying to get done early and beat the damned heat."

"If you call her to the phone, I'll only keep her a minute," Carver said. "Not even that long."

Vic Norton didn't answer for quite a while, letting Carver know he was mulling it over. Well, Carver understood; if Effie were his daughter, he'd want her helping around the house or marching in the school band instead of mixed up with hit-and-run murder and narcotics.

"Neither of us wants to get Effie hurt," Carver assured Norton. A bead of perspiration ran down his forehead, menaced the corner of his eye, then tracked down his cheek without veering. "All I need from her is some information."

"I'll go get her," Norton said. "But I'd like your promise you'll keep her outa your business from here on in."

"Done," Carver told him.

Distant plastic clattered as Norton laid down the receiver.

Carver waited and sweated, wishing he'd switched on the air conditioner. Finally Effie came to the phone.

"Dad said you had a question to ask me."

"Your friend Bobby who works at the Texaco station on Marathon Key, would he be on the job today?"

"Should be. Other'n Sundays, he works every day from eight to five. It'll be that way till school starts."

"Thanks, Effie. That's all I needed."

"How come you didn't just call Bobby at the station?"

"I like to talk with people face to face, and without advance notice. I learn more that way."

"Bobby wouldn't mind talking if you called, and he wouldn't run out on you. I told you, you can trust him."

"I'm more concerned with whoever else might know I'd called."

"Oh, I see what you mean. You don't trust many people, do you?"

The question made him feel unaccountably ashamed. "A few. Only a few."

"Mr. Carver, what'd Dad say to you?"

"We talked," Carver told her, "and we decided you getting involved in what I'm doing isn't a good idea. Your dad and I agree on that."

"Yeah, well, you would." She sounded petulant, as if she'd been denied permission to watch MTV.

"You've already been a help, Effie. You've done enough."

"The other day you asked me not to go snooping around, and I promised I wouldn't. No need to lie and say I solved the case."

He smiled. "I didn't exactly say that. Or even that anything was solved."

"Guess you didn't. You want me to come by like usual and clean today?"

"Sure."

"It'll be a while. They got me working in the prison yard here."

''That's okay, Beth's still asleep. She was up late last night, so the later you get here the better.''

''She stayed awake trying to help you figure everything out, I bet.''

''That's it. I'll be gone part of the morning. Maybe you'll still be at the cottage when I get back. You can have lunch with Beth and me if you want.''

''Sounds super. And don't worry, I won't wake Beth up if she's still asleep when I get there.''

After Carver hung up, he wondered if Effie's father would mind her staying at the cottage for lunch. Then he shrugged. Bullets didn't figure to fly over sandwiches and potato chips.

He left Beth a note, switched on the window unit so the cottage would be cool when she woke up, then limped outside and got in the Olds. The sun was already on a rampage, so he set the car's air conditioner on High and left the canvas top up for shade. The moody air conditioner decided to do its best today. In his bubble of cool air, he drove fast along Shoreline, past the Oceanography Research Center, then across the narrow bridge to Duck Key and on to Marathon Key.

CARVER REMEMBERED the Texaco station from his drives north. It was equipped with over a dozen pumps, half of them under a slanted fiberglass roof. All the pumps were self-service, and the cashier was inside a little square brick building that doubled as a modest convenience store specializing in canned soda and packed snacks. There were two bays for oil changes and repair work. One of the overhead doors was open. Carver could see an old white Cadillac up on the rack, the kind with tail fins. A boy in blue work uniform with baggy pants was bustling around beneath the car, giving it a lube job. Every few seconds Carver heard the snakelike hiss of the air gun forcing grease into the fittings.

After parking the Olds alongside the building, near a Dumpster piled high with trash, he walked to the service bay with the open door. The air gun's intermittent hissing was surprisingly loud now that he was so close, echoing in the barren brick and cinder-block bay.

The boy doing the work looked about sixteen, not fourteen, as Effie had said. He was short and stocky and had a wild thatch of blond hair above a round, guileless face with grease strains on it like Indian war paint. His blue uniform shirt was spotless, but his darker blue pants looked stiff with accumulated grease and oil. He noticed Carver, wiped his free hand on the front of his leg and smiled. He had teeth that were bad beyond redemption.

"Help you?"

"Maybe," Carver said, limping into the shade of the service bay. The smell of oil was strong. A long, viscous strand of it was draining darkly from the Cadillac's crankcase down into a wide, flat pan on a metal stand. "You Bobby?"

The blond boy nodded, held the grease gun to a ball-joint fitting, and braced his legs as if he were about to open fire with a machine gun. *Sssst! Sssst! Sssst!* The car's owner was getting his money's worth; a tubular glob of grease oozed from the overflowing fitting and dropped to the painted concrete floor, where it lay like an inert snail.

"I'm a friend of Effie Norton."

The boy's eyes flicked to the cane. He seemed more curious than pitying. "Carver?"

"Right. I wanted to talk to you about the black van."

Bobby resumed his work. "The one that creepy Davy guy drives?" *Ssst! Ssst!*

"That's the one. How often's he stop in for gas?"

"I'd say around the middle of every week, usually. Fills up the tank, always pays cash, goes on his way."

"When he pulls outa the station, does he always turn north on the highway?"

Ssst! "Seems to, the times I can recall watchin' him."

"This station must do a lotta business. What would make you watch him in particular?"

"I dunno. I suppose 'cause it's such a neat van. Then there's his tattoos and all. And once he gave Linda at the register a hard time 'cause she couldn't change a hundred. Then I noticed the way, after he fills up, before he walks inside and pays, he always drives the van to the far end of the lot, like he don't want anyone to peek into it. He does that, he has to walk a couple hundred feet in the sun to pay for his gas. Not that it's that big a deal, but nobody else parks away over there before payin'.'' He made a vague motion with his greasy right hand.

"Effie told me you sneaked over and looked in the van one day when Davy was inside at the register."

"Yeah." Bobby continued working while he talked. "After she talked to me"—*Ssst!*—"I got curious, figured what the heck. So when I saw there was four people waiting to pay in front of Davy, I kept the number-five pump between me and him in case he happened to look outside, and I got around the other side of the van and got my nose right up to a window." *Ssst! Ssst!* "Couldn't see much, though. It was a bright day, and those windows are tinted so dark it's hard to see inside." Again he made the motion with his arm, as if half-heartedly pointing. "Just the rug and the big wood box, like Effie told you."

"Better not try anything like that again," Carver said. "Davy's a rough man with rough friends."

"Effie told me that. I ain't scared, but don't worry. She said you didn't want me or her nosin' around any of them Key Montaigne people. She was plain on that."

Carver was pleased Effie had delivered the message.

The crankcase was finished draining. Bobby laid down the lube gun, wiped his hands on his thighs, and went over to replace the drain plug.

"When was the last time you saw Davy gassing up the van?" Carver asked.

"You mean before today?"

Carver's grip tightened on his cane. "Davy was in here today?"

"Not *was*," Bobby said, "he's inside payin' Linda now." He motioned with his arm again. "Hey, I thought you knew that."

This time Carver looked in the direction of the arm movement and saw the back of Davy's van at the far side of the lot. There were no other cars within fifty feet.

"Thanks, Bobby," he said. "Don't mention I was by and we talked, okay?"

"Don't worry about that," Bobby said, deftly screwing in the drain plug with blackened fingers. A dark rivulet ran down the back of his hand.

Careful not to place the tip of his cane on grease or oil, Carver left the service bay and got back in the Olds. He started the engine and switched on the air conditioner. The vents pulled in the sweet rotting stench of whatever was in the Dumpster.

A few minutes later Davy emerged from the square brick building, swaggered to his van and climbed inside. The van rolled slowly to the exit drive and stopped. When there was a break in traffic, it pulled out onto Route 1 and turned north.

Carver waited until another few cars had passed, then followed the van, figuring, Back to Miami. The thought made his burned nose hurt.

NOT MIAMI this time, though.

Davy didn't even leave Marathon Key. Half a mile from the station, he pulled off the highway and parked in front of a low clapboard building with a sign that said: BAIT, BEER, BOATS.

Carver stopped on the gravel shoulder and watched.

Davy got out of the van, puffed out his chest and tucked in his sleeveless T-shirt. He didn't enter the building. Instead he walked around it, underneath a thick cedar trellis enmeshed in vines with pink blossoms.

Carver shifted the Olds to Drive and let its idling engine roll him closer. He guided the car into the lot of a souvenir shop, found a parking slot between two other cars so the Olds wouldn't be noticeable, then braced himself for the glare and heat of the sun and climbed out. The Olds was angled nose toward the shop, its rusty rear bumper only a few feet from the highway.

The tumultuous hot wind in the wake of a speeding eighteen-wheeler almost bowled him over. He saved himself from falling by instinctively stabbing the ground with the cane. Better keep an eye out for those bastards, he cautioned himself, watching the square back of the trailer glimmer and grow smaller in the vaporous heat of the highway. His bald pate felt ready to burst into flames in the relentless sun, his nose was throbbing now, and already he could feel the thin leather soles of his moccasins warming. He was truly miserable, and for a second wondered how he'd come to be here. What an occupation, he thought. What a world. What a life. What was the purpose of it all, really?

No answer sprang to mind.

He limped over baked gravel toward the place that specialized in bait, beer, boats.

37

WHEN HE got closer to the low clapboard building, Carver saw that a smaller sign above the door proclaimed it to be ZIG'S FISHERMAN'S LOUNGE. He walked along an uneven stone walk that ran outside the building, and found that it led to a patio with some tables and chairs outside.

A faded green canvas awning supported by a rusty iron framework provided shade, but this was the void between breakfast and lunch, and no one was at any of the tables other than a few gulls pecking disdainfully at crumbs. At the far corner of the building a gaunt teenage boy stood shirtless in the sun, holding a garden hose and directing a meager stream of water on something beyond Carver's view. He seemed uninterested in his task as he absently bent to drink from the hose, then wiped a skinny bare arm across his perspiring forehead. A weathered wooden sign pointed the way to the dock, down a narrow dirt path that cut through tall grass, untended bushes that had once been a garden, and wind-gnarled date palms. Carver set the tip of his cane on the hard earth and began walking.

Within a few minutes he could see the ocean. There was a rickety dock, and a sloping concrete ramp where trailered boats might be put in the water. A gravel road ran parallel to the shore, then curved out of sight with the angle of the land.

Half a dozen open fishing boats with outboard motors bobbed at the dock. A pelican sat unconcernedly on the bow of one of them. The only person in view was Davy, standing on the sunny dock with his hands on his hips and gazing out to sea. About half a mile from shore a boat rode the glimmering ocean. Carver could see two men in it, unmoving as a sculpture, two fishing poles like jutting antennae. Beyond the boat, on the horizon, dense clouds were layered to a majestic altitude, more a mockery than a promise of rain.

He moved off the path and behind some bushes with huge pink blossoms that gave off an acrid, unpleasant scent. Leaned on his cane and watched.

The wavering drone of an outboard motor became audible through the clear morning air, and an open boat came into view. It was moving fast, skipping along the surface so the prop was clear occasionally and the motor snarled free of the water's drag. One man sat in it, hunched over the outboard in the stern, his neck craned as he twisted his body so he could see above the raised bow.

The V of white wake disappeared as the motor coughed and settled into a determined sputtering, and the boat veered toward shore. There was a muted thumping as its gray aluminum hull settled against the tires lashed to the dock as buffers, and the man in the stern cut the motor and scrambled forward to loop a rope over a cleat and secure the boat. The pelican had seen enough and flapped away.

Davy dropped his hands to his sides and stood without moving. A waiting attitude touched with impatience. For the first time Carver saw something familiar about the man in the boat. He leaned forward over his cane.

After clambering from the boat, the man made his way along the dock to where Davy stood. He was wearing khaki shorts and a loose-fitting red and gray striped pullover shirt, a white baseball cap with an oversized bill. He needed a shave badly, or he was cultivating a beard. As he shook hands with Davy, Carver realized he was looking at Frank Everman.

The two men stood talking in the sun for a few minutes,

then Davy drew a brown envelope from beneath his shirt and handed it to Everman. Everman opened the flap and looked inside, then he began thumbing through a thick stack of green bills, counting them with the brisk efficiency of a bank teller. Halfway through the bills he stopped and shrugged. He grinned at Davy, who was staring at him without expression.

They shook hands again as Everman tucked the envelope beneath the waistband of his shorts, then gave it a gentle, possessive pat. As if it were something vulnerable and alive he was protecting.

Davy watched as Everman climbed back in the boat and unfastened the line, hunkered down in the stern and yanked the pull cord three times on the outboard motor. The motor turned over and sputtered to life, and Everman gave Davy a vague wave and began maneuvering the boat slowly clear of the dock.

Davy stood as he had before, fists on hips, and watched as the motor snarled loudly and the boat's bow rose high and spread a curving white wake. Everman didn't look back as he aimed the bucking bow away from shore and set a course north over the gently choppy sea.

When Davy turned away and started up the path, Carver retreated farther into the sharp-scented foliage, out of sight.

Davy passed within twenty feet of him, gazing at the ground and wearing a grim smile. He plodded with his fists balled like sledgehammer heads at the ends of his muscular tattooed arms, as if he'd enjoy punching out anyone who got in his way. Popeye gone bad.

Instead of following him, Carver moved through high grass parallel to the highway until he could see the rear of the black van. He was afraid Davy might stay for a while in Zig's and drink a beer or two, but that wasn't the case. Less than a minute after Davy had passed from sight, the van reversed out onto the highway. With a faint squeal of rubber on hot concrete, it turned and accelerated south, back toward Key Montaigne. Carver saw no point in following.

He took his time limping back to the Olds. A swarm of

gnats found him and tagged along most of the way, but he barely noticed them. Something had taken hold in his mind.

After lowering himself into the Olds, he sat behind the steering wheel with the motor idling and the suddenly co-operative air conditioner blowing a hurricane, thinking about what he'd just witnessed at the dock. Putting it together with everything else he'd learned, and feeling his stomach plunge as he made some terrible sense of it.

It was cool in the Olds, but his mind and his gut kept churning and he was sweating. His body was coated with a nasty sheen of perspiration and the powdered dust that had risen from the dirt path to the sea.

Anger had joined revulsion by the time he swung the car onto Route 1 and drove for Key Montaigne.

HE'D BEEN back at the cottage only fifteen minutes when Millicent Bing called from Ohio. Carver told her what he'd figured out and promised to protect Dr. Sam's memory as much as possible, in exchange for one favor from her. She had to make a phone call to someone she was sure would pass the word to Walter Rainer that she was returning to Key Montaigne to meet Carver at eleven that evening at the research center.

She agreed. She really had no choice.

After hanging up the phone, Carver explained to Beth what they were going to do. Then he called Katia Marsh, did some more explaining, and got her cooperation in gaining access to the research center that night.

Then he cleaned his gun.

38

AT TEN-THIRTY that night, Carver left the Olds parked out of sight and limped along Shoreline toward the research center. There was enough light to see fairly well, broken only by the passage of scudding black clouds across the face of the moon. He placed his cane carefully in the dark, making good time to the parking lot.

As he drew near the angular brick building, he slowed his pace, gathering his thoughts and resolve. Around him were only the night sounds of insects, the brief drone of a faraway plane, water lapping down by the dock where the dark form of the *Fair Wind* rode. He could sense on his right the vast mystery of the ocean. He was sweating, breathing raggedly, as he used the key Katia had given him and let himself into the research center.

After closing the door but not relocking it, he stood for a while waiting for his eyes to adjust to the dimmer light inside the building. Then he limped past the posters of sea horses and dolphins and opened the door to the lower level Tide Pool Room.

There were no windows in this room, so he felt for the light switch inside the door. Found its smooth protuberance and flipped it up. It made a sound like a sharp slap.

The overhead fluorescent tubes flickered like heat lightning then glowed steadily, and the shark tank's wavering illumination was also activated. The hulking form of Victor swooped toward Carver, surprisingly near, startling him for a moment. Then the shark swept in a graceful arc behind the glass and with a flick of its tail glided in the opposite direction, its image becoming distorted and deceptively small on the far side of the tank. Victor's world. Circling, circling.

"You'd think he'd get tired," a voice said.

Still poised on the black steel landing, Carver looked down and saw Walter Rainer standing near one of the tide pool displays. Like Carver, he'd gotten the idea of arriving early, before Millicent Bing was due. Early birds hoping they weren't worms.

Carver clomped down the metal stairs with his cane and saw Davy standing to Rainer's left, where he wouldn't be seen from the landing. Davy stared unsmilingly at Carver, his muscular arms hanging limply at his sides. Carver nodded toward the shark and said, "I'm told they have to keep swimming, keep feeding, or they sink and die."

"I find myself in the same position," Rainer said. He ran a hand over his hugely protruding stomach, as if to reassure himself he was prosperous and well-fed. He was wearing a cream-colored suit that made him look even more massive than he was. A beige shirt, no tie. The suit was wrinkled and baggy, and though the Tide Pool Room was cool, Rainer's fat-padded face glistened with sweat and looked sickly in the fluorescent light. Davy had on tight jeans and a loud flowered shirt, untucked. Carver had left his own shirt untucked to conceal the Colt holstered beneath it. He figured Davy was also armed, probably with his weapon of choice, the sharpened cargo hook. There was pattern and predictability to sadism.

Behind Rainer the shark kept circling, the only movement in the room. Then Davy hooked his thumbs in his side pockets and swaggered out to stand in the center of the floor with his feet spread wide, closer to Carver but not too close. He was playing cool but he was tense; the nude dancer on his forearm twitched a hip.

Carver said, "Millicent isn't coming."

Rainer shrugged inside the tent-sized suit. "That doesn't

surprise me, nor does it matter. I was sure *you'd* be here. Time enough to deal with Millicent, if indeed I must."

"You must," Carver said. "Otherwise you won't sleep well, worrying about when her conscience might bite her and then you."

The small square room was silent, insulated from the outside world as the floor of the sea. "I assume she told you everything," Rainer said.

"She filled me in on what I hadn't already guessed after seeing Davy hand over a payoff to Frank Everman this morning."

Rainer gave Davy an annoyed look. Davy's flat little eyes fixed intensely on Carver, like dispassionate radar-gun sights.

"You weren't smuggling drugs or anything else into the country," Carver told Rainer. "You were smuggling something *out,* into Mexico. You run a way station, part of an operation that supplies certain people in Mexico with abducted children for sexual exploitation in brothels and for private amusement. Dr. Sam knew about it but wasn't part of it, though occasionally he gave you use of the *Fair Wind* when you thought the *Miss Behavin'* might attract suspicion. The doctor had a weakness for young boys, which you supplied in exchange for his silence. Millicent knew but wouldn't talk about it and ruin her husband."

Rainer was nodding slightly as Carver spoke, agreeing with him. "That kind of appetite burns in the blood," he said. "Dr. Sam was weak, couldn't help himself. Millicent's also weak. That's why she isn't here."

"And why she might eventually talk if you don't find her and kill her."

"I honestly don't see that as necessary," Rainer said. "There's always a way to persuade people, and if they aren't persuadable, there are other methods. For instance, just before you arrived I got a call from Hector telling me your friend Beth Jackson was arrested by Chief Wicke for spying on my private grounds. Apparently she was supposed to phone you here when I and mine left for this meeting. Instead she's now in the custody of Chief Wicke."

"You phoned Wicke to come get her?"

"Hector did, after Davy and I left unseen and were well on our way. We didn't want her to become impatient and interrupt proceedings here. But do tell me what else you think you know, Mr. Carver."

Carver glanced at Davy, who hadn't moved or changed expression. The faint shadow of the circling shark played over his stolid features. "The Evermans are part of the operation that abducts the children and sends them south in Davy's van for you to transfer to Mexico," Carver said. "The boy who drowned was high on cocaine so he could be controlled, but somehow he got free, tried to swim to safety, and drowned. The Evermans were sent from Miami to Key Montaigne to pose as the boy's parents and claim the body before further police investigation revealed his true identity and that of his real family."

Rainer gently touched his protruding stomach again, making the gesture somehow sensual and obscene. He sighed. "You've done surprisingly well, despite our considerable efforts to discourage you."

"Henry Tiller was doing okay himself, which was why you had him murdered."

"Yes, we had to send Davy to handle that chore."

"Chore, huh? Like weeding the garden."

"Or taking out the garbage. But doing violence and making it seem accidental isn't exactly Davy's style, so old Henry lived long enough to draw you into the situation. And you certainly proved to be as stubborn as your reputation promised." Rainer's gold ring glinted as he waved a fleshy hand limply but quickly, as if flicking something nasty from his fingertips. "No matter, I'm a man who takes precautions religiously. Davy's in his element now, not behind the wheel of a rental car. He's at his best preventing someone of known obsessive and dangerous personality from harming his employer or himself, even if it means that someone's unfortunate but lawful death." Not looking away from Carver, he nodded to Davy and said, "This is finally good-bye, Mr. Carver. It's been stimulating if irritating."

Davy reached beneath his riot-of-flowers shirt and pulled

out his sharpened cargo hook. His expression was businesslike as he advanced on Carver. He'd handled Carver easily in Miami, and now it was time to get serious and finish the job. The routine chore.

Carver calmly drew the Colt from its holster, but the cargo hook arced forward with startling speed and slashed his hand. The gun dropped to the floor, landing at an angle and bouncing away from Carver. The back of his hand throbbed and dripped blood from a four-inch gash.

Davy stepped back, grinning now. His eyes had changed. Since Carver had been disarmed, business and pleasure could be combined. Carver had little doubt that if he stooped to retrieve the gun, Davy would be on him for the kill. They both knew Carver wasn't going to do that. Doomed men tend to cling to time. Davy was obviously relishing the leisurely sport of finishing off a cripple.

But this time Carver wasn't caught by surprise. He stood almost still as Davy approached him, shifting his weight subtly so Davy wouldn't notice. His good leg was set so firmly that inside his thin-soled moccasins his toes were curled down tight against the concrete floor. He waited.

As Davy crouched to close in with the hook, Carver lashed out and up with the cane. It missed Davy's wrist by inches, but Carver pulled it close to his body and, as Davy sprang, he shot the tip of the cane forward into Davy's sternum, using it as a jabbing weapon to drive the breath from his attacker. *"Ooomph!"* He felt the sour rush of Davy's exhalation on his face, and the point of the cargo hook snagged for a moment on his shirtsleeve, then tore free. Now Carver slashed down with the cane, and the deadly steel hook flew from Davy's injured hand and bounced clanging beneath one of the display trays. As Davy instinctively lowered his free hand to grip his damaged fingers, Carver flicked the cane up in his face, jabbing at an eye. Jabbing again.

Davy snarled and leaped back. Stood rocking on the balls of his feet. Glaring and battling his temper.

"Davy," Rainer said softly, cautioning. Almost a whisper. "Davy!"

But Davy lost his composure and charged.

What Carver was waiting for. He flicked the cane out again, like a nifty boxer using a stiff left jab. Davy stopped and tried to brush the cane away from his face or grab it. Carver drove it into his groin. Davy's hands dropped again. Carver slammed the cane across the side of his head, feeling and hearing the solid connection of walnut with bone. Nailed him again on the backswing, opening up a cheekbone. He was a fraction quicker than Davy, and now both men realized it and knew it made all the difference. Christ, this was *fun!* Terrifying but fun.

Davy retreated. Streaming blood was making a grotesque mask of his face. His glance shot to where the cargo hook had slid beneath the display tray.

Carver smiled and motioned with the cane for him to attack again. Silently mouthed the word "Please," urging him to come forward.

But Davy moved fast in the opposite direction, going for the steel hook.

Before he could reach it, Carver was down and struggling for the Colt. His hand was about to close on the gun before Davy could grasp the hook, so Davy reversed direction and scrambled up the steel stairs. He knew when the war was over. In a flurry of noise and desperate energy, he burst through the door and was gone before Carver could raise the Colt above shoulder level and fire.

Carver planted the cane and hauled himself to his feet, holding the gun aimed at Rainer, listening to his own rasping fight for air. His labored breathing was making the gun barrel waver.

Unruffled and unmoving, Rainer said, "You use that cane very well as a weapon. Interesting to watch, but indecisive."

"Decisive enough so you and I are driving into Fishback to see Chief Wicke."

"No, no," Rainer corrected, wagging a ringed finger with impatient amusement. "Didn't I mention I was a man who took precautions, Mr. Carver? Allow me to set you straight on a few facts, the first of which is that as soon as Dr. Sam committed suicide—and it *was* suicide, brought about by middle-class remorse and self-hatred—I ordered destroyed every scintilla of evidence that the child-smuggling operation ever existed. Dr. Sam indeed had the kind of sickness that compelled him to sexually abuse young boys, but Millicent was certainly enough of an accomplice that she'll decide to remain silent when I convince her of the consequences of a loose tongue. Especially if we speak with Davy present.'' He stood taller, turning slightly as if aiming his jutting stomach at Carver like the prow of a proud vessel. "You see, I'm not merely a part of the smuggling operation, I'm in charge of it, so I have enough control to protect myself. And naturally I've exercised that control. There's no way for you to advance any legal proof of what you know. No way at all.'' The fleshy pads of his cheeks bulged in a smile. His eyes glittered. "In short, Mr. Carver, a closure has been reached, but not of the sort you envisioned. What transpired here tonight simply doesn't matter.''

Rainer's words made a horrifying kind of sense. And probably all too soon, in another place, in another manner, he'd be back in his profitable and terrible business.

Willing himself not to tremble with the rage building in him, Carver said, "Don't you ever feel the same self-loathing that made Dr. Sam hang himself?'' He knew even as he spoke that his was a futile hope. The evil wouldn't corrupt and destroy itself. Real evil seldom did that, and Rainer was the bulky embodiment of genuine evil.

"Ah, Mr. Carver, you should try to move beyond your simplistic and inhibiting delusions of right and wrong. You need to learn what Dr. Sam came to know and couldn't live with because he was weak. The world's like the ocean he studied, an arena of prey and predator in endless succession. A food chain without moral meaning. Sappy sentimentalism aside, the abducted children are merely prey, nothing more. They simply fell prey to a larger predator. Despite the naive moral interpretation you put on it, actually nothing could be more natural and correct.''

As Carver listened to Rainer he was watching the huge torpedo shape of the shark gliding in circles behind the fat man, its image wavering and shrinking with distance, then growing into sharp and ominous focus.

"You're burdened with morality and an absurd code of honor," Rainer said confidently, "so you're not going to shoot me. You're not a predator. Not the sort who can slay a defenseless man in cold blood, anyway. And nothing criminal can be proved, so face the fact that the game's over. Henry Tiller lost when Davy ran him down. Now you've lost. But you get to live, lucky you." He folded his pudgy hands in front of him. "And that, Mr. Carver, is simply that."

Still staring at the shark, Carver was backing awkwardly up the stairs. He knew Rainer was right. About too much, but not about everything. He said, "Have you noticed, Rainer, that this room's smaller than the shark tank?"

Rainer appeared puzzled. He glanced around the square concrete room and shrugged. "So it is."

"About the size of a swimming pool. You swim as well as your wife, Rainer?"

Rainer cocked his head to the side, pursed his lips and raised his eyebrows. The thought was forming.

Carver said, "Time for you to be introduced to a larger predator."

That was when Rainer fully grasped it. Carver saw it on his face as he reached the steel landing and opened the door. Set the tip of his cane and emptied the Colt into the thick glass wall of the shark tank, spreading the pattern of bullets from floor to ceiling. He glimpsed Rainer's mouth gaping soundlessly as the wide expanse of glass behind him went milky and bulged. Carver hurled himself out of the room, slamming and locking the door.

As he limped away he heard the thunder of crashing glass. Water roaring into the tiny room. The thumping and flailing of the startled and ravenous shark.

Possibly a scream.

39

It was Rainer's widow, Lilly, the FBI finally persuaded to talk by allowing her to swim to immunity. She thought it wise to cut a deal with the law before Millicent Bing had the chance.

Arrest warrants were issued for Davy and Hector. Davy was shot to death during a car chase in Nevada the next month. Hector disappeared, probably into Mexico. Mexican authorities were cooperating with the FBI to clean up that end of the abduction operation, while in the United States arrests were made in cities along the eastern seaboard and throughout the Midwest. The Evermans were captured without resistance early one morning in a motel outside Tampa.

Chief Wicke had decided Walter Rainer's death was as much an accident as Henry Tiller's. He felt guilty for turning a deaf ear to Henry and a blind eye to what had been happening in his jurisdiction. Silently he'd dropped the spent bullets from Carver's gun into Carver's hand, eliminating the evidence that the glass wall had shattered as the result of gunfire, or that Carver had been responsible. The only court appearance required of Carver would be as a witness in the prosecution of the ring members. A repentent Millicent Bing, who'd surrendered to authorities in Ohio and also been promised immunity, would be an even more damaging witness than Rainer's widow.

Two days after Rainer's death at the research center, Norman Tiller, Henry's cousin from Milwaukee, showed up at the cottage and said he was in a legal hassle with the state of Florida over his inheritance, and his attorney had advised him to move into Henry's cottage. Carver and Beth introduced him to Effie and left for Del Moray. Effie's father needed a part shipped in before he could repair Beth's car so it would run dependably, so she left the LeBaron at Norton's Gas 'n' Go. She paid a transport service to drive it north when it was repaired, and traveled in the Olds with Carver.

On the sun-drenched highway just north of Miami, he slowed the car after passing a teenage girl hitchhiking on the gravel shoulder. Beth laid a hand over his on the steering wheel, then shrugged and removed it. Carver stopped the Olds, put it in Reverse and backed toward the girl. She snatched up a faded blue duffel bag and ran toward him, glad she had a ride.

Up close she looked even younger, no more than fifteen. Blond, pretty despite a fresh scar beneath her left eye. She was wearing dirty jeans and a T-shirt with VIRGINIA IS FOR LOVERS lettered faintly across the chest.

"Hey, thanks," she said, as she ambled the final few feet to Carver's side of the Olds, her charity-case Reeboks crunching on the gravel.

"How far you going?" he asked.

"Don't really matter how far or where."

"How about back to Virginia?"

She studied his face, and her expression changed to one of fear and wariness. She'd been awhile on her own.

"Climb in," Carver said. "I'll drive you to a bus station, stake you to your fare home. It's a promise."

She was slowly backpedaling now. She hooked a middle finger at Carver and yelled, "Fuck you!" Wheeled and began jogging away, her shadow stark in the brilliant afternoon sun.

"Hey!" Carver yelled after her, thinking of his own

daughter in St. Louis. St. Louis was no safer than Florida. "Get back here, please!"

Beth said, "Forget it, Fred. Maybe home's not so good for her, either."

The girl glanced back and made another obscene gesture, switching her hips deliberately as she stopped running and walked away fast.

"Jesus!" Carver said.

"It's luck she'll need," Beth told him. "It'll all be in her luck."

"Luck hell! Why can't she be *made* to see it's dangerous being fifteen and thumbing your way through life with strangers? Why can't she be made to understand so she'll go someplace safe even if it's not back home?"

"She doesn't wanna understand."

"Why not?"

Beth smiled and shook her head. "People don't know why they do anything, Fred, or why things turn out the way they do. Kids, adults, none of us. We think we know, but we don't. You shoulda learned that by now."

The sun was giving him a headache. "I don't like to think the world's that way."

"Nobody does. That's why it works the way I said."

He watched the girl's slim form disappear around the corner of a bridge abutment. Caught a brief glimpse of her cutting across a grassy field toward a cloverleaf. He felt helpless. Furious.

He slammed the Olds into Drive and pulled back onto the highway, spinning the tires until burning rubber screamed his rage. Drove too fast and didn't look back.

He almost made it. Ten miles outside Del Moray a state patrol car pulled him over and he was a given a lecture and a speeding ticket.

He thought, Just my luck.

ABOUT THE AUTHOR

JOHN LUTZ served as president of the Mystery Writers of America in 1991. He has twice won the Private Eye Writers of America Shamus Award, most recently for *Kiss* (1989), as well as the Mystery Writers of America Edgar Award. He is the author of five previous Carver novels—*Bloodfire, Flame, Kiss, Scorcher,* and *Tropical Heat*—and more than a dozen other suspense novels. He lives near St. Louis, Missouri.